Miranda Writes

Honor & Justice

Baxter Productions Inc.
308 Main St
New Rochelle NY 10801
www.baxterproductionsmedia.com

ISBN 978-0-9982773-1-8

Second Edition

Miranda Writes, Honor & Justice

Frank Santorsola

Dedication

To my wife Christina, whose loving support allowed me to be me. To Jennifer, Spencer and Andrei, who have laughed, loved and cried with me on our journey together through life, and to my daughters Danielle and Rachelle with whom I hope to reconcile someday.

—Frank Santorsola

Preface

In the 1970s, as a young man in my twenties, I decided to become a police officer instead of the school teacher I had studied to be. My life's values are centered on the family unit. These values of honesty and integrity, and that there's nothing more important than family, were instilled in me by my mom and dad throughout my childhood.

My parents were poor Italian immigrants from Rimini, a small town in Northern Italy. They came to America with hopes and dreams of a better life for themselves and their kids. After moving around from rental to rental in the New York Metropolitan area, they eventually saved enough money to buy a two-family house in Harrison, New York, renting out the second floor apartment. My father, Frank, was a tradesman who first learned the art of construction with stone, then worked with brick as the building industry changed in New York. He played a big part in building many of the apartment houses in New York City that are still standing today.

I recall my father's hands being cracked from working outside with cement in the cold weather. He never complained. He was a proud man and happy to put food on the family table. Years of strenuous manual labor and working outdoors in the hot summers and freezing winters took a toll on his body and in his sixties his health failed. He was forced to stop working. I thank God for the rental money coming in which helped financially sustain them.

My folks raised us to be honest, hardworking people and never to dishonor the family name. These values were reinforced around our family table on Sunday afternoons spent enjoying traditional macaroni and meatballs. We celebrated family togetherness and our Italian heritage. On many Sundays, our aunts, uncles, and cousins joined us for lunch or dinner, singing Neapolitan songs, playing cards, and just enjoying each other's company. In retrospect, I think I ultimately became a cop to honor my father and mother for all that they sacrificed for me and my brother, and to pay them back by being a standard bearer of their values.

When I joined the police department, I was an idealist. I was naïve. I'll admit it. I felt that the world was on the level and believed in the values I was taught, but as I've come to find out, the halls of justice are sometimes lined with people who have agendas other than to serve and protect.

I was surprised to learn that there were some officers in the department who looked down on Italian Americans thinking that in some way we were all connected to the Mafia. I hated that my colleagues could think that way. I was proud of my heritage and of the many second-generation Italian Americans I knew of who had become doctors, lawyers, congressmen, senators, governors, entrepreneurs, and other professionals who had nothing to do with organized crime. Italians had helped to make America great. It was difficult for me to accept my colleagues' prejudiced thinking, so I made my mind up to do everything I could professionally to change people's minds about Italian Americans by setting an example.

My brother, Rich, knew exactly how I felt. He's also on the job, working as a special agent/investigative accountant for the New York State Organized Crime Task Force. His job consists of finding illicit money and assets the Mafia has hidden from the government, and seizing it.

I think that for most people, justice is viewed as an inherent right given to us by our founding fathers. Justice, truth, and freedom—these rights were written in blood, sweat, and tears in our Constitution and Bill of Rights. Sadly though, a lot of people experience inequities and injustices at the hands of those sworn to serve in our criminal justice system.

In my thirties the fact that I was finally working out of the bag, which means working in plain clothes, meant a lot to me. It meant meeting the bad guys face to face on their own turf, and for a guy who loved to live on the edge, there was nothing better than beating these knuckle heads at their own game.

After working in patrol with the City of White Plains, New York Police Department, I was hired as an investigator with the Westchester County District Attorneys' Office, and assigned to the Organized Crime Squad. It seemed that I had an affinity for undercover work and soon found myself working deep cover, infiltrating a crew of one of the New York organized crime families. I soon found myself making choices that were uncomfortable, and struggling inwardly to hold onto the values that I'd been taught.

The following story is fact-based fiction. It's my version, true to my recollection, of events that occurred while I was assigned to work with a federal informant, Mike Baraka, who claimed that he was falsely arrested, indicted, and convicted for a crime he didn't commit. It's a story about family honor, a tabooed friendship, and a surgical look into the very essence of the criminal justice system.

Chapter One

It was back in 2000 and my office was interested in developing a criminal case against Michael Calise, a.k.a. Mickey, a capo in the Lucchese crime family. The Chief of Detectives, Sean Daniels, summoned me to his office along with Deputy Chief John Howell. I asked Howell what the meeting was about, but he wouldn't say. "You'll find out when you get there." Since I could tell by the Chief's tone that I wasn't about to be in trouble, something I often was, I figured it was going to be another assignment.

Chief Daniels is an Irish American, and at the time of these events he was in his late fifties, with snow-white hair. He was a huge guy, weighing about 260 and standing about six foot five. I guessed his ruddy complexion was caused by whacking down so much Scotch in response to all the aggravation he got from treating the guys under him like shit. The guys in the squad knew to stay out of his way when he wore his light-blue pinstripe suit to work.

Well, that morning, unfortunately for me, he was wearing that pinstripe suit, which by the way looked like it hadn't been cleaned in months, and it probably hadn't. Yeah, the guy was cheap. Believe me, to know this guy was to hate him, even if you happened to be one of the few in the office who could tolerate him or even the looks of him. Daniels had no sense of style; for example, that day he wore a paisley tie that didn't match the suit. His button-down white shirt stuck out around his waist because his shirt was too small to fit over his unsightly belly. Talking with him, I had to be careful how I couched things because of his irritability, and I had to do a lot of listening. The man could accelerate from zero to sixty in a heartbeat, raging at his detectives and, on occasion, assistant district attorneys who disagreed with him. Daniels wielded a lot of power in the office, and the District Attorney loved him.

He was so far up her ass, satisfying every politically calculated decision she made. As for Deputy Chief John Howell, we in the squad called him "Shake and Bake." Howell couldn't or wouldn't make an investigative decision unless he first spoke to the Chief. And if the Chief was belly up to the bar somewhere, then the wheels of justice waited, frustrating myself or any other detective who might be working a case that needed direction on some issue.

The Deputy Chief looked like his personality—shaky. He wore the same gray suit to work every day. He was short and fat, and wore glasses. His receding hairline, dyed brown, plus his weathered features, gave his fifty-plus years another ten. His appearance perfectly matched his emotionally strained personally. The guy was a basket case.

When I first got into the squad, I hoped that beneath the nervous exterior the guy might be somewhat intelligent. But I was wrong. Howell had no street smarts. And I heard from another undercover that Howell's lack of smarts had almost gotten him killed. In the middle of an undercover, multi-kilo cocaine buy, the dealer decided to change the location for the sale of the drugs. Just so you know, most dealers who use the cocaine they peddle become paranoid, a side effect of the addiction.

As I was told the story, the dealer had driven up to a prearranged location with two other Dominican hoods. The dealer and his cronies decided that they didn't like the location and gave the undercover ten minutes to drive to another location they named. Then they drove off. The undercover cop, with $28,000 in his trunk, radioed to Howell, who was supervising the backup team, reporting that the location had been changed. The undercover then gave Howell the new location and after receiving confirmation from Howell of the change, drove to the new location, which was only a few minutes away.

Instead of leaving for the new location immediately, Shaky decided to call an operational meeting. Little did the undercover know that he was on his own.

When he got to the other location the bad guys asked to see the money. But procedurally, the undercover would never expose the money for fear of a rip. A rip is when the bad guys have no intention of selling

you the drugs, but plan to take the money and most likely your life.

The undercover insisted first on seeing the product and testing its legitimacy. He knew, or thought he knew, that by the time the drugs were tested, the bad guys would be in custody. But this wasn't the case, because Shaky and the other cops hadn't gotten to the location yet.

Once the undercover tested the coke, and believing that the enforcement team was in place, he gave his prearranged signal for the arrest. But the cavalry didn't show up and there were no cops flooding the area to take these guys down. As a result of Howell's ineptitude, the undercover was forced to make the arrest singlehandedly, with Shaky and his team showing up several minutes too late. And guess what— the three Dominicans were carrying MAC-10 semiautomatic pistols. So much for Howell's street smarts. The undercover told me he considered himself lucky that he'd survived the day.

Howell and I took the elevator up to the fifth floor of the Westchester County Courthouse, got off the elevator, and walked down to the end of the hallway to the Chief's office. I opened the outer door of the office, which led into a waiting room, where secretary Ruth Williams was seated behind her desk typing from a Dictaphone. "The Chief will be with you shortly. Take a seat." Gee—no "Hello," no "Good afternoon." Not even a greeting for Howell, who looked a little taken aback. After all, he was the Deputy Chief.

Howell asked, "Ruth, how long before we can get in to see the Chief?"

She finally picked her head up. "Not long, John."

Looking out the large office window behind Ruth's desk, I could see the city skyline as I began to daydream. Howell sat there with his face in the *New York Post* as I wondered what Ruth was like outside of the office. She was definitely a sexy lady, in her early thirties, five ten, about 120 pounds, bright red hair tied in a bun, with some strands falling to the sides of her milky white face. She had the nicest pear-shaped ass that I'd seen in a long while and her bursting chest was amazing! How could Numb Nuts over here not be interested in picking up his head once in a while to give her a glance? Just sitting there reading the *Post*? What an asshole. Ruth turned her head and bent down to a low desk drawer to retrieve some papers. As she bent over, her light brown, V-necked sweater revealed more of her bosom. Wow! A diamond pendant dangled

between her breasts. I was fixated, not wanting to take my eyes off them. But I had to stop staring and force my mind somewhere else. I knew Ruth was extremely loyal to Daniels and would cut my balls off in a heartbeat if she got the chance. I'd never let this bitch know that I'd like to get into her pants, because if she did, she would use it against me when it came to me dealing with the Chief. I was too smart for that. The intercom finally sounded.

"Ruth, you can send them in."

"Yes, Chief." Ruth nodded to us, turning her head towards the door. I replied, "Thanks." As we walked into the office, the Chief was looking out of the window, seeming to be in deep thought. He turned to us and motioned for us to have a seat. We pulled the two mahogany armchairs located on opposite sides of his office to the front of his desk and took a seat. The décor of his office was a disaster. County government gave him a battleship gray metal desk and not much else. I didn't feel bad for him, as my desk was not much better. Besides a few filing cabinets, a 2-foot × 2-foot floor safe, a county flag, and the American flag, there was a picture of him posing in golf garb with two other guys that hung on the left wall facing his desk. There was not much more memorabilia in the office. The only thing new in the place was the wall-to-wall beige carpet. And I found it strange that he didn't have any personal photographs of his wife or three grown boys anywhere in the office. I guessed this gave me an insight into his relationship with his wife and kids. They probably disliked him too.

Howell sat there not saying a word. So I figured that I'd break the ice.

"Hey, Chief."

He sat back in his swivel chair looking directly at me, "Frank, the District Attorney and I have been discussing a new probe into organized crime and she'd like to target the Luccheses. We've been in touch with the White Plains FBI and they seem to think that a crew run by Michael Calise controls most of the criminal activity in Westchester and the Bronx. I think that you're the detective that can get to Calise."

Howell chimed in, "We've been giving this a lot of thought, Frank. You're Italian; you know these people."

"What d'ya mean, 'these people'?"

"Ah, Frank, you know what I mean. I think that you could pull it off because you're Italian."

"Hey, I'm not the only Italian in the squad."

Howell, raising his voice: "Frank, you're it!"

I had no choice. I was now officially assigned. And they were right about one thing: I've got the tools that you need to get in with these kinds of guys. I know what they eat, drink, say. I know what not to say and I was going to enjoy beating these guys at their own game.

"Look, Chief, it's gonna take some time to get in with these guys.
I just can't fall out of the sky and introduce myself."

"We know that, Frank. We'll give you a false identity, Social Security number, and date of birth. We'll give you all the money that you need. A car, an apartment, and you can set yourself up as a second-story man. We have an evidence room full of seized jewelry; it's yours. Pick out a good Guinea name for yourself."

My blood began to boil because he used the word "Guinea." It's a derogatory word for Italians. I wanted to grab the son of a bitch by his neck and kick the cock off him. But I couldn't; I just glared at him for a moment and took a deep breath.

"Hey, do you know you just slurred the Italians? Don't use the word 'Guinea' in front of me again!" Daniels just rocked back in his chair and smiled. "I have to figure out how I'm gonna tell my wife and I'll have to find a way to see her and the kids from time to time."

"Fine. I'll inform the District Attorney; you and the Deputy Chief can work out the details."

Chapter Two

My wife Helen and I lived in a red brick, two-family house in the country club section of the Bronx. We rented a five-room apartment on the first floor with the kids. The furniture wasn't fancy, but Helen saw to it that it was nicely decorated. At the time, Francesca was five and Catie was two and a half. I remember that night I tried to tell Helen of my new assignment. I was trying to muster up the courage to tell her all night, but for some reason I just couldn't. It was July and raining hard; lightning was illuminating our bedroom and Helen was just about to fall asleep.

Helen wasn't thrilled that I'd become a cop instead of a teacher. This put a huge strain on our marriage. When I got promoted to the detective division and assigned to the District Attorney's Office, I was never home. The assignments consumed all of my attention and, after a few years, my marriage was on the rocks. Helen didn't have her mom and dad nearby to fall back on; they lived in Ohio.

Helen was half asleep and just as I was about to shake her, a crash of thunder shook the house to its foundation. Catie started screaming in the next room. Helen, startled, her body now rigid, sat up in bed, and was about to run to Catie, but I was already in the girls' room, picking Catie up.

"Shh. It's okay, baby. Let's get Francesca." Her sister seemed undaunted by the racket that the storm made. Still half asleep, I picked her up with my free arm and whispered that they would sleep with Mommy and Daddy that night.

Francesca whispered, "Okay," as I carried them into our bedroom and into bed. Now was not the time to tell Helen. I'd tell her in the morning.

It was Sunday morning, the sun was out, and I was off work for the day. It was a great day to be alive except I had to tell Helen about the new assignment. That day we were planning to visit my mom and pop. They lived a half hour away in a red brick, one-family Cape in Harrison, New York. My mother, Inez, was making macaroni and meatballs and we were bringing a bottle of red wine and a loaf of Italian bread. We always got together as a family on Sundays and I was hoping that my brother Richie would be there with his wife Jane and three kids: five-year-old Gerry, four-year-old Tommy, and Joey, who was one. Helen and the kids were excited to go because my mother always made a fuss over them and my father always slipped them a few bucks. Spending time with my folks was a reason for our families coming together and as my mom would say in her Italian accent, "Family is most important; always stay close to your brother."

My father Frank was the disciplinarian all through our young lives, but I knew he loved us deeply. I felt that I had disappointed him by becoming a cop instead of a teacher. But I liked living on the edge, even as a teenager, which sometimes got me in trouble. I was always getting written up for something at school or on the hot seat at home for breaking one of my father's rules. He was a stickler about our curfew; we had to be in the house by midnight or else we got the strap. I guess he gave up on the strap when we reached our fourteenth birthdays. His methods were a little harsh but hey—in the long run it paid off, in my opinion.

My mother in her early sixties was still working at an Italian- American grocery store in Harrison. She was fluent in her native language, which helped her to help the immigrants who lived in the neighborhood. She was feisty and argumentative, spoke broken English, and at the same time was intelligent, dressed well, and carried her five-foot-two frame with dignity. She was the peacemaker in the house. She kept a balance between my father and her boys and negotiated most of his punishments.

My father was forced to retire as a bricklayer at sixty-four due to a bad heart, and from that point on was homebound. It was painful for him and for us to see him that way. He went from a strapping five-foot- nine man with straight posture to someone who was frail and bent over when he walked. His robust, rosy complexion turned gray, as did his hair.

Once strong enough to lift twelve-inch cinder blocks, he only had enough strength to sit in his leather easy chair and read the newspaper. It makes me sad to think about this, but I guess that's life.

On that Sunday, Helen was making breakfast—pancakes for the kids and eggs over light for me. Catie was sitting in her high chair and Francesca was seated in the chair across from me. Sipping my coffee, which I liked black so I could taste the coffee beans, I felt that now was as good a time as any to tell Helen about my new adventure.

"Helen, it looks like I gotta new assignment."

"What new assignment, Frankie?"

"Well, the other day I got called into the Chief's office and was assigned to try to infiltrate a certain criminal group. It looks like it's gonna take some time and I'm gonna be away from home a lot."

Helen froze for a minute and then threw the spatula down into the frying pan, screaming, "No! No, you can't! Frank we can't survive this; the kids can't survive this!" She began to cry, running out of the kitchen and into the bedroom.

Francesca and Catie then began to cry. Catie held her arms out and motioned for me to take her out of her high chair, hysterically crying. Francesca ran into the bedroom with her mother. I picked up Catie and briskly walked into the hallway that led to our bedroom. I stood in the doorway, holding Catie.

"Helen, please calm down. I have no choice. I have to."

Helen sobbed. "You have a choice, Frank. You've chosen your job over us, damn you! And I'm not going to your mother's! I think you should leave! Get out of the house!"

"What do you mean get out of the house?"

Gasping for air as she tried to speak, a river of tears flowed down her face. Helen yelled, "Frank, you and I are not gonna make it, get out!" Catie and Francesca were crying uncontrollably, not knowing what really was going on. They looked bewildered. Francesca was wrapped around her mother's legs, tugging so hard that Helen almost fell to her knees.

"For Christ's sake, Helen, it's my job! What do you want from me?"

Helen wailed, "I want you to be a husband and a father, not a fucking cop!"

I was overwhelmed with the anguish on Helen's face. "I'm sorry, Helen. I'll get some clothes together and stay with my mother for a few days." I put Catie down, grabbed an overnight bag from the hallway closet, packed a few things, and walked out. Little did I know that I would never return.

Driving up to Harrison, I think I was in a fog. I just couldn't believe what had just happened. I knew that Helen and I were having problems, but I didn't think that it was this bad. We'd been married for seven years. I didn't think that it would ever come to this. I was hoping that Helen would calm down and understand what my job and I were all about. Ringing the doorbell, my mother answered the door dressed in her housecoat. As she opened the door and looked down at the overnight bag, not seeing Helen and the kids, I think she knew what was going on.

"Where's Helen and the kids?"

"Helen threw me out."

I'll never forget what she said to me.

"Frankie, I have two sons; one is the good one and one is the bad one. Guess which one you are?"

"Ma, I need a place to stay for a few days. Can I come in?" She just stared at me. "It's just for a couple of days, Ma."

"Frankie, you know your father's sick; what will he say?"

"Nothing, he'll just be disappointed in me as usual."

In Italian, "*Vieni a casa*, Frankie."

Walking into my old bedroom, looking around, I thought, *I'm right back where I fucking started from.*

Chapter Three

It took me six months, but I found the weak link into Calise's crew. After moving into my Hughes Avenue apartment in the Fordham section of the Bronx, I began to hang around in the South Yonkers, New York neighborhood where Calise's social club was located. I'd met Freddy Spina, a.k.a. Far Away, while enjoying a hot dog at a stand at the end of Parkhill Avenue. Freddy was a numbers runner who was always looking for new customers. The guy was right out of *The Godfather*. He wore a fedora hat, stood five six, weighed about 175 pounds with an olive complexion, dressed in slacks and a sports shirt, with sixty-plus years of wise guy experience. Freddy wanted to know who I was and where I came from, since he hadn't seen me in the neighborhood. I told him my name was Frankie Miranda and that I had just come up from Florida.

"So where you living?"

"I'm living in the Bronx."

"And how do you make ends meet?"

"I do a little bit of this and a little bit of that."

"And what's a little bit of this and a little bit of that?"

I stuck my hand into my pants pocket, pulled out a fourteen karat gold Gucci lady's bracelet, and handed it to him.

"Do you know anybody who's looking for one?"

"I'll ask around; how much you want?"

"It's worth about $6,000 retail, but I'll take twelve hundred."

"I'll look around."

What I've found is that money blinds most people, especially wise guys. Now Freddy wasn't a made guy; that is, he wasn't formally inducted into the Mafia, but he was an associate of Michael Calise and a big earner for Calise in the numbers racket. Freddy was my way into Calise and his crew.

If you don't know the numbers racket, it's an illegal lottery run by the mob with some of the profits invested into the purchase of narcotics, criminal usury (which is sometimes referred to as loan sharking), political corruption, and infiltration of legitimate businesses.

At the time, there were two illegal numbers drawn every day. One was the New York daily number, which was derived from the monies or handles bet at Roosevelt Raceway. It was calculated in three steps, first by adding the total monies bet on the first three races, and then moving the decimal point that separates dollars and cents to the left. This number became the first number. For example, if $324,179.89 were bet on the first three races, the first number to the left of the decimal point is "9," so "9" became the first number. The second number was calculated by adding all monies bet on the fourth and fifth races, then adding that figure to the handle of the first three races. So if $204,567.00 was bet on the fourth and fifth races, adding $324,179.89 plus $204,567.00 gives you $528,746.89. Therefore the second number would be "6." The third number was obtained from the total monies bet on the sixth and seventh races, adding it to the totals bet on all previous races, and then taking the last number to the left of the decimal point. So if $415,865.63 was bet on the sixth and seventh races, this amount is added to the total monies bet on all the previous races, and again, the third number would be the digit to the left of the decimal point. Therefore $324,179.89 plus $204,567.00 plus $415,865.63 equals $944,615.52. The third number would be therefore be "0," and the New York number for the day would be 962.

Bettors didn't have to pay New York state taxes on their winnings, and their payout was six hundred to one.

Now the Brooklyn daily number was simpler to calculate, and was taken from Aqueduct Racetrack. This number came from the total monies bet at all nine races. If for example, the handle was $1,000,500.75, the number was derived from moving the decimal point one place to the left of the handle. Therefore the Brooklyn number for that day would be 075.

Bettors could also make combination bets on any number that they decided to bet on. For example, bettors could place a combination bet on the number 357. It's called a three-way number. They bet the number in combination and indicated the particular track. The runner then wrote down the letter C in front of the number, indicating that it was a combination bet. So, for example, if 537 comes out (with the "3" and "5" transposed from the original bet of 357) then the payout for the bettor would drop to thirty to one.

One could also place a bet on the first or second number, which was referred to as making a front or back "bolita" bet, but the payout was only ten to one. People love to play the numbers, sometimes referred as Pari-Mutuel Racehorse Policy because there is action throughout the nine races. Little did I know that I would become one of Calise's biggest earners in the policy business, but before I was accepted into the life, I was tested on a daily basis for almost a year.

My apartment was broken into to see if I was who I said I was. My phone records were checked to see who I called and Mickey also had some dirty cop check me out to see if Frank Miranda really existed. We later found out that this shitbag of a cop, who was later arrested, ran a criminal history and motor vehicle check to see if I had an arrest record, and who the car I was driving was registered to. At one point Calise's right-hand man, Nick Galgano, a soldier, handed me a few thousand dollars, telling me to take the money and to leave them the fuck alone.

"Frankie, we know that you're a cop."

My knees buckled as I made a grab for the money and turned to walk away. Nick grabbed my arm, pulling me towards him and knocking me off balance. He grabbed the

13

money from my hand and barked, "Frankie, we just wanted to make sure. You know we gotta be careful. The circle that you're traveling in now is exclusive. Remember, every other guy works for the FBI."

Chapter Four

Mickey Calise and Nick Galgano were sipping drinks in the back room of Calise's social club on Maple Avenue as Freddy and I walked in one late afternoon. They were sitting where Mickey always sat, around a small, white, kitchen-type table with four chrome framed chairs with yellow vinyl seat covers. I'd been in with Mickey and his crew for almost two years at that point and it was a tough two years. My marriage was over and my ex did everything she could to keep the kids away from me. Helen told my girls that I was no good and just like the criminals that I locked up. It broke my heart.

Calise and Galgano were discussing Sami Hassan's obsession with an Italian card game called Ziginette. They were scheming on how to get Sami to pay back the hundred large he owed them and laughing that they had him in their back pocket. Mickey's reputation preceded him by those who had crossed him. God forbid you were late on an interest payment, or he found out that you were cooperating with the cops— he'd put you in the hospital or he'd see to it that you were never seen again.

Mickey, in his late fifties, a big brut of a guy, weighed in at around 250 pounds, and stood about five foot seven. He worked out regularly to keep fit so he could tune you up when he had to. Mickey loved expensive apparel, wearing designer suits and sport clothes. His salt-and- pepper hair gave him a rather distinguished look, if you could disregard his ice-cold facial expression, which sent a shiver up your ass when he looked at you with his piercing black eyes.

Nick Galgano, on the other hand, loved Mickey and was loyal to a fault. Nick served as Mickey's eyes and ears on the street and was good at reeling in the suckers like Sami Hassan. Galgano stood six foot four and 230 pounds. He enforced all of Mickey's rules and God help the poor bastard who broke them. Nick loved to hurt people. He'd rather tear

15

your arm off and beat you to death with it than make love to a woman. Nick was a classic psychopath. In his early fifties, Nick was completely gray, keeping his hair length to an army-style flattop, which accented his creased face and dark blue eyes. His name on the street was Nicky Blue Eyes. All of the guys have nicknames. I was called Frankie Cheech. Cheech is slang for Frank in Italian.

Although the feds had never been able to prove it, Mickey was involved in a number of illegitimate enterprises: drug trafficking, cargo hijacking, extortion, sports betting, loan sharking, murder, and as I described, the numbers racket. The club offered Mickey and his crew a private place to discuss their illegal business activities. It was nothing more than a two-story, red brick building that blended into an urban residential neighborhood. Mickey turned the interior into the ultimate men's lounge. As soon as you walked in you entered the main gathering room. The fully stocked bar was on the left, with leather barstools and a large espresso maker on the far left of the bar. Hugging the right wall of the room was a buttery leather, brown, three-seater couch. In the middle of the room stood a large felt poker table. The red velveteen wallpaper and the soft beige acoustic tile muted the activities of the guys who hung around the club playing cards or the occasional craps game. Plush, forest green carpeting accented the floors throughout, including the back room, where Mickey held court. There was also a roulette wheel and a Murphy bed for Mickey or Nick's *gumar*. *Gumar* means girlfriend in Italian. All the married guys had gumars, and their wives knew it, but couldn't say anything. Mickey usually sat at the small, circular kitchen table in the back room. The table was next to a door that led to a hallway connecting two apartments upstairs.

As I said, Mickey spotted me and Freddy walk in and waved me over. He asked me to sit down. He said that Sami Hassan was coming in to give him a tale of woe about not paying his vig this week. Vig is slang for interest on money owed. On the street it's called vigorish interest. Sami was a degenerate gambler who'd lost thousands playing Ziginette, a high-stakes Italian card game played at the club on Sunday nights from midnight to 7 a.m. Three hundred dollars bought you a seat at the table, and it was not unusual for each hand to tally into the thousands. Similar to Punto Banco, or Baccarat, Ziginette is played with three decks of cardsdispensed from a shoe, nine cards per hand, one for each player, face up on the table. Bets are placed on the cards and then after the bets close the dealer draws another card from the shoe. The drawn card has to match one of the cards on the table for the bettor to win; otherwise the house takes the original bet. The winners win double their money, but at Mickey's the house never lost, as it got five percent of the original pot bet. The deal could pass from one player to another only if a player could bank the game, usually to a sum of $500. The advantage of being the bank was that the player who held it could bet on his own card or against the house on the chance of the next dispersed card not matching his. Players without a seat could bet from behind the table, and the minimum bet normally was $10 or more. Those standing still had to buy a seat when and if a seated player went bust.

Hassan imported oriental rugs from the Middle East, retailing them to a steady stream of customers from the New York metropolitan area. His store was on the corner of Nepperhan and Yonkers avenues in a small storefront. Besides the rugs, there wasn't much else in the store aside from a desk and a few chairs.

I could see that Nick and Mickey had something up their sleeves for Sami. They were salivating waiting for him to arrive. Mickey told me that Sami would arrive in a few minutes and wanted me to sit in on their meeting and learn.

Sami had issues and everyone but him seemed to know. Or I guess that like a lot of people, if he did know about his issues, he didn't want to admit to them. His compulsion to gamble had driven him to the brink of bankruptcy. His tall, slender appearance, handsome features, and exotic Jordanian accent with deep brown eyes and dark black, wavy hair charmed many well-heeled women into bed using the excuse of measuring their living rooms for a new oriental rug while their husbands were at work. I guess he thought that the rug business was not enough to support several simultaneous affairs, so he played Ziginette, hoping for the big score, neglecting his wife and three small children at home.

Because of the feds' numerous past investigations into Calise's operations, Mickey figured that he was always under surveillance and that the club might be bugged, so when he discussed business he always would turn the volume up on the radio so that his conversations could not be understood or overheard. One thing he didn't count on was me.

Two years into my investigation, the NYPD, the DEA, and the detectives from the Westchester County District Attorney's Office gained access to the club by posing as Consolidated Edison workers operating in a manhole up the street from the club. Borrowing equipment from New York State Department of Environmental Conservation, the Task Force tunneled into the club's basement, setting up high-tech, amplified microphones through the cement foundation all the way up to the interior drywall. They then picked the lock on the front door to gain access to the club, installing additional listening devices in the electrical outlets. Of course this was all done by court order, with me being the instrument for the probable cause to do so. This was the beginning of the end for Mickey and his crew.

As we waited for Sami to arrive, Mickey and Nick ordered rye on the rocks from the bar. I ordered a Campari and soda with a twist of lemon. Peter Franco, the bartender, brought the drinks over, setting them down on the table along with a supply of fresh mixed nuts, cocktail napkins, and a small bucket of ice. Mickey gave a slight nod to Peter and a wink of approval. Franco, in his late fifties, balding, gray on the sides, was small in stature, only five foot two, thin build, and maybe 140 pounds. Peter had saved Mickey's life in a Mafia war in the early seventies by taking a bullet in the right lung. He saw the guy coming at Mickey, gun in hand, and knocked Mickey out of the way during an ambush on a side street near LaGuardia Airport. In return, Mickey looked after Peter and his family. He kept Peter out of the rackets, even sending his kids to private school and college.

At five o'clock Sami walked into the club and was escorted into the back room by Peter Franco. I noticed that Sami was fixated on the poker game that was going on and he nodded to some of the neighborhood guys as he walked past the game and into the back room. We finished sipping double espressos laced with sambuca as hands were shaken and Mickey motioned to Sami to have a seat.

Galgano got up and closed the door to the back room; that indicated to everyone in the club that Mickey was holding court. The pendulum-style electric light hanging over the table illuminated the room with a feeling of isolation for those unfortunate enough to be in Sami's predicament.

Knowing very well what brought Sami to the club, Mickey said, "So, Sami, how's the family? How's the kids?" Sami said that they were all fine but that he was in financial trouble.

Calise snarled, "So what do you want from me?"

"I need a loan to get back on my feet. I'm broke. I owe you over $100,000 and I'm really desperate. Just need a tide-over to get me through to pay the rent. I got no money for food for the family, even. I need some help."

Mickey threw his head back and laughed. "Hear this guy, Nick? Sami needs a loan."

Nick laughed. I just listened to the conversation intensely. Nick chuckled, "Yeah, he must think you got barrels of money in the basement."

Sami pleaded. I saw the sweat running down the sides of his face into his collared shirt. "Please, Mickey, I got no one else to turn to. Without a loan, it's over. I'm fucked, my family, my business, my life." Sami's eyes filled up, tears coursing down his cheeks, his face beet-red, flamed by his humiliation. Finally he hung his head, sobbing.

Calise, realizing he had Sami by the balls, zeroed in for the coup de grâce. I'd seen Mickey in action before, but what was to follow really put the finishing touches on the investigation. I hoped that the bugs were getting it all.

"Sami. Hey, Sami." Mickey stood, reached over and gave him a slap on the side of his head. Sami jerked upright in his seat, forced attention replacing his self pity. "You know you got a fuckin' problem, right? You know it got you in this deep shit with no one to blame but you. So if I give you a loan, how you gonna pay it back? I'll tell you up front, pal, you can't. There's no way in hell you can pay back a loan plus the vig you owe. Let's be straight with each other for once. You admit to what I'm sayin' here, and maybe, just maybe, we can all figure something out. Any relationship begins with honesty, something you been lackin' lately. So, let's get off to a new start, beginning with you admittin' ya fucked up. *Capisce?*"

Sami, realizing that his bullshit wouldn't fly anymore, for the first
time probably in his life looked directly into Mickey's eyes, contritely. "You're right, I'm so deep in debt, I can't pay you back."

"Well, now, that's better, my friend," purred Calise. He stood up, came around the table, and put his hand firmly on Sami's shoulder. "I think I got a solution to your money problems. I been giving it a lot of thought. You interested?"

Sami's eyes widened, hope beginning to replace self-pity. "Yes, Mickey, I am."

Calise, speaking softly, divulged that he and his associates had a contact in Damascus capable of smuggling high-quality heroin from Afghanistan to Syria. What Calise needed was for someone like Sami to recruit other Arabs to mule the almost-pure heroin in from Syria to New York. Once the product arrived in New York, Calise said his crew would take it from there.

The initial cost would be two to three thousand a kilo, but he could wholesale it out at two hundred and fifty thousand per key.

Galgano piped up laughingly to Sami. "Can you believe the fucking money with this shit? You'll have more money than you can spend, Sami."

I jumped in. "It's perfect, Sami. Since you're already in the rug business, you can travel back and forth to the Middle East without raising eyebrows. The feds will never suspect you. You can build a network of couriers and continue to grow your rug business."

Mickey chimed in. "What's to lose? Everything to gain."

Sami, with excitement in his voice, nodded. "When can I get started?"

Mickey knew he had him then. He hadn't discussed Sami's cut, much less any of the other details. This was the part he liked best, when he broke his victim's cherry, bending them to his will.

"Your end is ten grand for each key you bring in. We use a middleman to pay the couriers, so the ten grand you get is free and clear. The ragheads grow this shit for chump change over there, so no one gets stiffed here, and we help the farmers over there make a living. Hey, we're the ultimate entrepreneur, ya know?" We all had a good laugh. Mickey gruffly asked, "So Sami, we got a deal?"

Sami nodded his head yes.

Mickey and kissed him on both cheeks, surprising Sami, who wasn't suspecting this apparent display of affection. Little did Sami know he had just received the kiss of death if anything went wrong.

Nick suddenly took Sami by the bicep, his grip hard, his

fingers digging into the soft underarm tissue, making Sami wince. "No fuckup, understood? The feds ain't stupid and no one wants to spend the rest of their lives in the joint, especially me. So no loose ends, no fuckups, ya got it?"

"Got it. No bullshit. I already know the right people to contact." "Great," said Mickey, slapping Sami on the back. "Just remember, never let your right hand know what your left hand is doing."

"No problem, Mickey. You can depend on me."

Mickey walked back to his seat. "I want you to leave for Damascus in two weeks. We'll take care of the airfare. You'll meet Nadir Soufanieh when you land. He's a friend of ours and will be running things for us on our end over there. He'll be holding a chauffeur's nameplate with your name on the cardboard."

Nick, sitting quietly across the table, took an envelope from his jacket pocket and threw it on the table in front of Sami. Sami retrieved and opened it; his eyes widened as he thumbed through $10,000. Mickey and Nick looked with anticipation at their freshly caught fish while I sat there knowing that this was one more nail in their coffins. I knew my investigation was nearing an end.

Mickey, setting his hook as deep as it could go, said, "It's an advance. Put it in your pocket, have some fun." Nick then buzzed the bar. Peter came in and took an order for two bourbons and water, one for Nick and the other for Mickey. Sami ordered a glass of Taylor's Champagne and I ordered a Dewar's White Label, straight up. Thusly, an unholy marriage was born between the Lucchese crime family and the opium producers of Afghanistan. Little did Mickey know that this alliance would be short-lived because of my work and the work of the task force of local police and federal agents.

Chapter Five

My time was growing short in this double life I was living and most nights I had trouble sleeping. I'd lay awake, alone with my thoughts, in this dump of a one-bedroom apartment I'd rented in the North Bronx. I often worried what was next after this assignment. What would I be doing? Would I be able to adjust back into the squad? Could I patch up my relationship with Helen and the kids? There was my mom, dad, and brother Richie. I hadn't seen them for any length of time in years and I needed to reconcile with them. Would they understand? But how could they really understand what it's like to lead a double life, not knowing who the good guys are and who the bad guys are supposed to be?

There are only a few cops like me who've infiltrated the mob. To describe my life back then is to describe a life with no schedules and no regular reporting system. I was only responsible to myself, living by my wits with no backup, an island unto myself. I ended up trusting no one, sometimes even the people in my own department, not necessarily because they wanted to hurt me, but because their priorities were not mine. It would be too easy for one of them to slip up inadvertently, putting either me or the operation at risk. So the only real thought I had was to survive and succeed.

I'd been self-medicating for a while and hated the after effects. The up-front buzz wasn't worth the price to get to sleep. I was haunted by the same thoughts every night. Where did my sense of family go? What happened to everything my dad said about my family being the most important possession in life? What about losing Helen and the kids? Would I be able to live without them? I loved my job but hated it at the same time. I felt that it was killing me emotionally.

One night, after drinking a half bottle of Scotch to get to sleep, I was awakened by Nick Galgano at 2:15 a.m. Half asleep, I picked up the phone. "Hello."

"Cheech, this is Nick. Mickey wants to see you at the club in a half hour."

"What about?"

"You'll find out when you get there." The phone then went dead. Dazed, clumsily reaching to find the switch of my nightstand lamp,

I turned it on and sat up, transfixed on what I should do. I became anxious and apprehensive about why Mickey wanted to see me at that hour. It didn't make sense. For a moment my mind raced, wondering if somehow Mickey had discovered that I was a cop. If I wanted to preserve the integrity of the case, I had to meet with Mickey; there was no way out of it. I thought, *Should I call for backup?* But I knew that if I called, the office would be obligated to send a few carloads of detectives to cover their ass. I knew that Mickey would have people on the street looking for any strange cars that didn't belong in the neighborhood, especially at this hour in the morning. My backup would be spotted and Mickey would know that someone tipped the cops off about the meet and that the someone was most likely me. Besides, what good would backup do me while I was in the club and they were out on the street, sitting in unmarked police cars? If I did call, at the very least Helen and the kids would know what happened to me. Either way, unless this meeting was mundane, which I doubted, I had no choice but to go it alone and pray that I wasn't going to be hurt or killed. I got dressed quickly and left.

It was a little after 3 a.m. when I pulled into the municipal parking lot that was down the street from the club. Nick Galgano had already pulled in and was getting out of his car. As I got out of my car, I remember stepping on a broken beer bottle, which I heard pop under my foot, crushing into the pavement. A mild June breeze blew through the leaves on the few trees that were left in the neighborhood. All my senses were on high alert. Nick, smoking a cigar, walked over to me as I locked my car. I had to calm down and relax or Nick and whoever else was in the club besides Mickey would know that something was wrong with me and I wasn't my confident self.

I asked again, "Nick, so why does Mickey want to see me at 3 a.m.? "Cheech, Mickey wants to talk to you himself."

It was a fifty-foot walk to the club and I hoped that Nick didn't see my knees shaking with every step. As we walked past the tenements that lined the street, the stench of the garage emanating from the trash cans in the alley filled my nose. In that moment, I hoped that I wouldn't end up in one of those cans. If Mickey planned to kill me, there probably would be someone waiting to greet me at the door and as soon as I entered, I would be shot in the head.

As I reached the front door, Nick was behind me. The club was dimly lit, as I could see through the translucent windowpane in the door. Opening the door, I took a deep breath and walked in. Mickey and the crew were standing at the bar, Peter Franco pouring drinks. Well, I wasn't dead yet. I walked over to the bar and some of the guys greeted me with a handshake. What a relief so far. Mickey then walked to the middle of the room.

"You guys are wondering why I called you in. Well, what I have to discuss, I want to discuss as a group. Today, Eddie Campone was locked up at his numbers spot and I feel that he and the spot were given up by a rat. The reason you're here is that I trust all of you guys and I want you to keep your eyes and ears open. We need to find out who the rat is and deal with him. Understand?"

We all nodded yes. So, in retrospect, I'd made the right decision about coming that night. But at what cost?

Chapter Six

I remember sitting one morning on the edge of my bed, under the slow-turning ceiling fan, a ball of dust splattered on the bedsheet, having disengaged itself from the top of the fan blades. The last time the fan had been cleaned was before I'd moved in, a few years earlier at this point. The wastebaskets in the living room and kitchen were overflowing with empty beer cans and liquor bottles. All the ashtrays were full of burnt butts, left by the degenerates who on occasion visited me. Dirty pans on the stove and dirty dishes on the kitchen table were scattered alongside empty pizza boxes. Mickey told me a few times to clean the apartment up. He wouldn't set foot in the place anymore.

Laughing to myself, I thought how I'd be locking Mickey up soon. What did I care what he thought? But I knew that for my own sanity, I had to get a grip on myself and move on from this lifestyle that was ruining me. The first thing I needed to do to preserve my mind was hire a cleaning service and get the dump cleaned up. Then I needed to stop feeling sorry for myself. I had to remember why I chose this life.

I think what kept me going and wanting to continue to do the kind of police work I did were the ethical values my father instilled in me. He set an example, always trying to do the right thing no matter how tough it was or what the consequences were. He always said, "When all is said and done you need to feel right about yourself and remember that nothing is worse than compromising what you know is the right thing to do."

My father taught me that if one stands up for what's correct then there would be no regrets in life. But I was old enough and world-wise enough to know that sometimes the hard road of life got in the way of pure and noble precepts. It was a hard lesson to learn, but I just had to stay true to myself and do what I knew to be right.

Running one of Mickey's numbers operations gave me a

sense of accomplishment. I know it's hard to understand, but as I said, I loved beating these guys at their own game. I loved being out there on my own and, for the most part, having no one to answer to. Maybe this was why my personal life was so fucked up? Maybe this was why my marriage was doomed from the start? I really don't know.

Every couple of weeks I'd meet a detective at a prearranged location and hand him a scribbled report written on a lined piece of paper. I was making a lot of money for Mickey as a big earner and that gave me the respect and power I craved. Unfortunately for me this came from him and the guys, not my wife, kids, or family.

My numbers operation was run out of a storefront on 153rd Street and Third Avenue in the South Bronx. It fronted as a fruit and vegetable store and my office was in the back room. People from in and around the neighborhood would bet with me every day. I got to know my customers well and some became friends. It was going to hurt when they found out that Frank Miranda was a cop.

After the day's bets were in, I'd telephone Sal Pastier with the day's receipts. Sal ran the numbers bank for Mickey and tabulated the bets from all of Mickey's runners.

Sal would know who won by 4 p.m. and the winners would be paid the next day. My business was grossing $10,000 a week and growing. Thirty percent of every bet I took belonged to me. Seventy percent went to Mickey. Mickey loved me because he loved money and I was money. Money was Mickey's god and, as the saying goes, money makes the world go round.

The next several months proved that Sami Hassan was true to his word in at least one sense. He was able to establish a sophisticated heroin importation route from Syria to New York. It turned out that Nadir Soufanieh was able to put his hands on plenty of high-quality heroin for distribution, muled by a handful of trusted Jordanians from Damascus to Amman. From there, it was delivered by two sky marshals who worked for Alia, the Royal Jordanian Airlines. The marshals would tape two to four kilos to their bodies, under their clothes, three times a week. Upon landing at Kennedy Airport, they were able to walk past Customs without being checked, as their clearances were supposed to have been previously vetted by the airlines. Each flight netted Calise between four and eight kilos of pure heroin. The sky marshals were picked up at the airport by Sami or someone sent by Sami, and driven to the Holiday Inn on Queens Boulevard in Jamaica, Queens, where they checked in, engaging in an immediate weight-loss program, turning over the drugs to Mickey's people.

Unbeknownst to Sami or the other guys, the information provided over the bugs had established enough probable cause for a federal judge to authorize eavesdropping surveillance on Sami's home and business phones. By now, twenty additional detectives from the NYPD and the Westchester DA's squad and another fifteen DEA agents were involved in the expanded investigation, now named Operation Black Widow. The investigation was headed up by Assistant United States Attorney (AUSA) John Kenny, who oversaw the investigation from his office in Foley Square, near One Police Plaza in southern Manhattan. This investigation had now gone global, with implications far beyond the penetration of an organized crime family. At this point, it had evolved into a story of the international heroin trade funneling money into the various terrorist groups in the Middle East.

As the case progressed, and with the U.S. government being sensitive to any purported disgrace that could be embarrassing to the Jordanian government, the United States Attorney's Office at the highest levels sought out the U.S. Department of State. They conferred with the Jordan's royal family about the crimes being committed by two of its employees on Jordanian and U.S. soil. The Jordanian government proceeded to give the nod for the investigation to continue.

Mickey wholesaled the kilos at $250,000 per kilo and at eight kilos a week was racking up approximately $8 million per month. It wasn't long until Sami Hassan considered himself to be one of the main beneficiaries of the heroin trade.

As I found out later, the feds had dropped the ball, letting a side deal of Sami's slip through the cracks. Sami was partying at nightclubs every night and bedding down a different lady on a nightly basis. He had been skimming a kilo every once in a while from the shipments and selling to Yousef Nebor, an Egyptian national who owned Petra's, a popular Arabic nightclub on 34th Street and Tenth Avenue.

Sami frequented the club and had become friends with Nebor, eventually finding out that they were in the same side business. They

soon had their own heroin operation in full swing. I always wondered why Mickey didn't pay more attention to the shipments coming in. I guess he was making so much money that he got blinded by greed and felt that fear and intimidation were enough to keep Sami in tow.

So after two and a half years of endless surveillance, wiretaps, and bugs, AUSA John Kenny, Westchester County DA Annette Larson, the director of the DEA, and James Moore, commissioner of the NYPD, decided they had enough evidence to shut down Operation Black Widow. Kenny had been working with a federal grand jury for months and sealed indictments were about to be handed up. Search and arrests warrants were almost ready to be executed.

Chapter Seven

New York metro area traffic was a nightmare. I later learned that the Van Wyck Expressway was at a standstill. Construction reduced traffic to a single lane outbound, and a three-car pileup inbound, two miles from the Grand Central Parkway, held up the caravan of DEA agents and NYPD cops that were on their way to execute arrest and search warrants.

Supervising Agent Pat Donnelly, a red-faced Irishman, six foot two, about 235 pounds, thinning blond hair combed over to one side, and looking older than his forty-five years, was swearing under his breath with a carload of agents, who made their way to Mike Baraka's apartment in South Yonkers, New York. Special Agent Donnelly radioed the DEA group at Kennedy Airport, learning that the flight from Jordan was late due to problems on takeoff from Jordan.

An accident on the off-ramp of the George Washington Bridge had traffic backed up on the Major Deegan Expressway from the Triboro Bridge to the Yonkers border. The driver of the white van carrying another compliment of NYPD officers and DEA agents was told to take the breakdown lane to 233rd Street, where they'd get off and take the side streets to Mickey's club.

I knew what was coming down in a few minutes and couldn't take my eyes off the clock in the club. The shit was supposed to hit the fan at 6 p.m. None of the enforcement officers knew that there was an undercover in the club and the plan was to release those of us that didn't have an arrest warrant or weren't named in the indictment.

I hoped that there would be no fuckups, especially when it came to protecting my undercover status. To the enforcement guys, this was just another bust; but for me, if this got fucked up my usefulness as an undercover cop would be blown for good. For all I knew, I might be back in the bag again shaking storefront doors on the midnight-to-eight tour. While Freddy was watching the poker game, I couldn't help but concentrate on the wall clock. I knew that it was just a matter of time before all hell was about to break loose.

Agent Donnelly's two carloads of agents, NYPD detectives, and detectives from the DA's squad pulled up in front of 153 Landau Street, home of Sami Hassan and Mike Baraka. Baraka and Hassan didn't know it yet, but they were about to be swept up and arrested for heroin trafficking involving the Lucchese crime family.

Baraka, age twenty-six, worked as a bouncer at Club Zazu, a nightclub in the Bronx. He lived at home with his parents, who happened to own the building in South Yonkers and the building adjacent to it. His sister Delia was married to Sami and they lived in a large apartment across the hall from Baraka.

On a few occasions, the feds had seen Sami out in front of his apartment stuffing money into Mike's shirt pocket after a night of carousing. I learned later that Mike had tried to get Sami to be more careful in his behavior, knowing full well that they could be under some type of surveillance by the police. Mike told me later that he smelled the cops around the neighborhood. But not Sami—he was too caught up in the life to pay much attention to detail.

At one point the agents had even watched a late-night shoving match between the two in front of their building. Then, making up, Sami stuffed more money into Mike's hand. Pictures were snapped of the incident, with Mike walking into the building and Sami following. Mike later said that he'd considered giving Sami the money back, but money was money.

My office later informed me that the takedown at Kennedy Airport went without a hitch. Muffett Kadar and Hanni Saige, the two Jordanian sky marshals, were taken into custody while skirting Customs in the baggage claim area. Ten heavily armed DEA agents ordered the sky marshals to the ground. The marshals immediately dropped to the floor as pandemonium broke out amongst a group of onlookers. Kadar and Saige were then handcuffed and read their rights.

At the same time, in Amman, Jordan, the police arrested Nadir Soufanieh and the other traffickers. Our government tried to have them extradited to the United States but the Jordanians wouldn't hear of it. They were subsequently tried and convicted, then hung publicly from a scaffold in a public square in front of an old Roman amphitheater. It was reported that their bodies were left dangling there with a sign on the scaffold crossbeam stating "Heroin Dealers" in large block letters for two days as a lesson to those who might want to follow the same path.

The front door at the club flew off its hinges with a loud bang at 6:10 p.m. I know the exact time; I was looking at the fucking clock. Running in yelling "Police!" were NYPD's Tactical, a swarm of DA detectives, and several DEA agents.

Calise and Galgano made a bolt for the back door, hoping to escape, but the door had been flattened by a battering ram and a team of cops and agents had already stormed into the room. More agents ran up the stairs in the hallway behind the club to secure the apartments above. We were all told to keep our hands where they could be seen and to remain where we were. I remember pistols and pump-action shotguns being shoved into our faces. Jacob, Freddy, and I, along with the other ten or so people in the club, were told to lean against the bar with our hands stretched out on the countertop. Mickey and Nick were brought into the front of the club and handcuffed while the rest of us were asked to show our driver's licenses.

After they took our names and addresses they told us to leave the premises. Mickey and Nick were searched and later walked out to a waiting van where they were shackled around the ankles to chains welded to the inside of the van. Freddy was let go so that I could maintain my cover.

While all of that was going on, warrants were being executed at Baraka's building. What I'm about to tell you was told to me by Baraka. When Hassan's door flew off its hinges from the force of the guys wielding the battering ram, he was sitting in the living room talking to Delia. Delia and Sami shot up from the couch in shock, expressions of fear and panic imprinted on their faces. Their children came running from one of the bedrooms grabbing onto their mother. Sami yelled, "What's going on?" as handcuffs were placed on his wrists and he was read his Miranda Rights. He subsequently submitted to his arrest. Delia, on the other hand, had to be calmed down by one of the detectives before she could stop shaking and hyperventilating.

Delia didn't look the way most people would think an Arabic woman should look. She didn't have dark hair or olive skin. She was small in stature, with green eyes and stood five foot two, approximately 120 pounds, with reddish blond hair and a light complexion. Looking at her, one would think that she was English or of Irish decent. She was a pretty woman and seemed to be devoted to her family. Sami really fucked everything up for her.

There was a problem. It seemed that the wrong apartment, one across the hall, had been targeted for Baraka. A Chinese immigrant named Min Chen was flattened under his steel apartment door attempting to stop what he thought was a home invasion. He couldn't stop the door from giving way to ten agents who stormed through the doorway in total disregard of the half-naked man. Chen's nose was crushed and blood streamed out onto the floor. He lost consciousness as Quai Chen, his wife, cowered, screaming, in the corner of the living room, holding her five-month-old daughter. The baby began to wail uncontrollably, its nurturing surroundings shattered by the mayhem caused by the agents dressed in their black assault fatigues as they mistakenly secured the wrong apartment.

I often wonder if a kid that young would ever remember such an incident. It was traumatic for her parents to say the least, but I hoped that because she was only a few months old, she wouldn't have any memory of her family's nightmare.

Months later, the Chen family eventually won a $3 million lawsuit against all law enforcement agencies involved in the tactical operation. I found out that the two agents whose job it was to ensure they had the right apartment for the execution of the warrants were brought up on departmental charges and lost two weeks' pay.

While hell visited the Chens, Supervising Special Agent Pat Donnelly walked up the landing huffing and puffing to the Chens' apartment. Immediately seeing that a potential career-ending blunder had taken place due to poor police work, he yelled over his radio for an ambulance while the door next to the Chens' apartment opened. The head of Mike Baraka peeked out and was told to reinsert itself into the apartment and not to interfere in police business. More bedlam ensued once the ambulance arrived and Baraka's door once again opened. This time he came out into the hallway, asking what the hell was going on. Two detectives ordered him back inside, telling him that this was a police action and that a fugitive was being sought. Baraka asked who they were looking for and one of the cops said, "Mike Baraka."

"I'm Mike Baraka! Why are you looking for me?" I later learned from Mike that the detectives had looked at each other, dumbstruck, before grabbing him by the arms and throwing him against the hallway wall. They handcuffed him and then dragged him into his apartment. The detectives sat Mike down at the kitchen table and began pressuring him to tell them where he had hidden the heroin.

All the while, Baraka repeatedly shouted that he'd done nothing wrong and there were no drugs in the house. Sami's door was open; Delia was on the couch holding a handkerchief to her face, wiping away the tears. Quai Chen was yelling at the top of her lungs in Chinese at the agents as emergency medical people were trying to stop the blood from pouring out of her husband's nose. Police radios were turned to the maximum so responders could at least make an attempt to hear their own voices, and the Chen baby, red-faced, was sobbing, propped up by pillows on the Chens' living room couch.

Pat Donnelly was trying to assert some control over the situation; he was trying to comfort Quai Chen, who reared back, slapping Donnelly so hard that the detonation issuing from the slap of her hand to his right cheek and ear momentarily stunned all in the room to silence. Quai Chen then attempted to lunge at Donnelly when one of the DEA agents inserted himself between the two, restraining her, telling her to take care of her baby, trying to take her mind off of Donnelly and the assault. After a brief struggle with the agent, she was placed on the couch near her baby.

Quai Chen's moaning husband, still bleeding, was strapped onto a stretcher and taken out of the apartment to a waiting ambulance. Quai Chen now gazed wildly around the room, doubled over, and began vomiting onto the floor in front of the couch, her color alternating like a neon sign between pale white and fire-engine red. Donnelly directed the medical technicians remaining in the room to give her something to quiet her so that she didn't succumb to a stroke or a heart attack. He then radioed for assistance to the Psychological Services Unit at DEA Headquarters in Manhattan so staff could attend to Quai Chen and also provide assistance in helping her care for her baby while she mentally convalesced. He also detailed two agents to remain at the apartment until the door was fixed and secure.

Having done all he could for the Chen family, Donnelly then went to Baraka's apartment, where Deputy Chief Howell, who was supervising the DA's detectives that night, had Mike secured in the kitchen. Mike's parents and his other sister, Hanna, were told to remain in the living room. Assessing that the situation there was under control, Donnelly, needing to address what went down in the Chen apartment, told Howell to meet him out in the street.

According to Mike, his apartment was full of officers, with teams of two searching every room. A detective walked into the kitchen with a clear plastic bag full of white powder, telling Howell that the bag was found in a dresser in Mike's bedroom. Howell dangled it in front of Mike's face and Mike squawked back that it was not his, that he knew of no drugs in the house, and why were they doing this to him? The detective read him his rights, then stood him up and walked him out into the hallway. Adel, Mike's mother, had to be physically restrained as she grabbed for her son, while her husband, Shafke, made an attempt to comfort her. Hanna just sat with her head in her hands, no doubt saddened that Mike had never listened to her warnings to keep away from Sami and the rest of his worthless friends.

One of the guys later told me that Donnelly, too, needed some medical attention after being slapped by Quai Chen. The next morning he had his doctor check his ear, which had turned a reddish purple color and was swollen.

Baraka later described the scene in the West Street House of Detention in Manhattan. Everyone that had been arrested was placed in a large holding cell, then systematically fingerprinted and photographed. This went on most of the night, with prisoners arriving from the various locations as operations were concluded.

Mike seemed to stand out from the rest of the prisoners, constantly milling around, breathing hard, the sweat streaming down the sides of his face onto his polo shirt. At some point he walked over to Sami, who was engaged in a muted conversation with Nick and Mickey and, grabbing hold of Sami's shoulder, spun him around, yelling, "I got to get out of here! Why did they lock me up, Sami? You gotta tell them I had nothing to do with it!"

Sami growled, "Keep your mouth shut, you fucking idiot! We're all gonna beat this; the government's got nothing."

Then Mickey grabbed Mike by the throat with one hand and put his other forefinger to Mike's lips and whispered sinisterly, "Shut the fuck up." Pulling his finger away, he placed it under his own chin, drawing it across his neck, indicating to Mike that he'd slit his throat.

Galgano asked Mickey what he thought of the "fuckin' mess" they were in. Calise told him he thought they'd had it. He said that, judging by the group of guys who were in the pigpen with them, the bust was a coordinated effort by the government. Otherwise, how would the feds know to bust them all at once? Galgano intimated that he thought that Sami and his big fat mouth were responsible for them being there and the feds probably had managed to get enough on them to fry them.

I couldn't wait to go after Yousef Nebor, who unfortunately was not picked up on any of the conversations seized over Sami's phones. I'd have loved to see Mickey and Nick's faces when they finally found out that Yousef and Sami had been ripping them off. I would have given a week's pay to have arranged that scene, but it was not to be, not yet. Nebor would have to wait.

Chapter Eight

I'd learned in my short thirty years on this earth that human beings have the ultimate capacity to hurt one another—call it man's inhumanity to man. There's nothing left to the imagination, from a twenty-year-old Hispanic girl who had a butcher knife sticking out of her chest because of a jealous boyfriend, to a traffic accident caused by a drunk driver where I had to pick up someone's face that had been sheared off by his windshield. I know now, but didn't know then, that these things pile up mentally and come back to haunt you at night.

I'm getting a little ahead of the story and want to tell you a little more about Mike Baraka. In Arabic, his name is Ayman. His father, Shafke, the owner of the building in which he lived, was the first ambassador from Jordan to the United Nations, working directly for the royal family. As I've mentioned, Mike was a bouncer/doorman at Club Zazu in Westchester Square in the Bronx. Prior to his arrest, he'd worked at the club for almost a year and a half. He was accepted and trusted by the half-assed wise guys that frequented the club. At twenty-six, he was knocking down $200 to $500 in tips from these guys every night. On the weekends he did even better, as these knuckleheads would stuff hundred-dollar bills into his jacket pocket to impress the girls they were with.

Mike was dark-complected and handsome. He was charismatic and dressed well. As I've come to find out since, he's also extremely intelligent. His jet black eyes and hair contrast his slick appearance. Although he's Jordanian, he can pass for an Italian from the neighborhood. Almost six feet, and framed like a bull, he carries himself with a sense of confidence.

Shafke wanted more for his son, hoping that he would continue his education after high school, go to college, and end up a productive professional in a field of his choosing. However, that was not to be. Mike gave his father heartache, and unbeknownst to his family, had become seriously involved with Cindy Galgano, Nick's daughter. She lived in a two-bedroom apartment on the fifth floor of Mike's building, and soon after they met a budding relationship ensued.

Mike told me later that Nick found out about their relationship and almost killed him by pistol-whipping him to near unconsciousness, putting him in the hospital for a week. Mike received thirty stitches and had a concussion. Cindy was by his bedside throughout that week in the hospital, a fact that enraged her father further. Mike's parents weren't pleased about their relationship either. They only wanted Mike to date and end up with an Arabic woman.

I have to admit they made a handsome pair. Cindy was a knockout, with straight brown hair, hazel eyes, a stunning figure, and a creamy olive complexion that radiated a delicate sensuousness. When I later got to know them and saw them together, they were real head-turners.

Hanna, Mike's sister, seemed to be the only one who could talk to him. She had tried on many occasions to warn Mike to stay away from Cindy. She complained bitterly about their relationship and told him that Cindy would bring him and their family down.

Mike, being totally in love, felt he knew Cindy and was convinced that he could rise above it all and that eventually Nick would have to accept him.

One thing a cop misses in deep undercover assignments is closure. The protection of my cover was essential for future undercover operations. It was obvious that I would be missing the arraignment and sentencing of Mickey and his crew. I knew that I would have to testify in open court, but the Judge ruled that I could testify behind a screen to keep my identity protected as much as possible. Obviously, by the time the trial came around, Mickey and the crew knew who I was, but anyone else that the Luccheses had planted in the courtroom wasn't gonna get a look at me.

I learned from John Kenny that it was quite a scene in the courtroom, with Judge John Sposato, a no-nonsense individual, presiding. All the defendants' families were there, including Cindy Galgano, who was sitting next to Adel Baraka, attempting to comfort her through her tears. It must have been an eyeful for Nick to have seen the two consoling one another, while Mike was sitting at the end of a long defendant's bench, shackled to all the other defendants by the waist and ankles.

They all were charged with conspiracy to distribute heroin. Baraka had also been charged with possession of a controlled substance, heroin. Mike was admonished by the Judge because of an outburst in the courtroom protesting his innocence.

Judge Sposato assigned a former prosecutor turned defense attorney, Joan Connelly, to defend Mike. Connelly asked for a short recess to confer with her client. After the Judge reconvened court, Mike entered a plea of not guilty.

The Judge then stated that he would review Connelly's request for bail after he had a chance to study Baraka's criminal history and substantive reasons presented for advocating bail. Baraka was then remanded to the Federal House of Detention on West Street in Manhattan, until such time the Judge could rule on bail.

The other defendants, per the government's request, were denied bail because of the seriousness of their charges and the fact that they posed a flight risk.

Several days later, Baraka's bail was set at $2.5 million, meaning that a $250,000 bond (10 percent) or the same in cash would be required to release him. Connelly was successful in persuading the court to accept
$250,000 in cash, which came from a bondsman who had used Shafke's apartment building as collateral, along with the fact that Mike was a first-time offender.

Nine months later the case went to trial. All were

found guilty, with Mickey and Nick each sentenced to twenty five years to life, while some of the others involved received lesser sentences. Ayman "Mike" Baraka was sentenced to ten years in federal prison.

Jacob Staton, an assistant district attorney from the Westchester County District Attorney's Office, was cross deputized as an assistant United States attorney to assist AUSA John Kenny at trial. He told me that upon pronouncement of sentence, Baraka collapsed and had to be helped out of the court room by U.S. marshals, with his mother screaming "Ayman, Ayman!" from the gallery. After the courtroom calmed, due to the repeated banging of Sposato's gavel, Connelly asked for bail continuance during the appeal process. The Judge scheduled a bail hearing in two weeks' time.

Mike and Joan Connelly conferred frequently in the months that followed. Their discussions centered on his fear of confinement and the actions he could take to eliminate, or to at least reduce, the time he would have to spend in prison. They'd met several times with John Kenny and Jacob Staton, in Kenny's Manhattan office, to determine the parameters pertaining to the cooperation agreement that Mike would sign with the U. S. Attorney's Office, Southern District of New York. He eventually signed on as a confidential informant, with the hope of reducing or eliminating his prison time by making prosecutable narcotics cases. Both Kenny and Staton came away from this agreement more than enthusiastic.

The U.S. Attorney's Office then notified Judge Sposato of the agreement and, at the appointed time, the court was reconvened. Judge Sposato had the agreement read into the court record, thereby joining Mike Baraka, the U.S. Attorney's Office, and the Westchester County District Attorney's Office in a marriage of sorts. Baraka's bail remained at $250,000, which placed a financial and emotional burden on Mike's father, who had obtained a second mortgage on his property in support of his son. However, as fate would have it, the excessive stress placed on Mike's father overwhelmed him and two days after the cooperation agreement was signed Shafke collapsed onto the kitchen floor and died of a massive heart attack.

Chapter Nine

Reinsertion into the DA's detective division would take some getting used to. Most of the guys assigned to the unit were happy to see me back, especially Detective Joe Nulligan.

Joe and I had a history going back to when we first met at the police academy. We instantly liked one another and enjoyed spending some of our time off together with our families. He had a great sense of humor, but more importantly, I knew that I could count on him to watch my back in the street. So when Chief Daniels reassigned me to the narcotics squad, I took an empty desk next to Joe's.

For the first few weeks back, the squad supervisor, Captain Larry Christopher, left me alone. I guess he wanted to give me some time to integrate myself into the squad. But it was only a matter of time before he would assign me to work with one of the detectives in the squad. I hoped that it was either Nulligan or another streetwise detective, Angel Serrano.

One afternoon, Captain Christopher stepped out of his office and motioned for Joe and me to come into his office. His office was located at the very end of the squad room. The squad room was a large rectangular space with thirty or so battleship-gray desks, separated by a center aisle. Half the desks sat on one side of the aisle and the other half sat on the other side. Up against the off-white walls (that needed painting) sat a number of olive green filing cabinets containing departmental forms and old case files.

The Captain was forty-something, six five and approximately 180 pounds. His short-cropped, light brown hair contrasted his deep-set blue eyes and light complexion. He traditionally sported blue jeans, a polo shirt, and a sidearm in a shoulder holster. His disposition was calm and he exercised good judgment. The entire detective division trusted and liked him.

Joe Nulligan, on the other hand, was thirty and built like a fireplug, with an Irish disposition, quick to laugh, and quicker to anger. This bulldog of a man at five foot ten, 215 pounds, brooding blue eyes, blond hair, and fiery temper, had gotten into trouble with the department on a number of occasions.

Upon entering his office, Captain Christopher asked that we shut the door and take a seat. We pulled up the two chairs that were hugging the wall and positioned ourselves in front of his desk. The Captain's office had a large window behind his desk that overlooked Martin Luther King Boulevard and the city skyline.

"Look guys, I'm assigning you to work together. You know the drill; start making street level buys and let's see if we can work our way up the food chain. Starting tomorrow, you'll work a steady four to twelve and time off when you need it. Just let me know when overtime is needed. If the case warrants it, you'll get it. Oh, and we'll talk about working weekends."

"Fine, Cap," I responded as Joe and I got up to leave.

Joe, grinning from ear to ear, saluted the captain as we slid the armchairs back against the wall and walked out of his office.

"Guys, please leave the door open. Thanks."

It was now lunchtime. Catching Joe's eye, I flicked my head towards the door, indicating that we should grab a bite to eat. He nodded in agreement. We decided to go to a local place, Jake's. I noticed that there were three new people in the squad room, guys I didn't know, so before walking out I stopped by their desks and introduced myself.

Joe and I walked down the back stairwell four flights to the rear parking lot and got into his car, a deep blue Ford Galaxy, soon to be auctioned by the county. Dented and scarred from its 135,000 miles, it had served its purpose, traversing the five boroughs and southern Westchester for eight years. When Joe turned the key, the car sputtered to life, its eight-cylinder Interceptor engine growling as Joe pushed the stick shift into first gear and we drove away.

Jake's Bar & Grill was and still is in the Chester Heights section of New Rochelle, down the Bronx River Parkway to the Cross County Parkway, east to the Hutch, and exiting at Exit 10-New Rochelle. The owner, Jake McDonald, has a son who works out of the 45th Precinct on Barksdale Avenue in the Bronx, making the restaurant cop-friendly and not a hangout for wise guys or shitheads. I hadn't had lunch or dinner there in years. The last time I was there was when I took Helen and the kids there for dinner. Since my divorce and the Calise case ending, female companionship had been nonexistent for me. I was so torn up inside from losing Helen and the kids, I couldn't bring myself to think about dating other women at that point. So, maybe lunch at Jake's was my reentry into the real world and improving my social life.

Jake's offered comfortable booths for relatively private conversations, unlike sitting at the bar where the guy sitting on the barstool next to you could easily eavesdrop. As soon as we walked in, Jessica, Joe's girlfriend, greeted us from behind the bar. She leaned over the bar and kissed Joe on the cheek. Jessica and Joe had been dating for several years, meeting when she first started tending bar at Jake's. They became instant friends and not long after that, they were exclusive to one another. Jessica Carbone was young and beautiful, in her mid- twenties, with a sensuous figure. She stood five four, with dark black hair, blue eyes, and a milk white complexion. Jessica was a stunning woman. If Joe wasn't dating Jessica, I'm sure that there would have been a bunch of guys lined up to take her out.

"Frankie, it's nice to have you back. Joe told me all about it. Sorry to hear about Helen and the kids."

"Yeah, well, if I had it to do all over again, I wouldn't. The sacrifice was too great. It wasn't worth losing my family over a few knuckleheads." Jessica didn't know what to say. But how could she? Only I knew what it felt like to lose everything.

"Frankie, I hope to see you here a lot. And I hope we can all spend time together. So what will you have?"

"I'll have a White Label neat."

Jessica had Joe's drink already poured, and slid him a Blue Point Lager across the bar. We picked up the drinks and took a seat in one of the booths opposite the bar. The waiter walked over and placed menus in front of us.

"Jessica has the first round. Look over the menu and give me the high sign when you're ready."

"Thanks, but I think we know what we want. Joe, I know what I'll have; how about you?"

"Yeah, I'll have the bean soup and a blue cheeseburger, well."

"Okay, then. I'll have the minestrone, baby back ribs, and a Guinness to chase the White Label down. Thanks."

"Thanks, guys. Be right back with the beers."

Jessica had the beers waiting for him. He grabbed the beer from the bar, walked back to the booth, and set them down. "The food will be ready in a few," he said as he walked back towards the kitchen.

Neither Joe nor I said much at first, just sitting, enjoying each other's company while sipping our beer. Just then my cell phone rang. It was Captain Christopher, who said that he'd just gotten off the phone with the Deputy Chief and apparently one of defendants in the Calise case wanted to cooperate.

Joe asked, "What was that about?"

"It was Christopher. We got a meeting at the United States Attorney's Office at four. A defendant from the Calise case wants to cooperate."

"Oh yeah? And you're telling me he's ours?"

"Can't tell yet—maybe the feds', maybe ours."

"Who needs him?"

"Well, we might need him, never know. We'll see."

Joe, chugging half a glass of beer, replied, "Yeah, right, we'll see."

Just then the waiter came through the swinging doors of the kitchen, setting the plates in front of us. "Thanks," I said.

After noshing down half the ribs, I looked up at Joe, who was gnawing on his burger, and asked, "When you first married your ex-wife did you ever think you'd divorce?"

"No, but I don't think about it. I think about the alimony and child support payments every month and that I don't see my kids much."

"I know; it sucks. Helen's keeping the girls away from me. I don't understand why."

"Yeah, it doesn't make any sense."

"I guess it's the job and the life we live. It's not worth the tossing and turning every night, trying to get to sleep, or the guilt about the kids. All that shit."

Joe took another slug of beer. "You think too much. Shit like this'll drive you nuts. Me, I'm buzzed every night so I don't have to think. Thinking about the shit you just spewed is exactly what I don't want to do. Listen, Frankie, right now, all I want out of life is to just get through it. There've been nights that didn't sit too well, you know? I've lost everything, just like you have, because of mistakes I've made not once, but multiple times. I hear my ex is living with some pencil-neck dentist from Scarsdale, but she won't get married, so I'm still footing the bills. But at least the agita's gone." We proceeded to finish our lunch after another round of drinks. Splitting the tab, we decided it was time to head to Kenny's office.

When we arrived, and after checking our weapons in a weapons locker off the main lobby, we found Kenny sitting on the edge of his large wooden desk as Joan Connelly, Baraka, a swarthy, dark-haired male looked on, watching Kenny as he studied some papers in a manila file folder. As we walked into his office, Kenny stood up, greeted Joe and I, and then introduced us to another man in the room. John Kenny was a rising star in the U.S. Attorney's Office at the young age of thirty-two. He motioned for us to take two seats next to Connelly and the dark- haired male. John towered over us at six three, 210 pounds, an intimidating figure, with sandy blond hair and dark blue eyes, and he was appropriately attired in pleated, well-cut, sand-colored slacks. His navy blue sport jacket hung on an upright coat rack in the corner behind his desk. Wearing a soft orange and beige tie against his white, button- down shirt, John could have been a model for *GQ* magazine.

Connelly was dressed in a navy blue suit over a white blouse with an appropriate neckline for court and black high heels that looked to be around the three-inch mark, all accented by white pearl earrings and a pearl necklace. Her deep brown hair tied neatly into a bun accentuated her stunning features, although they were hardened by her stern demeanor and the granny reading glasses balanced on the edge her nose. Kenny sat in the chair behind his desk, expressing that Mr. Baraka had signed a cooperation agreement to work with the narcotics squad as a confidential informant on investigations.

Joe, leaning forward in his chair, motioned a question with his hand. "I don't understand—why us? Why not the DEA?"

I piped up. "Yeah, why with the Westchester County DA's narcotics squad?"

Kenny responded, "Frank, you helped develop the Calise case. With that said, I felt that it would benefit everyone involved to have you assigned."

Joan Connelly turned to us. "We feel that it is in my client's best interest to work with the local authorities."

I looked over at Joe, who seemed to be thinking about what was just said. I knew he recently had a bad experience with John Martin, an informant who was double-dealing him. Joe was negotiating a half-kilo coke buy with a Colombian drug dealer. Martin decided to give Joe up to the dealer as a cop. They planned to steal the money and kill Joe. Shots were fired and Joe was nearly killed. John Martin wasn't so lucky; he took two in the chest and had been killed instantly. He died face down in a putrid pool of water that had collected in a depression near some garbage dumpster that had leaked its refuse onto the pavement during recent rains. For Joe, the betrayal just reinforced the fact that you can never wholly trust an informant.

Baraka was studying Joe and me intensely. "Listen," he said, "it's my idea to work with you guys, not theirs. Frank, I saw you on the street and never thought that you were a cop. For that matter, I guess no one else did either. I'd rather take my chances with you than rot in prison. If I go to jail, I'll die. That's no lie. At least this way I'll be home to keep an eye on my mother. She's got a heart condition and since my father died she's not doing well, especially with me going to prison. Now I'm the head of the family and need to be home for her. I won't disappoint you guys, I promise."

Kenny then interjected. "I'd like to remind Counsel that good-faith efforts will not help mitigate Mr. Baraka's sentence. Only prosecutable cases will be presented to the Judge."

Connelly retorted, "We are well aware of the stipulations in the agreement." She turned to Joe and me. "So, gentlemen, do we have an understanding?"

Joe and I looked at each other and nodded yes.

We both got up. I stood looking at Kenny. "So, what's next? Anything out of your office?"

John shook his head no. "Nothing on the front burner for the moment. Work within your own agency to develop leads. Joan, could you and Mike stay for a moment? I need to go over some additional details with you. Gentlemen, will you excuse us? Thank you."

I took a final look at Connelly, so prim and proper with not a curl out of place, always looking over those fucking glasses like a spinster schoolteacher lecturing to her students. In spite of her radiating an iceberg façade, she was one of the best-looking women I'd come across lately, but truthfully I hadn't been looking. I had a fleeting thought of what she'd look like in bed with nothing on other than a filmy negligee. I quickly put that thought out of my head as Joe and I walked out, unintentionally giving the door a little slam, listening to the window rattle as we walked down the corridor.

I punched the elevator down button. Joe glanced at me, turning his head slightly. "That went well, don't ya think?" he remarked, and chuckled.

"Yeah, just great."

The elevator arrived, delivering us to the lobby, where we retrieved our guns. We drove back to the office and opened up a case file registering Baraka as a confidential informant. His C.I. number was 252.

Chapter Ten

It was the evening of November 17, 2003. A cool autumn breeze chilled the air. As Joe and I waited in the car, I was thinking of Helen and the kids and what they might be doing that night. The thought depressed me, so I made myself not go there. Instead I thought about what I was going to do on the weekend. Maybe I'd call my brother, Rich, and see if he wanted to get together on Saturday night for dinner out at one of our favorite restaurants on Arthur Avenue in the Bronx, or perhaps see if he was available on Sunday for macaroni and meatballs at Mom's.

There's nothing better than my mother's gravy served over her homemade macaroni. As a kid, the memory of waking up to the smell of my mom frying meatballs on Sunday morning will stay with me until I die. This sensory thought brought me back to my meditations on what was really important in life. I really needed to reconnect with my family, or what was left of it.

Just then, Mike Baraka walked out of his building and over to our car. The game plan was to pick him up at 7 p.m. and drive around some neighborhoods in the Bronx and northern Manhattan so he could get a feel for how we work. This time, we were in a supercharged '94 Trans Am with a hopped-up 420-cubic-inch engine, something that didn't have cop written all over it. A large, gold Firebird was displayed on its black hood. The car had been seized from a drug dealer, along with money and cocaine.

Joe opened the door, climbed out, and held the door for Mike as he pushed forward the bucket passenger seat and climbed into the back. Joe then got back into the car, bringing the door with him via the door pull, as he settled into the front passenger seat. He looked over at me, shaking his head from side to side, with a look of *Here we go again.*

I knew it was going to be a long night.

With an energetic voice, Baraka piped up, "Okay, detectives, ready when you are. Where to?"

I put my head down, hand over my face, knowing what was coming next. Joe blew, turned in his seat, and grabbed Baraka by the front of his shirt, pulling him face to face. I turned to make sure Joe's gun was still holstered, knowing full well where his temper could lead. So far both hands were occupied, one on Baraka's shirt and the other pushing against the console, balancing Joe in his seat.

"Look, you're just a street punk. You don't set the agenda. We do. So keep your fuckin' mouth shut unless you're spoken to, got it?"

Visibly shaken and wide-eyed from this unexpected violent behavior, Baraka said, "Sure, anything you want."

"That's better." Joe released his grip from Mike, allowing him to settle back into the seat behind me, a noticeable departure from his previous position. Jesus, we were only ten minutes into it and already I was longing to be sitting at the bar at Jake's, sucking down a glass or two of Dewar's White Label.

We made the circuit through the streets and Joe's abuse turned into a never-ending tirade about how Mike needed to be on time every day, that he'd better not bite the hand that fed him by double-dealing us, and that he'd better hustle and come up with a drug dealer soon, or he'd have his bail revoked.

Finally, I'd had enough. I pulled to the curb and stopped the car, looking back at Mike, who was stone-faced. The muscles in his jaw were twitching. I glanced over at Joe. "Okay enough. You've made your point. I think by now Mike knows what's expected of him."

Joe expressed a look of betrayal. "Yeah, okay, he'd better understand."

I pulled back into the traffic. We slowly cruised the streets, sometimes pulling to the curb, and more often than not double-parking, watching the action develop. In several instances we saw actual buys. Using a night-vision camera, Joe snapped a few photos of the dealers. Observing one of the dealers, he said, "Remember these guys, Mike. They're good guys to key on. We can work our way up to their suppliers."

Mike nodded his head yes, not wanting to cause any more problems.

It was past midnight, so we decided to call it a night. I drove back to Mike's building, pulling to the curb in front of his entrance. This time I got out of the car, as he'd been sitting in the rear on my side of the car the entire evening. Joe also got out, leaving the door open, as Mike walked around the front of the car with me to the sidewalk. Extending his hand to me he innocently said, "Look, detectives, I was wondering . . ."

Joe interrupted. "What? What were you wondering?"

"I was wondering, since I haven't been able to work for a while, and well, it's my girl's birthday tomorrow, I was wondering if I could get a few dollars to take her out."

Joe yelled, "I don't think I heard this right! You what?"

Mike straightened up. "Can I borrow some money to take her out?"

Joe screamed, motioning with his hand in the air toward me, "Can you believe this fuck?"

Then, turning to Mike, he roared, "You think the taxpayers want to shell out money so a dirtbag like you can take out Galgano's daughter? Are you out of your fucking mind?"

Joe's face was red under the streetlight, the muscles on his neck pulsing as his blood pumped under the surface of the skin surrounding his neck.

I knew that there was something wrong with Joe. This behavior was uncharacteristic of the Joe I knew, and certainly unprofessional. I got between them.

"Joe, take it easy."

Mike, having had enough, exploded, "Cindy has nothing to do with her father's business. Frank, you know that. And neither do I. The heroin they found in my dresser wasn't mine. Sami put it there because my sister didn't want the shit in their apartment, so he stashed it my place without telling me. I've never dealt dope and I've never been involved in it in any way. The cops fucked up. They didn't want me; they wanted my cousin Ayman, who split to the Middle East. So this whole deal's a big fucking mistake and I'm going to do time for my scumbag cousin who doesn't have the balls to come back and stand up for me."

Joe, somewhat calmer, said, "Yeah, sure, and the Pope's not Catholic." He reached behind him, took out his wallet and pulled out two dollars, throwing them at Baraka, where they hit him in the chest and fell to the sidewalk.

Mike stared at Joe for a few seconds and said, "Look, that's okay. Don't worry about it. I'll figure something out on my own." He turned to go into the building, leaving the money on the ground.

Joe began yelling as he made a move toward Mike, "Don't worry about it? You got some fuckin' nerve." Mike was caught off balance by the suddenness of Joe's lunge. As Joe got behind Mike with one arm around his throat, grabbing Mike with his other hand, he cranked Baraka's arm up at a right angle toward his shoulder blade.

I jumped in, trying to separate them, yelling at Joe, "What the fuck is wrong with you? Relax, Joe, let him go! The money's not coming out of your pocket." Joe released his grip as I came between them. Then Joe made another grab for Mike, but I pushed him back as he spit at Baraka, narrowly missing his left shoulder, with some of the phlegm grazing my forehead. I wiped it off, glaring at Joe, furious.

I turned to Mike, "Are you all right?" He was shaking, with clenched fists, and said nothing as he went for Joe, his temper having been brought to the boiling point.

Suddenly I found myself between them again, grabbing them by their shirt fronts. I said to Joe, "Get back into the car before this gets bad." It was already out of control, but I didn't know what else to say.

He actually listened and put his bulk back into the front passenger seat. I released Mike and asked him again if he was okay.

"I'm fine. I don't want any trouble, so keep that fuck away from me. This isn't gonna work."

I continued to try to calm Mike down, saying that Joe was just on edge with some of the cases we were running, but Baraka would have none of it. I then pulled out one hundred dollars in twenties from my wallet and handed the money to Mike.

"I don't want the fuckin' money. Forget it," he said.

I shoved the money into his shirt pocket and walked back to the car, glaring at Joe. I opened the door and climbed into the driver's seat, praying that Joe would stay calm and stay in the car as Mike walked into his building. We pulled away from the curb as Baraka's entrance door slammed shut.

As we drove down the street, I yelled at Joe, "What the fuck is wrong with you?" I was so angry I thought that I would pull over and throw him out of the car. But I took some deep breaths and kept driving. Joe snapped back, "Don't think that this puke won't try to jam us up. He'll say that we pocketed expense money that was supposed to go to him, or some other bullshit. Remember, he's fucking Galgano's daughter and she's probably got the cock out for you after what you did to her father, for Christ's sake!"

Just then a car swerved in front of us, nearly hitting us. Joe yelled, "Look out, Frankie!"

Jerking the wheel enough to avoid a collision, I calmly said, "I see the asshole; take it easy."

"Look, I'm sorry. I know I was a little rough on Baraka tonight." "Yes, you were. What's going on with you?" "Ah, I think I'm just tired, tired of all this shit." "Maybe you need some time off?" "Yeah, we'll see."

Again, the same asshole who almost sideswiped us before

jammed his brakes on in front of us and this time I nearly rear-ended him. Joe asked, "You got the dome light? You want to stop him?"

"Yeah, what the fuck. But you do the paperwork."

I pulled out the light from the console and popped it onto the roof of the car, hitting the siren. We chased the fuck for two blocks before the car pulled to the curb. Jumping out of the car, we cautiously walked towards the vehicle. Almost simultaneously, a short fat fireplug of a woman appearing to be in her mid-thirties exited the old, beat-up Ford Taurus with a scowl on her face. She could have been a candidate for the female Olympic wrestling team. This gal had black curly hair, closely cropped, and stood around four foot seven with an eight-foot attitude. She yelled, "What the fuck do you want?"

Joe pulled out his shield, waving it towards her, and said, "License and registration." As Joe and I walked closer, his shield almost in her face, she gestured with one middle finger, then the other, so that both simultaneously were aimed at 90-degree angles midlevel on our chests.

She shouted, jerking each upended finger in succession up and down, "Here's my license and here's my registration. Stick 'em up your ass."

Joe and I looked at each other, dumbfounded, shaking our heads as we pondered our predicament. Without a word, we walked back to the car and got in. I took the light off the roof and put it back in the console. Pulling away and into traffic, Joe and I looked at each other and almost in unison we both said, "Not even fuckin' worth it."

We began to laugh so hard that the tears rolled down our cheeks. Maybe that stupid little pit bull had done us a favor. I asked Joe the time.

"It's almost 1:30 a.m. Why?"

"Let's stop by Jake's for a nightcap. Is Jessica working?" "Yeah, she's working tonight."

We were headed to Jake's, making small talk, when Joe

said, "Did Staton tell you about Baraka's girlfriend's old man? The shit he put himself into last week in the slam?"

I glanced over at Joe. "No, I haven't seen Jacob. What happened?" "Staton said that Nick almost beat an inmate to death."

"Oh yeah?"

Joe then told me the story. Galgano had been on the phone in the day room with Calise behind him, waiting his turn for the phone, when a big black inmate behind them in line yelled for Nick to hurry the fuck up. Then, from what Corrections related to Staton, Mickey got into it with the black dude, turning around and asking the guy who the hell he thought he was, telling Nick to hurry up.

"I can see it now."

Joe began to laugh, me right with him.

He then went on to say that the inmate, now nose to nose with Mickey, had called Mickey a bitch. So Mickey punched him in the throat and kneed him in the balls and yelled something racist like, "You big fuckin' monkey!" as the guy lay there moaning on the floor.

We both laughed. "I don't get it. What's Galgano got to do with this?"

"Well Nick's screaming on the phone that he'll decide who's harmless and who isn't and that he wants an eye kept on her."

"I guess we know who he's talking about, huh?"

Joe continued, "Anyways, Nick turns around, rips the receiver off the phone box, and beats the guy, who's already prostrate on the floor holding his nuts, over the head until the guy is half dead."

"I knew that fuckin' Nick was crazy."

"That's not all. Jacob said that Nick threw the receiver at the guy, calling him a stupid mulligan. Mickey and Nick walk away, Mickey yelling that the guy's a fucking animal. Then Nick grabs his own chest and collapses to the floor."

"Is he okay?"

"Who knows? Jacob's still waitin' to hear."

We pulled up to Jake's, parked out front, and went into the bar. The scene at Jake's was the usual. Jessica was tending bar. As soon as she saw us walk in, she had our drinks lined up. "Hi, Joey. Hi, Frankie. How'd it go tonight?"

Joe gave Jessica a sour look. "I don't want to talk about it. Just keep pouring."

Looking as if someone had just slapped her face, she shot back, "Okay, another of those nights. Forget I asked, asshole."

I thought to myself, *Way to go, Joe. Most guys would kill to have a girl like Jessica love them, let alone like them. If you had any hopes of getting laid tonight, you might as well forget it.*

We moved to a booth, the conversation centering around Baraka and the fact that we needed to use him. The drunker we got, the more heated the discussion, until we were both so drunk that we weren't making sense. Jessica, seeing that it was time for us to go, had the people from the cleaning service herd us out to her car. She made sure that Joe and I didn't end up as a highway statistic, in a wreck, or arrested and losing our jobs. Lucky for us, Joe and I didn't have to get to work until late the next afternoon.

Chapter Eleven

We arrived in the squad room at 3:45 p.m., bleary-eyed and still hung over from the night before. The thought of keying in on last night's report made my headache feel even worse. I knew that Joe felt the same way. It was tough enough for Joe and me to follow up with reports when we were sober, much less when we were hung over. Nevertheless, what transpired the previous night with Baraka had to be put into a police report, so I began to bang away on the computer. But between my headache and the noise in the squad room, it was hard for me to concentrate. Angel Sorrano, sitting across the aisle, was on the phone screaming at his lawyer about his ex-wife breaking his balls because he was late with the month's child support payment and how she was about to take him to family court.

I don't know what it is, but divorce seems to be a disease that comes with the job. For cops, the late nights, the drinking after work, the available women, and the pressures to take care of your family all contribute to a high rate of divorce. More than 50 percent of the guys in the detective division were divorced.

Joe coached me on some notes he'd taken but that was all he was going to offer, other than his signature on the document once it was completed. We were nearly finished when my desk phone rang. Joe, standing over me, picked it up.

"Narcotics, Nulligan. Yeah, sure, just a second." He looked down at me, putting his hand over the mouthpiece. "It's Staton."

I took the phone. "Hi Jacob, what's up? I'll be right up."

Joe mumbled, "Try to make it short and sweet. I want to get out of here."

I wondered what this was about. Staton wanted to see me in the DA's office, but not Joe. How come?

The DA's office, at that time occupied by Annette Larson, was one floor up. As soon as I walked off the elevator into the outer office, Christina Weaver, Larson's secretary, motioned for me to hurry into her office. Something was up, because Christina hit the buzzer to the door before I had a chance to say hello. The door opened to Larson sitting behind her oversized mahogany desk, flanked left and right by Chief Sean Daniels and ADA Jacob Staton. They reminded me of two bookends propping up law encyclopedias. Larson had on a navy blue suit with a white ruffled blouse accenting her lapels, and a short pearl necklace offsetting her matching pearl earrings. I wasn't about to let her petite stature and baby doll complexion fool me, because her harsh demeanor made up for any misgivings I might've had about her edginess. Her light brown shoulder length hair swirled slightly when she moved her head, softening her sharply refined facial features. It must be a legal thing, perched on the end of her nose were granny glasses that gave her a scholarly look for effect. She was just another politician who surrounded herself with self-serving cronies all of whom had their own agendas in mind.

Jacob Staton, half Jewish and half African American, was wearing a beige summer suit with a white shirt and pale blue tie that accented his shaved head. He was six feet tall and had played tight end for the New York Jets before he became a lawyer. His dark brown eyes reflected his innate intelligence, although Jacob told me that it had taken him three times to pass the bar exam. Jacob was a serious guy, especially when it came to putting the bad guys away. There was something about Jacob that I liked. Maybe it was because he carried himself as a regular guy and because of that I felt that I could talk to him as one man to another.

As usual, Chief Daniels looked like an unmade bed. He wasn't wearing a jacket, but his pants were blue pinstripes, so I figured that he was in a bad mood, and his matching jacket wasn't too far away. I had to be careful how I answered him because this backstabbing excuse for a human being could turn on a dime, and I knew I could end up back in uniform with one false move.

The Chief motioned impatiently for me to take a seat between him and Jacob. My senses were heightened and you could have cut the air with a knife. As I seated myself, I asked, "What's this all about and why isn't Nulligan here?"

Staton, the only one in the room who I really trusted, began. "We're here because of what occurred last night."

"I don't get it. What happened last night?"

"Ayman Baraka is extremely valuable to us, Detective," responded Larson.

"Baraka's attorney called me this morning," Jacob remarked. "She told me that Mike was extremely upset with Joe. She said he'd rather go back to jail than work with him and that's saying something. He only wants to work with you."

My heart sank. "He only wants to work with me?"

"That's right, but don't worry, Frank," Jacob said too quickly. "You'll have a lot of latitude on this. You know, he wants to be a player, to help out, but he's not comfortable working with Nulligan. I think you get my drift on this."

Sweeping me further into the corner, DA Larson gave a push with her broom. "We would like you to consider working alone with him. I understand the irregularity of the request, but as I said, he's valuable to us."

I was upset with how this was going. "So, you're telling me that Baraka will only work with me? I don't like it. What if there's an integrity issue? It'll be his and his lawyer's word against mine. What about backup? What about time off? You know what happened to my marriage. How's everything going to work with no partner? There are a lot of issues here."

Chief Daniels, picking up on the cues in the room, continued, "We'll pull out all the stops. You'll call the shots. Whatever you need, whenever you need it, it'll be there. I'll see you get it. We'll still pick up the rent on your apartment. You'll report directly to me and I want Deputy Chief Howell to run the field operations. This is gonna work, Frank, just trust me. What do you say?"

My mind was going a hundred miles an hour. I'm thinking, *Trust you? Jesus, I wouldn't trust you with my worst enemy. Shit, I'm fucked. I don't know Baraka, have no partner, no one to cover my ass, and Howell running the field operations. I'm fucked! I'm between a rock and a hard place. If I say no, I'm fucked. If I say yes, I'm fucked. Either way, I'm fucked.*

Chief Daniels saw that I was taken back. "Jacob feels that Baraka can connect with major importers. We don't want to lose him because some burnt-out cop can't keep his big mouth shut. What do you say?"

"If I say yes, what happens to Joe?"

"Nothing," responded the Chief. "I'll reassign him to another partner until this is over, then you two can go back to working together again."

I had to say yes. I had no choice. "Okay, I'll work with him, but it's got to be on my terms, on how I do things in the field, or the deal is off." Baraka I could control, but the Chief was another matter. His ethics were already in the toilet, so I'd have to use Staton as a buffer, still knowing that Chief Daniels was my boss. I looked over at Staton, then back at Daniels for confirmation. They both shook their heads yes. Larson folded her hands together with a slight smile, saying, "Okay, then I guess we're all in agreement. Gentlemen, thank you."

I got up from my chair, nodding my head yes as I left her office and headed for the staircase at the end of the hallway. On the way back to the squad room, I was thinking, *Joe, a burnt-out cop?* What the fuck did they think I was? I wondered how they viewed me if they had that perception of Joe. I also wondered if Baraka was telling the truth about his cousin being involved with Calise, and not him. Then, frankly, he wasn't the prize they thought he was. If Mike wasn't involved, how could he develop cases—at least, any major ones? Although, I knew it was very possible that Mike knew more than he was saying. The wise guys must've trusted him, or they wouldn't have hired him to bounce at Club Zazu. I was sure the guy had overheard many drugs deals discussed and planned at the club. And to boot, he was dating Cindy Galgano. What was that all about? I'd need to stay as far away from Cindy as I could. She could really fuck things up. All she had to do was to tell her father that Mike was cooperating and working with me. If that happened, the government could kiss everything goodbye, including me and Mike. The question was, if I could figure all this out, why couldn't the powers-that- be? I began to think maybe there was something rotten in Denmark, and definitely more here than met the eye.

That morning Joe was reassigned to work with Angel Serrano, who had grown up on the streets of the South Bronx. His parents had moved from Puerto Rico when he was ten and he had learned to survive on the streets, at the same time keeping out of serious trouble due to a strict upbringing. Fluent in Spanish, undercover work was a snap for him. He had friends who owned bodegas where he could stash his weapon if he felt that he might be patted down by a dealer. Short and wiry, with an aggressive personality, he had a knack for developing informants, but like Joe, had a short fuse. Not knowing how long the Baraka situation would last, Joe and Angel had an arranged marriage they had to make work. We all did.

That night I purposely went to the Melody Club, a club on the Yonkers/Bronx border where Denise MacKenzie danced from time to time. I didn't want to risk a scene with Joe that night, and knew that I wouldn't run into him at the Melody Club because he hated the place. There were a lot of things to talk about with Joe, but Jake's wasn't the place. We'd have to hash things out in the squad room.

Denise was in top form that night. Actually, she was in

top form whenever I saw her, clothed or unclothed. She was five eight, had long shining blond hair, green eyes, and what I had determined to be a perfect body. She wore a green sequined bra and a G-string, along with a set of smoky stockings and five-inch patent leather black stilettos, which caught reflections of the overhead jeweled-up disco balls as she undulated around a pole onstage to some Etta James. When she saw me sitting at the bar she flashed me a smile, her beautiful white teeth framing two sculpted, medium-full lips. Her top lip curled slightly upward to one side when she grinned or smiled, giving her a come-hither look. She was one of the sexiest women I'd ever met. Why she took a liking to me is a mystery. We hadn't progressed far enough into our relationship that I could tell her what I did for a living. I didn't know who Denise knew and since she worked as a dancer I figured that she must know a few bad guys. All she knew about me was that I was divorced, in the newspaper distribution business, and made a few bucks. So for now I figured some things revolved around the chemistry between two people, and let it go at that.

I had found out that Denise was a PhD candidate at Columbia, working in geologic studies. I'd actually met her at Jake's while she was having lunch at the bar. I sat down next to her, offering to buy her a drink, which she accepted, and two hours later it was like we'd known each other all our lives—although, as you know, I hedged when she asked me what I did for a living and changed the subject back to her. She told me about her dancing to support herself while she pursued her studies, impressing me with her determination to get ahead. It was my good fortune that I met her at Jake's and had not taken a shot at picking her up at the Melody Club. She'd had enough of lonely hearts chasing one-night stands. She invited me over to the club and from then on I began frequenting the place. I figured it was time to get back into the dating game even though my heart wasn't into it.

Being somewhat philosophical, I figured things would

happen between me and Denise when they were meant to, so why push it? Besides, maybe she knew better than I what I needed at the moment, decent companionship without entanglement, so I accepted her explanation of early-morning classes the next day without resentment. I ran into Joe midmorning the next day, in the squad room's locker room. His face was blood red and the anguish in his eyes reflected how upset he was. Unable to contain his rage, he launched his tirade, nearly eye to eye with me, thankfully not at Daniels.

"We're partners. Daniels shouldn't have split us up! He backed a fuckin' informant and never gave me an opportunity to defend myself. I'm sick of this shit!"

As calmly as I could, I replied, "Daniels didn't split us up. It was Staton. Baraka complained to his attorney, who called Jacob. Once the cat was let out of the bag, there was no going back. Jacob had no choice but to yank you off the case. Baraka's that important to them. The Chief was just the bearer of bad news."

I thought that Joe was about to explode, his neck pulsating at a rapid rate. He was just able to get the words out of his mouth. "You're crazy to work without a partner! This prick will get you hurt! You can tell Daniels and the rest of them to go fuck themselves! You'll see I'm right!" He then turned and stormed out of the locker room, no doubt as angry with me as he was with everyone else in his life, including himself. I sat down on the locker room bench, upset about the whole situation. It seemed that Joe's comfort zone revolved around me, but I wasn't sure I had a comfort zone to revolve around anymore. I'd been undercover so long sometimes I thought my comfort zone was the danger zone, being a part of the mob. But then, in reality, my only happiness revolved around my family, and that joy was gone. Now I was on my own again, just after reinserting myself into the squad. I wondered how this was going to shake out.

I got up to go to my desk to lay out a game plan with Baraka. My phone rang just as I was pulling out my desk chair.

It was Daniels telling me to hustle up to his office. He could barely contain the excitement in his voice. I wondered what was so important that the fat fuck couldn't tell me on the phone instead of me running up the stairs to his office.

I soon found out. Baraka had developed a lead already and our relationship was only a few days old. It was a coke dealer named Hector Cruz. I thought to myself, *Hell, maybe this guy's got more to him than I think. I can't wait to find out.*

I mentioned before that Chief Daniels wore his pinstriped blue suit to accommodate his mood swings, which were usually bad. Well, we all have our superstitions, and mine revolved around a brown suit. I wore this suit on all major undercover operations, and it had never failed me. I hadn't received a scratch over the course of ten years wearing that suit and I planned to keep on wearing it until I retired. It was medium-weight worsted wool for any season. I know it sounds crazy, but I felt that the suit kept me safe. It was my lucky brown suit, and I didn't go on anything with hair on it unless I was wearing it. I'd never wear it out for mundane activities, like trying to get lucky with Denise. It might spoil the karma.

Chapter Twelve

It was Sunday, late afternoon, and I was stuffed after leaving my folks' house. My mother had cooked macaroni with meatballs, sausage, and rolled beef stuffed with pine nuts, Parmesan cheese, parsley, bread crumbs, garlic, salt, and pepper. As we ate, Richie and I reminisced with my folks about our younger days, but the conversation soon turned to me. They were upset and disappointed about the way my life was turning out. Frustrated, they began to speak over each other. My mother railed about missing Catie and Francesca. My father voiced that Helen had no right keeping the kids away from them and me, while Richie augured that I didn't fight hard enough for Francesca and Catie, and would regret it later on. Little did I know that he was absolutely correct.

I was one story. My younger brother, Richie, was another story. He could do no wrong as far as Mom and Dad were concerned, and he had his act together. Rich was doing well; he knew what he wanted in life and saw to it that he got it. He'd met a girl who was a prosecutor at the New York State Organized Crime Task Force, where he worked as an investigative accountant. They hit it off from the beginning and loved the same things. In their off time, they hiked, traveled abroad, and loved to eat out a lot because she didn't cook. My mom winced when she heard the no-cooking part.

As I left the house, my mother was at the front door waving goodbye. At that moment, I couldn't shake the thought of Helen and the kids, so I drove to a florist on Harrison Avenue in Harrison and bought a bouquet of assorted flowers to bring by the house. As I've said, the house was located in the country club section of the Bronx and had a two-family occupancy, with Helen living on the first floor. It's a strange feeling to knock on your own door, knowing that you're not free to just walk in. I was wearing a starched white shirt, with a small gravy stain on the collar left over from my mother's, a brown, checked sport coat, charcoal gray slacks, and newly shined tassel loafers. I looked as well as I knew how. I'd even trimmed my mustache the night before. I could only hope she noticed.

I began the motion of knocking, holding my arm half-cocked in the air, looking in the side window next to the door, wondering if she was home and if she would open the door when she discovered that it was me. As I knocked, I thought that maybe I should turn around and just leave the flowers on the stoop, but I wanted to see the kids, so I knocked again gently on the door.

I noticed the curtain in the side window part as Helen looked out toward the front door with a frown on her face. That didn't sit well, but I hoped that she would at least give me a chance to see the kids. She cracked the door open, peeking her head out. She looked as beautiful as ever, the blond curls bobbing on her neck, her radiant blue eyes, and her China-doll complexion sparkling in the sunlight reminding me why I was attracted to her in the first place.

She gazed at me as if I were someone from her past she was trying to remember. "What, Frank?"

I looked into those blue eyes unable to speak for a second. "I was passing by . . ."

"Frank, don't! Don't you understand? We're not a couple anymore!
It's over! I don't want to see you!"

"Helen, I need to at least apologize and I need to see my kids." "You know that the lawyers are working out visitation. You'll be
able to see the kids. But I know that you'll never have time for them." "I'll see them."

"My God, Frank. You weren't even there when Francesca was born. What kind of person does that? Maybe you should apologize to her. Jesus, Frank!"

I pleaded. "Please, Helen."

"Damn it, Frank, what kind of father does that? I ask you

that."

I had tears streaming down my cheeks. "Just let me see Francesca and Catie for a minute. I won't stay long."

Helen was now crying as well. "I thought we'd . . . " she paused, sobbing, ". . . grow old together. All I ever wanted was you and the kids." She stepped back out of the doorway and into the house, shutting the door gently behind her, as if to say, *Sorry, but now you've made your own life; I suggest you live it.*

I turned, looking down the walkway to the street, a path I'd taken many times. It now looked alien and out of character. Propping the flowers up against the side of the house near the door, I walked out to the street, looking back momentarily to see if Helen was looking out the window, perhaps offering a glimmer of hope for reconciliation, but there was no movement anywhere from the house. I got into the car and drove away, knowing that it was all over for us.

Later that night, about 10 p.m., I got a call from my brother to meet him and Mom at New York-Presbyterian Hospital. My father had just suffered a heart attack and was waiting for surgeons to arrive to perform triple bypass surgery.

He came out of surgery at 1:20 a.m. We were all by his bedside,   looking down at his weak, exhausted frame in the intensive care unit. The respirator clicking with each breath of life it dispensed. His skin color was a gray-white, contrasting with the rosy hue I always remembered, especially after he had had a few of glasses wine. I took his hand, whispering to him that I loved him, begging him to not die, that there was plenty of life to live yet, and that we needed him. There was an overwhelming feeling of emptiness that penetrated my very bones thinking of life without him and the love he gave us. What would we do without him?

He died the next day of a massive seizure; his body was unable to cope with the damage done to his arterial system due to rheumatic fever he had had as a kid.

We were at his side when he took his last breath. I

remember grabbing my mother, hugging her small, five-foot-four frame tightly as she stroked my hair. "I'm so sorry, Ma. I'm sorry that I was such a disappointment to him. I tried my best. I loved him."

Richie surrounded us with his arms; his head lay on my mother's shoulder, weeping in pain, crying, "Ma. Ma. Daddy's gone. Daddy's gone."

We cried in each other's arms, not caring who saw us, Mom whispering, "It will be okay, shh, it will be okay," like she used to say to us when we were kids. When we finally separated, my mother walked over to his bed and bent down, first caressing her husband's face, then kissing him gently on the cheek. Richie and I held each of his hands, weeping as we told him again that we loved him. Exhausted, we took hold of our mother and gently walked her out of the room. We had funeral arrangements to make.

Chapter Thirteen

Baraka was a number. Chief Daniels kept his confidential informant file in his office safe. As I mentioned, the number assigned to him was 252. This number system was implemented to protect the identity of informants. Even within the detective division, his safety could be compromised by referring to him by name rather than by number. In all police reports, he was identified by his number instead of by name, as these reports were later to be given to the defense attorney if the case should go to trial.

Working with an informant is a complicated matter. There is a feeling that none of them can be trusted. Most are on some substance, self-medicating, and all of them will do or say anything to stay out of jail. Most informants have a short life expectancy. The very streets that they live on will catch up with them, cutting them down. I wondered if the cycle would ever end. Unfortunately, informants, male or female, are necessary tools used by the police to get criminal information.

Baraka and I were having a light early lunch at the White Plains Diner on Westchester Avenue in White Plains, New York. Mike had a BLT in front of him with an iced tea and I had just taken my first bite of a hamburger with fries on the side. It was only 11:45 a.m.; the place was not yet exploding with customers, but it would soon be. I got the sense that Baraka was different from other informants I'd worked with. He cared for his family; he was not using drugs from what I could tell; and he had a regular job before he was arrested. Other than Cindy Galgano, he was not connected to any organized crime figure, yet he seemed to know more of them than his station in life should have warranted. I asked him why this was.

"What gives with you? How do you know Hector Cruz?" "You remember Club Zazu, where I worked?"

"Yeah, sure, I always wanted to stop in for a drink. Some of the guys from Mickey's crew hung out there. So tell me about Cruz."

"Well I got to know a lot of people at the club. They liked me; I always kept my mouth shut. Johnny Migliacchi, you know him?"

"Yeah, he runs a crew for the Bonannos."

"Well, Migliacchi wanted me to come work for him, telling me to give him a call if I were ever interested in making more money than I was making at the club."

"What did he want you to do for him?"

"I don't know, he never said. It never got that far." "So tell me about Cruz. Did he hang out at the club?"

"Not really. He hangs out at a dive in South Yonkers. One of my friends at the club told me that he hangs out there regularly. I've made it a point to start hanging around that bar so I could meet Cruz. I think he's connected to one of the South American cartels. I overheard him the other night on his cell talking to a guy named Lopez. He mentioned Cali, Colombia, and said "Pepe" a couple of times, so I think he was talking to Pepe Lopez."

I almost choked on my fucking hamburger. "You keep your ears open, don't you?"

"Yeah, I do."

I'd heard of Lopez and if Mike had this right, this could be good. The Cali Cartel was one of biggest groups of cocaine smugglers in the world, controlling both the production and distribution of cocaine. The organization recruited farmers from Bolivia, Colombia, and Peru to grow the coca leaves from which the drug was manufactured. Labs were erected in the jungles for processing, and then transportation routes were established through every type of terrain imaginable, including land held by various rebel factions that were aided financially by the cartel, to buy guns and fight against regional authorities and their central governments.

The cartel was ingenious. Through cash payouts to manufacturers of items, the items would be filled with cocaine and then shipped to various destinations in the United States for distribution. They used coffee cans labeled "Colombian coffee" that were actually filled with cocaine to bypass U.S. Customs. Not only were these guys smart, but they were also ruthless. If they suspected that any of their people were cooperating with the police, those people and their families would be killed.

Mike finished eating his BLT and, swallowing the last few sips of his iced tea, listened as I said, "If Cruz is connected to the Cali Cartel, you know what we're into here."

Baraka put the ice tea down. "Yes, I know."

I leaned forward towards Mike so no one could hear me. "If they find out who we are before we wrap them up, we're fucked. Not only us, but everybody connected to us. Do I have to explain myself, or do you get the picture?" These guys were fucking nuts and they didn't care who they took out. "So, we have to be careful and get these assholes clean so they never figure out who we are. *Capisce?*"

Baraka leaned forward as I sat back. "When I agreed to do this, I knew the risk. You have to understand—I'm innocent; I had nothing to do with any of it. And don't roll your eyes; I know what you're thinking. Yeah, yeah, you've heard this before. That may be the case, but with me it's true. Sure, Cindy's Nick's daughter, but when I tell you that she hates what her father does, that's the truth. How do you turn your back on your father when you know he thinks you're the only thing worthwhile in his life? He hates me because I'm an Arab, but let me tell you, she could do a lot worse. I love her and would never do anything to hurt her. So I've got a lot to do to clear my name and jail can't get in my way, so here we are."

There was silence between us. I didn't know what to say. After a minute or two, I asked Mike, "I heard Nick had a heart attack?"

"Yeah, he's in the intensive care unit in the prison hospital. He's still in a coma and they don't know if he's gonna make it."

"Huh—how's Cindy doing?"

"Not well; she wants us to visit him, but I told her if I go, it will upset him. What if he wakes up when I'm there? He might croak on the spot. I couldn't deal with that, so I told her she needs to see him on her own. Plus last night she told me that she's pregnant."

"Jesus, you really have a knack for stepping in some shit. Under normal circumstances, I'd say congratulations, but you need this like a fucking hole in the head. I don't have to tell you that Cindy could blow us out of the water. She has to keep her mouth shut not only around Nick, but everyone else. If word gets out that we're working together we're both fucked and you might as well pack your toothbrush."

"She knows. She's not going to say anything. Cindy loves me and now that we're going to have a baby, she'll be more careful than ever."

"Let's keep it that way for everybody's sake. I know Nick and he'd slit his own mother's throat if he thought he had to."

"I understand."

"Okay, then let's get out of here."

I didn't even signal for the check. I left forty dollars on the table, figuring that would cover the tab plus tip. I got a receipt from the waiter and then we left. I needed a receipt so that I could document the expenditure in Mike's informant file.

We walked about fifty feet down the street to the car. We got in and I pulled out into traffic. I then told Mike, "I'll take you home; not much going on. What's the name of the bar where Hector hangs out?"

"It's the Red Rooster Lounge. It's a dump, but Hector feels comfortable there."

"Good. Do you think that you could set something up for Friday night?"

"I'll try."

"Tell Hector that I'm a connected guy with some serious backing. Tell him that I can do things in Atlantic City."

"Okay, Frank. If he asks me your name . . ."

I interrupted him. "Frank Miranda, my name is Frank Miranda. Remember it. Wipe the name Santorsola from your mind. It could get me killed. We clear?"

"Okay, I understand. When you get to know me better you'll . . ." I swung the wheel sharply, stopping his conversation abruptly, as I pulled the car to the side of the road.

"Look, look at me when I talk to you." Baraka turned his head, looking directly at me. "That's better. Let's get something straight. I've been assigned to work with you. That's the extent of our fucking relationship, you understand? I'm under no obligation to get to know you better. I have no fucking interest in developing anything other than a cop-informant relationship. There's no crossing the line here. As far as I'm concerned, you put yourself in your own shit. You gotta dig yourself out. Am I clear?"

"Yeah, you're clear." Mike hadn't taken his eyes off me. "Frank— can I call you Frank, or should I call you 'Detective'?"

"Call me Frank."

"Frank, just one thing."

"What?'

"I'm innocent. Remember that!"

I studied Baraka for a few moments before I pulled back into traffic. I wanted something to latch onto that would strip away the bullshit to assure me he was as dirty as the guys we were attempting to put away. But what if the son of a bitch was telling the truth—what then? None of the informants I'd worked with in the past insisted on their innocence as sincerely as he did. Why?

I decided that I wanted to stop for a drink, so I asked Mike if he had any plans. "No, just seeing Cindy later and checking on my mother, but right now, no."

"Good, you're coming with me." Perhaps I was about to cross my own previously defined boundaries, but I had to find out where this guy was coming from and what made him tick. Casey's on Randall Avenue, in the Bronx, was a bat-and-ball joint off the beaten path. No one I knew went there, so I could relax and have a cocktail or two with Mike. We arrived about two o'clock in the afternoon. The parking lot was empty, so there wasn't a problem finding a parking space. After locking the Firebird, we walked into the bar and took a seat at one of the booths. I guess that most sports bars are similar, as the layout of Casey's is similar to Jake's.

One Scotch turned into four or five. At that point I was unable to distinguish who I was sitting across from, much less figure out personality traits. I'd definitely crossed the line by getting drunk in front of Baraka. I made a big mistake; now he had an up-front and personal glimpse of who I really am, a guy who can't handle his personal demons, so he self-medicates himself with alcohol.

Mike was in control; he just had a few beers. It must have been somewhere around 5 p.m. when the bartender decided that I had enough and cut me off, seeing that I could no longer lift my glass. As Mike had no cash, he somehow persuaded me to dig into my pocket for mine, assuring me that he'd paid and left the bartender a good tip.

Since Mike was the only sober one, I was forced to let him drive. If Chief Daniels found out that Baraka was driving my undercover car I'd be fucked royally and brought up on departmental charges. Let's see how many departmental regulations I would have time to break. It was only five o'clock. It was rush hour and it would take us a while to get to his place, which probably was fortunate, because it might give me time to sober up. When we pulled up to the curb outside of his building Mike suggested I come up to the apartment for some coffee. I said absolutely not. He insisted. Again I told him no. He insisted that I needed to sober up and have a cup of coffee.

"Frank, what could it hurt if you came up? You can't drive like this. What are you gonna do, sit here for a few hours until you sober up enough to drive? Come on up."

I sat in the passenger seat for a minute staring straight ahead out the windshield, too drunk to function, but at least the inside of the car had stopped spinning. Mike's hands gripped the steering wheel tighter and tighter as he made each point as to why I should come up to his apartment. I thought, *What the fuck, what's the difference?* At least I wouldn't have to sit in the car and sober up.

"Okay, Mike, but just for a little while." I struggled out of the car, looking at the building, which seemed to be moving on its foundation as we walked toward it. He helped me up the entrance stairs, opened one of the double doors, and then helped me up three steps to the hallway and down the hall to his apartment.

Mike yelled out, "Ma?" but neither she nor Mike's sister, Hanna, was home. Mike pointed me to the living room and told me to have a seat on the couch. He walked into the kitchen to make the coffee. A few minutes went by and he brought out a tray of cookies covered in powdered sugar and placed them on the coffee table in front of me. He said that his mother and sister were out shopping for dinner, as she only cooked with fresh ingredients each night. I liked that because it reminded me of my mother, who shopped every day for fresh food to cook for my dad. Mike went back into the kitchen to check on the coffee as I sat there thinking that this was a day I wouldn't forget.

As I looked around the room, I saw that it was filled with what must have been expensive Middle Eastern antique furniture. The beige couch I was sitting on was centered on the back wall facing windows that looked out to Landau Street. The couch had curved arms in what looked like expensive, hand-carved, scrolled mahogany. My feet were planted on a beautiful maroon oriental rug with a large sculpted medallion in its center. I could bet it was purchased from Sami Hassan. Mike brought the coffee into the living room on another tray, complete with what looked like a silver server, small espresso-like cups, sugar, and cream. He set it down on the glass, bronze-framed coffee table in front of me. He even had napkins and small spoons to match the cups. This really surprised me. He had enough class to entertain me and put this together. I couldn't see me doing the same in the shithole I lived in. Could you imagine: *Hey, Mike, want a drink? Grab the whiskey in the living room, wash out some glasses, and help yourself. Just make some room on the kitchen table; yeah, just stuff the empty pizza boxes in the garbage while I wipe the table off so we can sit down.* What a joke!

I poured a cup of coffee, putting in a little sugar. The coffee reminded me of the Italian black coffee that my father always drank. It was similar. Mike took his black, as did I. He sat in a matching chair diagonally across from the couch and asked me, "What do you think of the coffee?"

"Delicious. A little sweet, though; I put in a little too much sugar.
What is it?"

"It's sweet because I already put the sugar in it in the kitchen. I probably should have told you, sorry.

"It tastes like the coffee I had at home."

"We make the coffee from fresh beans from Turkey, grind it to a very fine powder, add some sugar, leaving the grounds in the coffee, which means we don't strain it. It's strong." I downed the first cup to get it out of the way. With the next cup I poured it without adding sugar and took a sip. Perfect. I eyed the cookies, picked one up, and took a bite. The cookie had a slight almond-and-lemon flavor. I took another. They were delicious.

Mike and I talked about how his father had come to America and how his father was the first ambassador to the United Nations from Jordan. Mike said that he had disappointed his father in many ways, and regretted that he wouldn't have the chance to make amends and make his father proud of him one day.

I was getting too comfortable and this made me feel uncomfortable. It was time to go and I was now sober enough to drive. Mike asked me to stay for dinner. His said that his mother was a great cook and always made plenty of food and that, besides, she wanted to meet me. He told me that his mother wanted to meet the person who was responsible for her son's safety and that she was frightened for both of us. You know, hearing him say that was the first time I'd thought of it that way. I was responsible for keeping him safe.

Thanking Mike for his hospitality, I said that I couldn't stay for dinner and had to go. He saw me to the top of the stairwell, asking me if I'd be all right.

"I'm fine; thanks again for the coffee." He offered me his hand and I shook it. "Let me know how you make out with Cruz."

"I'll try to set it up as soon as I can."

Down on the street, I looked around—a habit of mine— before I unlocked my car. Everything seemed all right. I slid into the driver's seat, realizing that I had no place to go. How pathetic. I took out my phone and dialed Joe, wondering what he was up to that night. He answered on the second ring.

"Joe, got any plans tonight?"

"Yeah, I've got a buy going down with Angel tonight. We're supposed to meet in an hour."

"Oh, I was hoping we could go someplace decent, someplace maybe for a good steak and a nice bottle of wine, somewhere where we don't get drunk and have to have someone drive us home."

"Sorry, Frankie, sounds good, but I have to save it for another night.
You okay? You sound down."

"Yeah, I'm fine. I'll talk to you later."

I started the car and headed for home. I decided to have a really big night, stay home, and order Chinese. I thought about Baraka on my way, about how he was a mystery to me. But I knew that I would eventually figure him out.

Chapter Fourteen

The bar was dimly lit. I figured the lights were low to either hide the filth or keep down the electric bill, maybe both. The red border tile from the bar to the floor was chipped, with whole tiles missing, probably from customers at the bar smashing their mugs into the tiles out of annoyance caused by the barstools being too close to the bar and their knees continually banging against the bar. The fake Tiffany lamps over the booths had a coating of dust accentuating their glass shades; the drab maroon carpet was threadbare and the brown leather seating in the booths was cracked, showing black-ringed holes from the many cigarettes that had been dropped there. Behind the bar, suspended from the ceiling, was a giant, ostentatious, red plastic rooster highlighted with a spotlight. Johnny Camerari, the owner of this bucket of shit, hadn't put a dime into the place since he'd bought it fifteen years ago.

It gets better. The bartender was a study from a cartoonist's imagination. His shaved head was perched on a 300-pound, pear-shaped frame, and he was only five foot four. In his late forties, this goofball sported black-rimmed eyeglasses, a red checkered vest covering a white tee shirt, and all of that with red suspenders holding up his brown corduroy pants. This guy reminded me of a barker at a sleazy sideshow in a traveling circus.

In the rear room of the bar stood four pool tables, where many arguments had led to shootings and stabbings. The dump was a true neighborhood sub-blue collar establishment, where most of the patrons knew each other and strangers stood out like a sore thumb. The name outside and above the entrance door in half-broken red neon lights said it all: "Red Rooster Lounge." The guys in the intelligence unit had identified it as a location frequented by drug and gun dealers and a place where a few documented shootings had taken place. I guess that is why Hector Cruz felt comfortable meeting there. Anyone who didn't belong would stand out, especially a cop.

I know Hector would have his people there that night to watch his back. If things got rough, they'd help him get out of the place. The only problem for me was that the only one in the lounge I'd know would be Mike, and I didn't think he'd be much help to me if the shit hit the fan. But all in all, I loved the excitement of being introduced to Hector and convincing him that I was a wise guy who could buy as much product from him as he could sell.

It was nine o'clock when Mike walked in. Spotting me sitting at a table opposite the booths in the bar area, he came over and pulled up a chair next to me.

"Hey Frank, how long have you been here?"

"Not long, about ten minutes. Where'd you park?"

"I got a space right out in front."

"You driving Hanna's car?"

"Yes."

"As soon as we get the waitress's attention, I'll order us drinks." "Geez, the music is awfully loud."

"Yeah, I think they got Toni Braxton blaring through the amplifiers."

Looking around, I saw some of the patrons get up to dance on the poor excuse of a dance floor between the bar area and pool tables. Believe me, these folks weren't bashful, and seemed intent on having a good time.

Finally a buxom waitress showing a little too much cleavage and a lot of life's wear came over to the table and took our order, a Bud Light for Mike and a Scotch and soda for me.

I wondered if I'd regret ordering out of a glass when tomorrow morning rolled around.

She was back with the drinks with a slight smile. I'd seen the guys at the next table place a $20 bill on her serving tray and one of them kiss her on the cheek. Like I said, everyone knew everyone. After setting the drinks down she asked if we wanted to run a tab, and I replied yes, that we were waiting for someone else.

"Fine, I'll be back," she said, and walked back to the bar.

We sipped our drinks for a while, making small talk, when Mike said, "Hector asked what you looked like, so I told him. I guess he wanted to know who to look for when he walked in."

"Oh, yeah? What'd you tell him?"

"That you look kinda like Andy Garcia, with a mustache." I laughed. "Hey, I'm moving up a notch."

We'd finished our drinks, so I signaled for another round. I'd have to watch myself, as two would be the limit. Even I have professional rules. Mike was getting fidgety, looking at his watch, looking at the door, sipping his beer, setting it down, and then engaging in the ritual again. His nerves were getting the best of him

Leaning over, he said, "Do you think something's wrong? He shoulda been here a half hour ago."

"Relax. Smile. Guys like him are always late. They're never on time. Just take it easy; we'll be fine."

Just as the waitress set the drinks on the table, the door opened and in walked Hector. He looked like something out of the movies. He stood about five feet nine, had a medium build, and looked like he was a regular at the gym. He was wearing a gray designer jogging suit, expensive black and white sneakers, and a large gold chain around his neck from which hung a diamond-inscribed pendant in the form of the letter H. His black hair was combed straight back, tied in a short pony tail. His eyes flashed around the bar, spotting us as Mike stood up, waving him over. I stood, extending my hand, which Hector shook.

"Mike's told me a lot of good things about you."

I looked down at Mike, who was worried, and evidently at a loss for words. Finally, collecting himself, Mike looked at

Hector.

"Hey, Hector, how's things? This is Frankie Miranda."

Hector replied nonchalantly, "You know how it is, busy running around." While still standing, he signaled the waitress. She immediately came over at almost a run. He ordered a rum and coke and another round for us. Now, I wished I'd not had that second Scotch. He sat down directly across from me for the obvious reason of keeping me in direct eye contact. The waitress hustled back, set the drinks down, and turned towards another table with another set of drinks.

"Hector, it's a pleasure. Mike's said good things about you too. He's always trying to do the right thing, except he coulda found a better place for a sit-down rather than this bucket of shit." I could feel Hector's eyes boring into me, trying to detect any deception. He was intent on every word I uttered. I thought, *Good-looking guy. I'll bet he has no trouble bedding a different lady every night. We'll see how he likes prison when he's bent over, taking it up the ass from some musclebound freak.*

Apparently I'd insulted Mike. "C'mon, this place is fine."

Hector just smiled. He looked at Mike for a moment, realizing that he was embarrassed. *Good*, I thought. It's what I wanted. Hector had to know who was controlling the meeting. Then Hector turned his attention towards me. He asked where I got my jewelry from.

"I like the bling; where'd you pick it up?" I explained that the diamond pinkie ring and gold-studded dice hanging from an eighteen karat gold chain were gifts from my *gumar*.

He asked, "Gumar?"

"Yeah, my girlfriend."

"Ah, every culture, it seems, has its words of affection. Ours is *novia* for our special girl, but we have many other names for not-so-special ones." He laughed, flashing brilliant white teeth, a contrast against his dark complexion.

I could see he was beginning to relax and feel comfortable, which in turn made me confident about accomplishing my mission. Between sips of his drink, he said,

"So, mi amigo, Mike tells me you're looking for some new product." Before I could reply, he leaned forward and with a riveting glare asked, "Who's been supplying you with *cocaína?*" Mike just sat there keeping his mouth shut.

Leaning towards Hector, my face grimacing from his question, I replied, "I don't discuss people I do business with and I don't fucking do business with nobody who discusses me, *capisce?*"

Digesting that statement, Hector seemed to look through me for a few seconds. Then, slightly nodding his head in agreement, he let out a belly laugh, saying, "I like that, Poppi, I think maybe we can do some business." We picked up our glasses and clicked them together. Mike raised his glass, a bead of sweat rolling down his face.

I reached over across the table and laid my hand on Hector's arm. "Hector, we're very serious people. We have connections to unload between five and ten kilos of coke in Atlantic City every week. But you gotta know one thing. If you decide to do business with us, no mistakes. amigo, me and my people don't intend to spend one day in the joint. *Comprende?*"

"*Sí*, Poppi, *yo comprendo.* Sounds like somebody got burned. I have the purest shit around and can deliver as much as you want anywhere. You tell me you can handle five to ten keys a week, well then, my friend, I'm prepared to offer you a good price. But we got to start off slow until we get to know each other better."

I looked at him square into those traitorous brown eyes. "And what's a good price, my friend?"

He lowered his voice to almost a whisper. "For you, you can have them for a few thousand below wholesale, fifteen thousand per key. We do one, two keys at a time, then, the sky's the limit." He laughed.

"Anyway you want it is fine with me."

Unable to keep his mouth shut any longer, Mike blurts out, "Yeah, we can . . ."

85

I immediately cut him off, raising my voice. "Shut the fuck up!
Don't ever interrupt me when I'm doing business!"

Mike looked at me as if I'd slapped his face. "Sorry, I . . ."

"What'd I just say? What'd I just tell you? Keep your fucking yap
shut." I stared at him, wanting to choke him. He slumped back in his seat, emotionally deflated, just staring at his drink.

I turned my attention to Cruz. "I want you to remember one thing, Hector, you can't spend cocaine, you can only spend money, and I got the fucking money. Fifteen large is too high."

"*Sí, comprendo*, we'll talk about price later. How does one businessman get in touch with another businessman? Because I have a gift for you, Poppi."

"For now, you can call me." I jotted down my undercover cell phone number on the napkin and handed it to him. "In the future, Hector, maybe you can come to my house and we can take care of business like gentlemen."

He must have liked what he'd heard. He took a small card from his shirt pocket, scribbled on the back of it, and handed it to me. "Frankie, here's my cell number and the phone number of a social club on 149th Street. You can always get word to me at the club if I don't answer my phone." The words "El Tres Dos, Hundred & Forty Ninth Street, Bronx, New York" were written on the front of the card that he handed me.

Hector waved to the waitress and shouted for the check as he finished the rest of his drink. As he got up, he asked, "Do you know South Yonkers, where Post and Livingston is?"

I looked over at Mike, nodding to him that it was okay to speak. He quietly said, "Yeah, I know where it is."

Then, speaking under his breath and looking at his watch, Cruz asked the time, and said, "You and Mike meet me there in an hour." He grabbed the check from the waitress and as he caressed her face with one hand, with his other hand he stuffed a hundred-dollar bill into her apron pocket, telling her to keep the change. "See you in an hour," he said to us, and then walked out of the bar.

We sat there for a while. I could see that Mike was feeling dejected after the dressing down I gave him.

"Hey, nothing personal, but you gotta learn when to keep your mouth shut. You slip up and Cruz sees that we're not on the same page, you could get us hurt. These guys ain't stupid. They can read you like a book, so let me do the talking. I know where I'm going with the conversation. Only speak when you're spoken to when there are bad guys involved, *capisce*?"

"Sorry, I understand. It won't happen again."

The waitress came over again, asking if we needed something. I shook my head no.

Changing the subject to lighten the mood, I asked, "So, how's Cindy's old man holding up?"

"He's out of intensive care. I think I should go see him. I need to get some things off my chest."

I looked over at him. "You know, that might not be a good conversation to have right now. You don't have a job and you're cooperating with the government. If he finds out, we're both fucked. I don't think it's a good idea. Maybe you should wait to see him until we've finished our business."

"Yeah, maybe you're right."

Looking at my watch, I saw it was time to go. We got up, walked through the bar area, and out the door to where my car was parked. I told Mike to leave his car at the Red Rooster. For the Cruz meet, I'd rented a black Lincoln Continental sedan. We slid into the car and pulled into traffic. I drove around the neighborhood to make sure that Cruz didn't have someone following us. Mike was still pretty sullen, looking around everywhere except at me. I wondered if he was getting pieced off by Cruz for setting up the deal. Fifteen thousand was a lot of

money for a kilo of coke. I decided not to confront him just yet. I wanted him relaxed. Besides, I needed to get my head together and focus on what I was doing. Daydreaming, my thoughts reverted to Daniels and Howell. They'd pop Valium if they knew what was coming down tonight, and I'd be in a world of shit. They'd say I'd had time enough to call for backup. But if I called them, they'd make me wear a transmitter and I couldn't take the chance that Cruz would find it if he decided to pat me down. Plus,
Cruz could have guys on the street and they'd pick up any strange cars in the area.

We arrived at the post at Livingston about 11:55 p.m. Mike nervously asked if I had a gun on me. I told him not to worry about it. The intersection and surrounding streets were brightly lit by halogen streetlights. On the left of the intersection were rundown tenements and on the right was an industrial park surrounded by a chain-link fence topped with razor wire. I continued through the intersection under the blinking red overhead street light, noticing that Hector was in a phone booth on the southeast corner, speaking on a pay phone. I slowly pulled the car to the curb, directly across the street from the phone booth, eyeing Hector. While Hector was on the phone, I reached under the front seat and pulled out a nine millimeter, placing it inside my pants, under my jacket, at the small of my back. I could see Mike's uneasiness.

He blurted, "I don't see anyone on the street, what d'ya think?"

Looking at Mike I said, "Maybe he has his people watching us from one of the tenements, or from one of the commercial buildings. You never know where they are."

It felt like Hector was on the phone for hours but in reality it was only minutes. Finally, he slid open the phone booth door and walked out into the center of the intersection, under the overhead street light. The blinking red light reflected off his long leather trench coat and slicked-back hair. He waved his hand for us to come over. I wondered if this was what hell looked like. Certainly it was the setting for it. No, this was worse than hell; at least you'd know where you stood in hell. Here, there was no telling.

I looked over at Mike. "Time to rock and roll."

We'd both exited the car when Hector yelled out, "Only you, Poppi, only you. My gift is only for you."

Mike took a deep breath, let out a big sigh of relief, and got back into the car.

The human body is an amazing machine and thank God mine was in good working order for the twenty-foot walk to the middle of the street. The old familiar symptoms kicked in. I felt the constriction in my stomach, the heave in my chest due to a need for more oxygen, with my heart thudding as the blood pounded in my ears, and the muscles in my entire body tightening. I had to consciously control my breathing— perhaps the most important thing of all. Because if I appeared nervous, Hector would be able to pick it up and know that I was scared and maybe not legit. And in his mind, there should be no reason why I should be afraid.

Hector had both hands in his coat pocket now and there was no doubt in my mind that one of those hands held a gun. His posture was relaxed as he intently looked up and down the street to see if I was alone. As I continued to walk towards him, my knees shook. My senses were so in tune with my surroundings that I could hear the electric current humming in the overhead wires leading to the streetlights and the muted crackling of the halogens. After what seemed like an eternity, Hector and I were face to face. Suddenly, he made a movement with his right hand and quickly removed a small, egg-shaped packet of tinfoil from his left jacket pocket. Then he said, as he fingered the packet, "Hey, good to see you, my friend. I've got a sample of the best stuff around. Let me know what you think."

I looked him straight in the eye. "If this shit hasn't been fucked with, I'll get back to you."

He shot back, "No, Poppi, you test it now."

I put out my hands, palms open, in an attempt at reasoning with him, "I don't use the stuff. I just sell it. I'll get back to you."

His left hand shot out of his pocket with lightning speed, holding a twenty-five automatic, pushing it into my forehead while his forefinger rested on the trigger. With the other hand, he pressed the tinfoil packet into my left hand, telling me, "You test it now."

Realizing I had little choice in the matter, I slowly opened the packet and took a small amount of the white powder secreted inside, placing it on my left palm. With the other hand I sealed the packet, putting it into my jacket pocket. Then, slightly turning my head away from Cruz, bending down, I took a pinch of the powder, and rubbed it onto my right nostril. Blocking the nostril with my fingers, I inhaled deeply through the other nostril. After shivering a little for the Hollywood effect, and praying he bought my act, I turned back towards him and looked him straight in the eye. He obviously saw the ring of powder left around the right nostril, looked at me for a second or two, then lunged forward, grabbing me in a bear hug, the silver automatic still in his left hand. My first instinct was to go for my gun, but that's tough to do when someone has both of his arms wrapped around you. I felt the strength of the man, his arms pressing tightly around me.

As he released me, Cruz laughed. "Hey, Poppi, its good stuff, no?" "Yeah, Hector, but what's with the fucking gun?"

"Oh, you know, Poppi, these days you can't be too careful. There's a cop hiding on every corner."

"Okay, Hector, I'll make sure to remember that. Let's stay in touch and set something up, but the price is still too high."

We shook hands. As I walked back to the car, I saw a man standing in a doorway a few buildings up from my vehicle. His silhouette was outlined in shadows by the streetlights. I was right again; I didn't have backup, but Cruz did.

I pulled away from the curb, swinging the car in a U-turn to go back down Livingston and eventually connect to the Saw Mill River Parkway. I looked over; Mike's hands were shaking.

"What the hell's wrong with you? You're shaking." "They couldn't pay me enough to do what you do."

I gave a stoic laugh. "You know what? They don't pay me enough." Laughing to myself, I thought, *I do it because it's my job.* But that's bullshit. I did it because I liked the rush it gave me. Man, there was something seriously wrong with me.

I continued to drive through a myriad of traffic lights and onto Nepperhan Avenue when it began to rain heavily. Mike began to regain his composure as the tension drained from his body. Making our way to the Saw Mill River Parkway a few exits later, I jumped onto Palmer Avenue. That's when Mike said, "Frank, I have some information."

"Oh, what have you got?"

"I know an Arab who couriers half a million in drug money about twice a week. I know his route. He drives it to a connection in Washington, D.C."

"Who's he working for?"

Mike looked straight ahead. "A heroin dealer named Khalid. I don't know his last name. This guy never carries a gun. I was thinking, we could stop him, you could flash your badge, and we take the money and leave. No one has to know."

Mike had just crossed the line. I swerved over to the side of the road, jamming on the brakes, screaming, "Get outta the fucking car!" I ran around to the passenger side of the car, opened the passenger side door, snatched Baraka by the collar, and dragged him to the center of the road. I forced his head to the double yellow line, grinding his cheek into the macadam. The cars and trucks honked their horns as they passed in both directions.

91

"You see that fucking yellow line? Take a good look at it." I released the pressure on his neck so he could gaze down the yellow double line. "I'm that yellow double line. I don't go to the left of it and I don't go to the right of it—you got that?"

I looked up to see an eighteen-wheeler barreling towards us, its horn blaring, its headlights blinding as it sped by. Through the driver's open window I heard, "Get outta the fucking road, assholes."

Infuriated by Baraka's suggestion, and keeping his head pressed to the road, I screamed at him, "If I ever hear anything come out of your mouth like that again, I'll pull the plug so fast you'll be in the slam before you can blink your eyes. Do you understand? Now get back in the fucking car."

Releasing him, we walked back to the car as more vehicles whizzed by and more insults were yelled at us. Back in the car, I noticed the front of Mike's pants were wet. I guess he pissed his pants. "Serves you right, you fuck. The night's over; I'm taking you home. I'm warning you, don't fuck with me. I meant what I said."

I started the car, jamming it into drive. Even Cruz hadn't gotten to me the way Mike just had. I figured now was as good a time as any to confront Mike about any side deal he may have with Cruz.

"Another thing is bothering me about you and Cruz." "What's that, Frank?"

"You have a side deal going with Cruz?"

Mike's jaw dropped; his eyes dilated. "What are you talking about?" "You taking smart money?"

"Smart money?"

"Don't play stupid with me. He wants fifteen thousand large per key. You taking anything off the top?"

"Shit, no! Cruz wouldn't be stupid enough to give me anything before the deal went down. And how the hell would I get it after?"

"Well, how do you know Cruz is going down on the first

buy?" "Look, Frank, I'm not taking a dime from Cruz. I
just want to work
my way out of the mess I'm in."

"How am I gonna believe anything you say now?"

"Frank, I just needed to know where you're coming from.
I need to be able to trust you. Right now, I don't know who to
trust."

"What the fuck, Mike!" I yelled. "So you're giving me a
litmus test to see if I'm a dirty cop? You're playing with fire
here, Mikey boy. Just do what you're fucking told and stay
out of my way. If you don't trust me, call your fucking lawyer
and forget about cooperating. Got it?"

Mike didn't say another word as I made it to his building
in record time. I couldn't wait to get him out of the car; he was
stinking up the car with the smell of urine. After dropping
him off, I swung by the office to field-test the sample that
Cruz gave me and secure it into evidence. It tested positive
for cocaine hydrochloride. Cruz was almost in the bag. Since
I was still all pumped up, I decide to head for Jake's, hoping
that it was still open and that Joe was there.

On the way to the bar, I thought back on some of the
lectures at the police academy I'd heard about how the body
reacts to stress and some of the constructive ways to cope
with it. Go to the gym, it gets rid of the adrenaline in your
system. Your body's chemistry will kill you if you don't keep it in
balance. Run, lift weights, do what it takes to stay in shape and
relax your mind. Above all, don't self-medicate with alcohol;
it's a lose, lose proposition leading to ruined marriages and
careers. Boy, didn't I know this? I was a casualty of that war
already. Out there in the streets, my life in the hands of
dirtbags; if I twitched the wrong way, I was history. So,
going to the gym in the morning just didn't cut it for me. For
better or worse, my gym was a place called Jake's and my
workout was in Joe's ear and I was flushing my system with a
good bottle of Scotch.

Of course, the fact that I'd built a stone wall around

myself, deflecting most advice I'd been given since I was a kid, pretty much said it all. I was mule-stubborn and probably looking at a radically shortened life span because of it. What really bothered me was the thought that I might make it through all the crap and then right at retirement, some fucked-up disease might strike me out of the blue, like a stroke, or pancreatic cancer. Going all this way inundated with stress and hardship racking my mental and physical well-being, believing in what I was doing, only to succumb in the twilight years to some bullshit affliction, probably caused by what I did for a living, didn't quite make sense to me. So, what is it that makes sense in life? Maybe it's doing what you believe in and doing it in the best way you know how. Maybe that's it? I pulled up to the curb outside Jake's, where there was plenty of parking since it was 3 a.m. I walked in to find Joe sitting at the bar with Jessica; they were sipping their drinks. Jessica ran behind the bar to pour me my usual, Dewar's White Label Scotch straight up. Joe asked if I had just finished up, so I proceeded to tell him what went down with Cruz that night.

He began to rant. "Frankie, you're crazy for not calling for backup.
When Daniels finds out, you'd better strap in. You're in deep shit." "Joe, I did what I had to do. Hector is a big fish and I wouldn't have
him in my back pocket if I didn't go it alone. I don't give a fuck if Daniels blows an artery when he finds out."

"How did Baraka hold up?"

"Fine, he sat in the car while I dealt with Cruz."

"Frankie, don't trust that fuck. He's out for himself. Don't give him a chance to burn you."

"I'll keep Baraka at arm's length. Believe me."

After throwing down my drink, I kissed Jessica on the cheek and said good night. Outside of the bar, it was quiet. I loved the quietness and the peace that the early morning hours brought. I took a deep breath, smelling the spring air

94

as I got into the car. I was finally relaxed as I made my way to my apartment.

Chapter Fifteen

I'd unplugged the phone so I could get some sleep before going to the office and meeting with the Chief the next day. It turned out to be the right thing to do, because when I plugged the phone in at noon, it rang instantly. Daniels's secretary told me that the Chief wanted me in immediately. She said that she'd been trying to get me all morning. I said that I'd been up all night and took the phone off the hook so I could sleep. I told her that as soon as I showered and dressed I'd be in.

I arrived at the office at about 1:30 p.m. Before heading up to Daniels's office I stopped in the squad room to see if there were any messages left on my desk. Joe was sitting at his desk reviewing an intelligence file obtained from the Intelligence Squad on Hector Cruz. He said that, as suspected, Hector was a player tied directly to Pepe Lopez. His name came up in a few investigations, but he'd never been arrested or prosecuted.

I told Joe that the Chief's office had been calling for me all morning; he must have found out from the evidence guy that I'd logged in the sample of coke that Cruz gave me the night before. The Chief was likely pissed that I hadn't called for backup. Joe said he would tag along with me to the Chief's office; he brought the Cruz file with him. We walked up to the fifth floor and walked into Daniels's office. His secretary, Ruth, buzzed the Chief's intercom. "Frank's here." "Tell him to take a seat; I'm on the phone."

Joe and I took a seat. I felt like a kid in grade school who'd misbehaved in class and then been told by his teacher to go to the principal's office. The slight eye roll that Ruth gave us as we sat down confirmed my feelings. Ruth's intercom sounded after a minute or two.

"Send him in."

"The Chief will see you now."

"Thanks." Joe and I got up and started for Daniels's door, half smoked glass, half wood.

Ruth interrupted. "I do believe the Chief just wants to see you, Frank. Joe, you can wait here, if you please."

I turned to look at Ruth, careful to reply civilly. "Joe's obtained information pertinent to this meeting. Both of us need to see the Chief." She shrugged, her attention now directed towards her computer.

"Well it's up to you, but don't say you weren't warned."

"Thanks for the warning, Ruth." Turning to the doorknob, I opened the door to see an open bottle of Pepto-Bismol sitting on the Chief's desk. Daniels's face did have a purple hue to it, the blood vessels plainly in evidence in his bulbous nose and in the puffy balloons of skin billowing out from his cheeks. His eye sockets had receded and were jaundiced under the rims, reminding me of two pissholes in the snow. He was typically disheveled; his brown print tie was loosened at the collar and resting on top of the white, button-down shirt protruding over the mound of fat that surrounded his midsection.

He was standing by his desk studying a file folder as he motioned for me to sit.

At the sound of two chairs scraping the floor, he looked up, surprised to see Nulligan. He raised his eyebrow, snarling, "What are you doing here, Nulligan? This doesn't concern you; get out."

"Look, Chief, I've got some intel on Cruz that I thought you might be interested in."

"Christ, if I needed intel on Cruz I'd have asked for it. But since you're here, what do you got?"

"Cruz is connected to Pepe Lopez and the Cali Cartel. We got a chance to get to Lopez."

"Is that right, Nulligan?"

Daniels reached for the Pepto-Bismol; opening the bottle, he poured out a handful of tablets into his hand and tossed them into his mouth like cocktail peanuts. "Okay,

Santorsola, tell me what I don't know about last night."

I told him what happened the previous night, including that Cruz had given me a sample of coke. Daniels was quiet at first, listening intently. But it didn't take long for him to explode.

"Frank, you're not out there on your own anymore. You had plenty of time to call for backup and you didn't. Pull another stunt like you did last night, Frank, and I'll have you out on your ass writing parking tickets."

I raised my hands in the air, frustrated. "Chief, Cruz was looking for cops last night. If I called for backup, I wouldn't have him in my pocket right now. I saw at least one guy in a doorway and I guarantee he wasn't there coming home from a party."

Daniels's voice rose. "Frank, I'm beginning to think I made a mistake signing off on you and Baraka."

Joe sat there not saying a word.

"C'mon, Chief, I'm sure I can get to Lopez if we let the first buyo."

"That's bullshit, Frank. I'm not going to let thousands of dollars
isappear without taking Cruz down right then and there. There's no way he's gonna do twenty-five to life. He'll flip on Lopez. I'm the Chief; I've made my decision. Now the two of you get out of my office."

"It's the wrong decision; Cruz won't flip."

Joe couldn't help himself. His street instincts were overriding his better judgment. "Frank's right; Cruz won't flip. He knows that his family back in Colombia won't be safe. You don't become a Hector Cruz without knowing that."

Daniels's face was a bright shade of red, the veins on his neck pulsating from anger. "I said that I've made my decision, now get out of my office!"

We got up and walked out of the Chief's office to the outer office where Ruth was smirking behind her desk with a look of *I told you so* on her face. As we exited Ruth's office, Joe slammed the door so hard that the glass echoed in its frame. I turned to Joe.

"The guy's got no balls. Like it's his money."

We walked down to the fourth floor and into the squad room, where I decided to give Baraka a call, telling him I'd be in touch shortly to discuss Cruz. I now had to put all my energy into arresting Cruz and hoping that he would take me to Lopez. The problem was that it was highly unlikely that Cruz would flip, and Lopez would eventually find out that Mike had set Hector up. If that happened, Mike's life and maybe mine would be in jeopardy.

It took some time to set up the buy/bust. We had to book several rooms in the Ramada Inn in New Rochelle, New York. One room was mine, where I could set up a lab to test the coke. The other room was connected and designated as the command center from where Deputy Chief Howell would supervise the operation. There were DA's detectives positioned in vehicles throughout the hotel parking lot. The streets may have been Cruz's, but we needed to control the hotel to make the operation a success.

The buy/bust room, 1021, had to be wired for visual and audio, with a pinhole camera secreted into the wall above the connecting room door to the command center. The pins on the door were removed so that detectives on the other side could break through on my signal with little problem. Communication had to be established with everyone assigned to the operation in order to avoid any potential screwups that might jeopardize the operation.

Howell was only concerned about the success of the operation, and never about the cops themselves. I always think that when supervisors don't care about their subordinates, it usually means they're out for themselves. That sentiment fit Howell like a glove. That night he acted like a Mexican jumping bean, bouncing here then there, asking if this and that had been done, getting on the radio when there was no need, and generally making a real pain in the ass of himself in a feeble attempt to ensure his own usefulness.

He was still in his gray suit pants, wearing his usual plain blue tie, which was pulled down from his collar and somehow hung below his waist. The sweat poured off him, soaking his armpits through from the stress he created for himself. Shaky Howell couldn't stay calm and cool if he were on top of the covers with the air-conditioning blowing onto him. Everyone tried to avoid him but somehow he was always in everyone's face.

A little after 9 p.m. I took the elevator down to the lobby to wait for Cruz to arrive. The lobby was bustling with guests arriving for a convention. Baraka was sitting in a chair next to the front desk, reading a magazine. He and I had arrived at the hotel about an hour earlier. I told Mike to keep his seat while I went upstairs to check things out. I hadn't told him anything about that night's operation. He was under the impression that the first one or two buys would be let go so I could deal directly with Lopez. It bothered me that it wouldn't go that way, but there was little I could do about it. What a bunch of bullshit. Lopez would only replace Hector with another guy. This fact was irrelevant to Howell and Daniels. All they were concerned with was looking good for the DA by chalking up another bust of a major player.

Three detectives were posted in the lobby, posing as hotel guests. Detective Cheryl Smyth, gray hair, matronly, early forties, her slightly wrinkled face peering into a magazine, was seated at one end of the lobby on a red velveteen couch. Jim Johnstone, medium height, totally bald, mid-thirties, athletic build, was writing postcards at the concierge station at the front desk. And John Dempsey, short, pudgy, mid-thirties, short cropped blond hair with a face like an English bulldog, was at the other end of the lobby sitting on a gold-colored loveseat.

When I came back downstairs, Mike walked over as soon as he spotted me. I told him to be calm and relaxed when

Cruz walked in, and above all not to say anything. "You do what you're told, no matter what, no matter what you think is gonna happen. Trust me, there's a reason for everything I do, so no fuckups. Are we clear?"

He looked around the lobby, then back at me. "Sure, Frank, anything you say."

I got closer to him, almost whispering, "Look, you don't have to be nervous. You don't have a major role here tonight. The reason you're here is so that Hector doesn't become suspicious, wondering where you are."

Mike stared at me for a moment. "How the hell do you do this every night? Jesus, I'm peeing every five minutes and you don't even break a sweat. What are you made of, stone?"

I laughed. "Not really. It's just what I do. Okay, enough bullshit.

Time to go to work. Stand next to me and that's all you do. Got it?" "I got it."

I checked the lobby again, making sure that everyone was where they were supposed to be. The most important thing that night was the communication. I needed to know that all units could hear me. Sergeant Steve Cook, the technical officer, set up the communications for the night's operation. Steve was a mild-mannered British guy. Standing six feet, premature graying hair, fifty-five or so, and built like a pug, he was an expert in his field. Steve knew everything would need to work flawlessly that night because my life would depend on it.

I had a transmitter hidden in a belt along with my cell phone and case. We'd checked and there'd been no area of the hotel where each transmission I made hadn't been crystal clear.

At 9:30 p.m. my cell rang. It was Hector, telling me that he'd be there in ten minutes. I hung up and updated the command center. True to his word, Hector walked in through the front door at 9:40 p.m. with another guy. Hector sported a brown, full-length leather coat with a white silk scarf wrapped around his neck. I thought to myself, *What a knucklehead. If he had half a brain, he'd dress like a Wall Street businessman, not something out of Superfly.* I wondered how many movies he'd watched to come up with that outfit.

Hector's buddy was short and stocky, of Hispanic origin, with piercing black eyes, slicked-back black hair, and a pencil-thin mustache. He wore a shiny gray sharkskin suit and overcoat. They walked directly over to us. Hector extended his hand and as I shook it, he said, "Aye, Poppi, are you ready on your end?"

Releasing his grip I said, "I'm all set. How about you?" "*Sí,* but I want to see the money first."

"I got twenty-eight thousand upstairs. We're talking about two keys, right?"

"*Sí,* Poppi."

"Hector, no problem, you can see the money, but I want to do business like gentlemen. No guns upstairs. No one's going upstairs strapped. Before we go upstairs, we need to go into the men's room so we can take a good look at each other. I've got nothing to hide—how about you?"

Smirking, he spat out, "Sure, Poppi, let's feel each other's balls.
After all, amigo, we're both honorable men, no?"

Mike and Hector's sidekick stood alongside us, saying nothing, but listening intently.

"Mike and your friend stay here. Is he carrying anything?"

"No, Poppi, he's clean. José will stay here with Mike until I'm ready for him. *Uno momento.*" He pulled José a few feet away; their hand gestures were like two traffic cops pushing traffic through an intersection. I couldn't help but notice the flash from the two gold front teeth in José's mouth.

Hector returned shortly, stating, "Okay, my friend, let's take a walk into the men's room and feel each other's balls." Once inside, we waited for a guest to leave, both of us primping in the mirror.

"Okay Hector, I'm first." I opened my suit jacket, gesturing for him to pat me down. He brushed and padded me up and down, especially around my ankles, groin, waist, and armpits, finishing with, "You're clean."

"Of course I'm clean. Men like us have each other's interest at heart, no?"

Then it was my turn to reciprocate. I began at his ankles, with Hector looking down at me. Moving my hands up his pants legs to his groin, thoroughly feeling around the groin area, I slid my hands around his waist and felt his pockets, able to feel a metallic object in his right front pocket. I inserted my hand, pulling out a twenty-five caliber automatic. Probably the same one he'd shoved against my forehead. Calmly, I asked, "Hector, what's this? Are you planning to hurt me?"

"No, Poppi. I thought I'd left it in the car."

I quickly removed the clip and racked the chamber back, forcing the round in the chamber out into my hand. Then, placing the clip and the round in my pocket, I handed him back the gun. I checked Hector's coat just to ensure there were no more nasty little surprises, and then we exited the men's room and took the elevator to the tenth floor.

Once in the room, Hector gave it the once-over, looking for anything out of the ordinary—like a gun or a pair of handcuffs, for example. He looked in the closet, under the bed, and even looked under the mattress. What he missed was the bug under the lampshade and the pinhole camera above the door that captured every action in the room. Glancing over at the glass beakers, test tubes, chemical reagents, and bottle of champagne along with two glasses that I'd placed on the table by the window, Hector commented, "Hey, Poppi, are you a chemist or something?"

"It's cobalt thiocyanate and hydrochloric acid to test the shit. You know, amigo, I wouldn't want to buy bad shit from you. Nothing personal, this is just business. Call it insurance for both of us. The champagne's for us, provided all goes well."

"No, Poppi, I understand. Now, my friend, I want to see the money."

"What about the coke, where is it?" "Don't worry, amigo, it's not far away."

I walked to the night table and picked up the phone, dialing 7- 1023, and the adjoining room. Howell picked up the phone. All I said was, "Bring it over," and hung up. Cruz was standing by the end of the bed, his eyes darting around the room, no doubt nervous because I was in control of this part of the melodrama. I'd seen it so often before. Take the scumbag from his own turf and, human nature being what it is, vulnerability and paranoia take over.

There was a knock on the main entrance door. I walked over asked who was there.

"Manny."

Cracking open the door slightly, a briefcase slid through on the floor. I quickly closed the door and handed the case to Hector. He placed it on the bed, opened it, and I swear I could see his eyes dilate as he gazed at the crisp stack of bills. The distrustful smirk had been replaced by a grin extending from one side of his mouth to the other. Immediately he started to count the money and by the time he'd reached ten thousand, he was so overcome with excitement, he lost count. I asked if he needed help. He threw up his hands in frustration.

"I trust that all the money is here. We're just wasting time." "Okay, it's your turn to play show and tell. Let's see the coke." "No problem, I'll go down and get it."

"Wait a minute, Hector. We'll do it by the numbers again. The same way as before, so that there's no surprises. Then we come back here, I test the coke, and we part as friends."

He nodded his head yes, his eyes centered on the briefcase on the bed, and then he left the room. I waited a few minutes, making certain he was observed walking out of the hotel. The case with the money was retrieved from the room to ensure that the twenty-eight thousand dollars didn't disappear and an empty case was put in its place.

Hector left the lobby with his gold-tooth friend, José, and walked to a late-model Mercedes Benz in the hotel's back parking lot. He popped the trunk as two other Hispanic males got out of the car and surveyed the parking lot. Cruz could be seen gesturing toward the hotel, pointing at his watch in an animated discussion with his associates. He then took out a brown canvas gym bag from the trunk and motioned to José to come with him. The other two men climbed back into the car.

As this was happening, I made my way down to the lobby and walked over to Mike, who was still sitting in the chair where I'd left him. As he stood up, I asked if he was okay.

"I'm fine. Hector and the other guy just walked out the back door." "I know. He'll be right back. Just relax."

Looking around the lobby, I was reassured to see Detective Cook and the others in place. A minute or so later, Hector and José walked back into the lobby and over to us. Hector and I fell into pace, telling José and Mike to wait there as we walked into the men's room. This time the men's room was empty. I searched Hector and the gym bag, finding nothing but two brick-like packages wrapped in brown paper and sealed with brown tapes. He then patted me down, finding nothing. We took the elevator up to the room. Hector handed me the gym bag and took a seat in one of the chairs surrounding the table with the drug-testing paraphernalia, his eyes riveted to the briefcase. I placed the gym bag on the bed alongside the briefcase and opened it. I took out one of the brick-size packages, and placed it on the table. Taking a small penknife off the table, I cut into the brown plastic tape and brown paper that sealed the substance inside. Exposing one corner of the package, I saw the material had a yellowish tint and was scaly in texture, like fish scales, as some in the trade call it. I dug into the brick with the tip of the penknife and dropped in into a test tube containing cobalt thiocyanate. It immediately turned pink, then blue. Bingo— cocaine! I quickly tested the other package, and it tested positive for cocaine. At this point, I knew the guys in the other room were chomping at the bit, waiting for me to single them to break down the door of the adjoining room and arrest Cruz. The magic words I had to utter were, "Let's break out the champagne," and Hector would be on his way to becoming a statistic. But for the moment I was having too much fun and wanted to continue the game.

Hector stood up from the chair, unable to control his nervousness, and twitching his body like a barnyard animal, blurted out, "Poppi, the money?"

Holding the test tube high in the air, I smiled at him. "My friend, we're going to do a lot of business together. I see we're going to become good friends."

Hector was now perspiring, the beads of sweat glistening on his forehead. He again yelled out, "Poppi, the fucking money!" and looked at his watch. Suddenly, he made a dash for the briefcase. Simultaneously, I gave a signal that would profoundly change Hector's life. I gave the signal. "Well, let's break out the champagne now!"

Within a millisecond, the adjoining room door exploded, landing on the bed and just missing Cruz. Hector's expression changed from nervous expectancy to one of disbelief. He lunged instinctively towards the onrushing cops with a straight razor in his hand, but before he could use it, he was smacked in the head with a blackjack, falling unconscious to the floor. Later, looking at the gym bag, we found out that he had squirreled away a razor in a pocket underneath the bag, which I had missed, and had slipped it up his sleeve. Hector was handcuffed as he lay on the floor. They also handcuffed me to confuse Hector. We didn't want him to know that I was an undercover cop or where the arrest came from. We wanted Hector to wonder who the police were looking at. I knew that it was just a matter of time before Pepe Lopez found out about the arrest, and if Lopez thought that I was also arrested, Mike might be insulated and protected for a time.

Events were happening rapidly in the lobby. Cruz's men exited the car and were just about to enter the hotel when teams of detectives jumped out of their cars and vans and quickly converged on them, yelling, "Police! Get down on the ground!" At the same time, detectives Cook and Smyth and the other detectives stationed in the lobby attempted to stop José as he pushed the up elevator button. They identified themselves and drew their weapons, yelling for him to freeze. He didn't comply, reaching into his belt and drawing out a pistol. They screamed, "Drop the weapon!" but it was too late. As he turned, raising his weapon, they unleashed a barrage of bullets, scattering his brains all over the shiny, gold-sheen elevator door.

Outside, the men in the parking lot pulled out semiautomatic pistols and aimed them towards the arresting officers. Thinking they could literally shoot their way out of a cordon of police was a big mistake. The cops in the parking lot were screaming for the men to drop their weapons, but when the first perpetrator opened up a staccato burst from his pistol, the officers did the same, literally cutting the men to pieces with a flurry of bullets.

Back in room 1021, Hector was coming to and looking around the room, yelling incoherently in Spanish, "I told them if I wasn't down in twenty minutes to come up and kill every motherfucker in the room."

The tapes were still running in the other room, so we were able to capture his statements from a translator a few days later.

Hector was then dragged to his feet and whisked away to the District Attorney's office for debriefing. In my heart of hearts, I knew he wasn't gonna cooperate.

I made my way to the lobby, but there was no sign of Baraka.

I asked Sergeant Smyth where he'd gone. She said he'd gone into the lobby men's room and hadn't come out. I went in to check on him and found him leaning over one of the sinks, wiping vomit off his face. His complexion was drained of color, and he stood staring in the mirror over the sink.

I asked, "Hey, Mike, you okay?" He just stared into the mirror, unable to speak. I stood beside him, placing my hand on his shoulder, gently massaging his shoulder muscles in an attempt to release some of the tension in him. "Hey, pal, talk to me."

He whispered, his breath reeking of bile, "I've never seen anything like that. The guy's brains are all over the elevator door. Jesus!"

I shook him gently, trying to bring him back to life. "Look, the stupid fuck had a choice and he made the wrong one. It's what happens. Better him than us. The son of a bitch wouldn't have hesitated a second to blow your fucking head off if he smelled a rat. So, my friend, out here it's survival of the fittest, and don't forget it. Now, finish wiping your face with that paper towel and let's get out of here. C'mon, let's go."

We went out to the lobby, where by now the pandemonium of guests screaming and diving for cover had been replaced by forensics and blue-uniformed officers taping off the area where José had been dispatched to a better place. The elevator door had been covered by a white cloth. The hotel had taken the elevator out of service so that it could be cleaned. José's body had been bagged and was waiting for transport to the Westchester County Medical Examiner's office. Baraka and I needed to get out of there before the press arrived, which would be any minute. The last thing I needed was our faces plastered all over the front page of the *New York Post*.

We made our way to the rented Lincoln Town Car parked in the back lot. Detectives and people from the Medical Examiner's office were bagging the guys in the lot. Mike glanced left and right nervously, unconvinced that we'd gotten all of Cruz's people.

"What's with you? You think that some of Hector's guys are still around?"

"Yeah, maybe some of his guys are still around. You never know, Frank."

"Forget about it. We've had our people out here all day. Trust me, we got them all. Besides, I'm wearing my lucky brown suit and nothing's gonna happen to us when I'm wearing this suit."

"What d'ya mean, lucky brown suit?"

"I wear this suit when things have hair on them. And it never fails me."

"Frank, what d'ya mean, when things have hair on them?"

"Like when you introduced me to Hector, and tonight, when the hit hit the fan. I got my suit on, so me and you are walking out of here. You got it?"

"You think that your brown suit keeps you safe, Frank?"

"Mike, everyone needs a good luck charm. Anyway, I'll get you home now."

We climbed into the car and I headed for Landau Street in South Yonkers. As I drove, I wanted to find out more about Mike. I asked him why he'd dropped out of college.

"Well, Sami fixed me up with the bouncer's job and the money was so easy, I decided to quit school. It was a mistake. Since I got into this mess, I've seriously been thinking that there's more to an education than I thought, so I may go back and finish up.

"Oh yeah, in what?"

"Well, don't laugh, but look at my situation. I mean, I'm wrongly convicted for a crime I didn't commit. How many other people are like me? If I didn't have you, no one would be helping me. I'd be sitting in a fucking jail cell and my life would be over. I'm telling you, Frank, if I have to go to jail I'll either kill myself or someone else will do it for me. That's how I feel. So if I get out of this, I'm thinking about finishing up my undergraduate degree in criminal justice, then going on to law school."

"Whoa, that's a switch."

"Yeah, well, we all have to wake up at some point in our lives, and I've had a rude awakening."

"Well, brother, I'll tell you one thing, there's no shortage of dirtbags, so you'll never be out of work. But let's see if you can get out of this fucking mess before you start thinking about the future."

"I know. But here's where I am. Cindy's pregnant and her father hates me, so it's never going to be like, 'Hey, Mike, bring the kids over for a barbecue on Sunday afternoon.' I'm fucked, with no way out but one, to keep working with you. I've got no future other than to go back to the club, depending on tips, but that's not going to pay the bills with a kid on the way. Frank, I plan to marry Cindy—I love her and I'll stand by her. She's not just some street trash I picked up for a one-night stand. I should have listened to my father and made something of myself. Now, I plan to."

"You know, you've got some set of balls, I'll say that much for you. My suggestion is to take it one thing at a time; otherwise, you might end up like me, losing everything important to you and sitting in a bar every night drinking your life away."

"Frank, I have to ask, what did you lose, if you can tell me?" "Well, Mike, I lost my family. I'm not going to get into it, but I haven't seen my kids in a while, and it hurts." "Sorry to hear that."

"Thanks."

"By the way, did I tell you that I went to see Nick in the prison hospital the other day?"

"No, you didn't. He doesn't know that you're working for the "Feds"?

"No, he doesn't know I'm cooperating, and Cindy hasn't said a word. Anyway, I guess he's getting better. I tried to explain about Cindy and me, but he threw me out. I left before he had another heart attack. Cindy stayed, and she cried, telling him she was pregnant, that he was going to be a grandfather, and how much she loved me. After he yelled at her to abort the baby because I was a fucking Arab who can't be trusted, Cindy told him that an abortion wasn't going to happen. Nick finally settled down after a while. When he calmed down, Cindy begged for his blessing, telling him how much he meant to her, that he was the only parent she had left, and how important he'd become in her life since her mother had died. She said that it didn't matter if he was in jail—that she would visit him as much as she could, especially when the baby came, having the joy of holding his grandson in his arms. The guards let her spend over two hours with him, and at the end of it, he grudgingly accepted the situation for what it is, although he told her straight up he didn't like her being involved with me."

"Hey, maybe there's light at the end of the tunnel."

"Yeah, maybe. Anyway, Cindy had one of those tests, and we think it's a boy."

We soon pulled up in front of Mike's building. As he got out of the car he nodded goodbye and I watched him walk inside. I headed for the office to make sure that the cocaine was put into evidence. The twists and turns in Mike's life were now beginning to entangle my life, but what could I do? We were working together and had just concluded a big case, which Mike would be credited for, most likely reducing his ten-year sentence to some extent.

Chapter Sixteen

It was almost 3 a.m. when I walked into the squad room. The two detectives that Deputy Chief Howell had assigned to bring the two keys of coke and the twenty-eight grand back to the office had already logged everything into evidence. The chain of custody was now established, if this case made it to trial.

As soon as I walked in Sergeant Cook came up to me. "It was a rough night; how's Baraka holding up?"

"He's doing okay, Sarge."

Most of the detectives that were involved in the shooting were milling around and quietly talking to one another. They were too pumped up to go home and most of the watering holes were closed, so they were in limbo until they couldn't stay awake any longer.

Nodding to the guys, I just walked over to my desk, where Nulligan was standing. "Good job, Frankie."

"Yeah, we did what we had to do. Too bad it wasn't clean."

Chief Daniels walked into the room, not wanting to be left out of any impromptu conversation. He came over to me and, before I knew it, had me in a bear hug while giving me a kiss on my cheek. Grabbing both my arms as he released me, he said, "Look, the shootings were righteous; it's too bad, but that's the game they played. We all need to move on, so congratulations, Frank, and good job. Take a break now, get some rest, we can deal with the details."

So, here we had it—the Chief, the schoolyard bully, showing his desire to suddenly become accepted by his subordinates, every one of whom he'd taunted and demeaned at some point, now wanting acceptance and praise that he could hold on to, like a branch overhanging a quicksand pit, before sinking back into being the poor excuse of a human that he was.

In retrospect, I was probably more repulsed by his actions and forced good wishes than by any other intrusion into my personal space that I could recently remember. In spite of his good will, Joe and I knew the real score of the evening. The Cruz bust stuck in my craw like a particle of freshly ground pepper I couldn't choke up. Lopez was the main stateside guy we should have been pursuing, but the Chief's modus operandi was so transparent, I wondered how he retained his job. But of course I knew—he only let the DA know what he wanted her to know, and as long as he remained politically correct, he was her golden boy.

Knowing that the Chief was the ultimate chameleon, I thought that now was the time for me to take a professional shot at him. Looking him in the eyes while his hands were still holding my arms, I said sarcastically, "Did Cruz flip yet? Are they still debriefing him or is he in lockup?"

His hands slid off me, as did his smile, which immediately turned to a scowl. His demeanor stiffened, the hatred building in his face until I thought he'd choke on his own bile. He turned on his heels and walked out, no doubt plotting how to get rid of me.

As I looked over at Joe, he shook his head in disbelief, and then laughed. "Way to end a perfect evening, Frankie."

The next morning, after a few hours of sleep, the phone rang in my apartment. It was Staton, requesting that Mike and I come into the office. I told him we'd be in shortly after lunch. He congratulated me on the bust and said he would speak with us when we got in. It felt good waking up without a hangover, not having to take three or four aspirins, and taking a shower without having to hang on to the towel rack in the shower stall. It was like having a new lease on life. After showering I called Baraka, telling him that I'd pick him up in thirty minutes and then we'd grab a bite to eat before meeting with Staton. He wanted to know what the meeting was all about. I could hear the nervousness in his voice. I said that we'd find out when we got there.

I picked Mike up at about 12:30 p.m. and drove to the White Plains Diner. As soon as he got in the car, he wanted to know what Staton wanted, and continued to question me even as we walked into the diner. I guess for Mike, now, whenever he was summoned by someone of authority, he figured it was for the worst. So trying to sit down and have a peaceful lunch was out of the question as he fidgeted and continued to question me all through the meal, until finally I said we should go, that he was driving me crazy. I threw down the money on the table, telling him to finish his Coke so we could get the hell out of there before I strangled him. I got a receipt from the waitress and then we left.

We drove over to the office, where Jacob Staton was waiting for us. His office door was open and he motioned us in, looking through a file while seated behind his desk. He stood up, shaking our hands, then asked us to have a seat. We pulled up two short-backed leather chairs from the rear wall of his office, placing them in front of his desk, and took a seat. Jacob and I could see the tension building in Mike's face. As soon as we sat down, Jacob got to the business at hand.

"You guys did a terrific job last night taking Cruz down. But Lopez may figure you set Cruz up, Mike."

Mike gazed at Staton, not quite sure he was understanding what was being said. "What does that mean, Mr. Staton?"

"It means I think we should present your work to the Judge. I feel confident that he'll reduce your sentence."

Mike was beside himself. He became emotionally upset. "Reduce my sentence? So I still end up serving time? No way!"

Jacob leaned back in his chair. His facial expression changed from casual to serious.

"Mike, I've got a moral obligation to let you know that your life could be in jeopardy, now more than ever. If Cruz figures out that you set him up, they'll come after you. Do you understand that?"

Baraka sat rock-steady in his chair. "Either way, I lose my life. I'm not going to jail. I'm innocent, except no one in the goddamned system will listen to me. It was my cousin who put me in this mess, and I need time to get him to admit it. If I'm in jail, I can't do anything to help myself. Do you understand that, Mr. Staton?"

Jacob looked at me. "Tell him,

Frank." "Tell him what, Jacob?"

"About the fact that his ass is on the line. Jesus, Frank, you can be thickheaded sometimes."

"You heard what he said, Jacob. It's his choice."

We got up, not saying anything else as we left Staton's office. Mike was more agitated than ever as we walked out into the street. He was railing that one case wasn't going to do it; what the hell did they think that he wasn't committed for the long run? Thankfully my cell phone rang, which interrupted his rant. It was Joe. He informed me that Cruz had been just arraigned and charged with criminal sale of a controlled substance, cocaine, in the first degree, and criminal possession in the first degree and felonious possession of weapons, a .25 caliber automatic and a straight razor.

"So, that's good news, right?"

"Sure, for the short term, but the word's out that he's trying to post bail and may just get it by the end of the week, so watch your back."

"Thanks, Joe. Talk to you later."

I distinctly remember the days of the week passing very slowly; hours of mundane paperwork were necessary to document the Cruz investigation for court purposes. Sure enough, Cruz made bail at the end of the week. Word had it that a wealthy Colombian real estate developer who bought and refurbished dilapidated buildings in Washington Heights had posted over $250,000 cash bail on Cruz's behalf. His attorney had said in court that the developer was a family friend, but we figured he probably worked for Pepe

Lopez.

That following Saturday afternoon, Cruz was leaving his rented brownstone in Brooklyn Heights when two men came up behind him, pumping six nine-millimeter bullets into his head and back, leaving him face down in a pool of blood on the sidewalk at the base of the stoop in front of his residence. Deputy Chief Howell called me that evening to relate the murder. As I hung up I thought, well, that's one way to save the taxpayers money. I didn't have any particular remorse for Cruz. I figured that he'd get it in prison or on the street, like he did. After years of seeing the violence that human beings can amass on one another, you eventually become numb and hardened to it. It comes with the territory, and you think that it doesn't have an effect on you, but it does. The violence sneaks up on you and somehow you become a person that you don't know or even recognize. You live and work in a violent world every day, and after a while it's hard to separate the two worlds—the one you came from, and the world you work in. Somehow these worlds have a habit of colliding, causing emotional havoc in one's life, as it has mine.

Sunday was a day off for me, and unfortunately left me with little to do but think about how miserable my life was. I wanted to call my mom or my brother, but I couldn't. I wouldn't know what to say to them. Telling them that I was miserable and depressed wouldn't fly. Perhaps the Cruz murder bothered me more than I thought, as it reminded me that we often were not in control of our own destiny. Maybe it was because Baraka now had to live under a constant threat and could be snuffed out just like Cruz at any time. Or maybe I was feeling my own mortality. Whatever the case, I thought I'd better snap out of it for my own sanity. In any event, I decided to stay put in my shithole of an apartment and watch TV for the rest of the day. I couldn't wait for the day to be over so that I could go back to work. The loneliness was a killer.

A day later, I saw that Baraka evidently was feeling better

than I'd expected. Having picked him up in the car earlier, I noticed a lightness of mood I'd not seen in him before. It was the Monday after the Cruz murder, and so far there'd been no fallout from Hector's arrest, but I had my eyes peeled when I was with Mike. If he kept bringing cases in, I'd be a very busy detective. I couldn't help it; I loved the excitement of the hunt. I was beginning to find out that being an undercover cop was more than a job for me; it was my own personal addiction. As we rode around, checking out some of the neighborhoods in South Yonkers and making small talk, I asked, "So, what's going on? You sounded excited on the phone earlier."

"Frank, I am excited. My friend from the neighborhood, Kareem, thinks he met a guy who sells heroin."

"Oh yeah—talk to me."

"Kareem hangs around an Arabic restaurant in Manhattan and met an Israeli who has a couple of kilos of heroin to sell."

"Is your friend Kareem a drug dealer?"

"No, but I trust him, and he knows I need help." "Go on."

"This guy, his name is Mordechay Zisser. He has two kilos of heroin stashed at his girlfriend's house in Queens, and she wants them out."

"Don't any of these fucks have any regard for anybody but themselves?"

"I guess not. But at any rate, he wants to sell them."

"How much did Kareem say he wants for them?"

"A hundred twenty-five thousand a kilo."

"What? Can't be, the price is too low. There's something wrong."

Mike looked over as if his trustworthiness was in question. "His girlfriend wants either the heroin gone or the boyfriend out, so it sounds to me like the guy is desperate."

"Yeah, well, we'll see about that. Don't be naive about these fuckers. Believe me, it's always about the money, so if this guy Zisser is the real deal, I'll know it. By the way, has Kareem met the guy's girlfriend?"

"I don't think he has." Baraka paused.

"Frank?" "What now?"

"My mother wants to meet you. She wants you over for dinner tonight. Cindy and my sister Hanna will be there, besides me. She wants to cook some Arabic food for you."

It takes a lot to shock me, but that did it. As I was driving, I began thinking that maybe Baraka was trying to set me up for something; sitting down to dinner with Nick's daughter would be something, and most importantly, breaking the golden rule of not getting involved in the personal lives of informants. *Shit, why'd you have to go and throw a fucking monkey wrench into everything, Mike? What the fuck is up with you? I know that you'll do anything to stay out of prison, even at my expense. Right now, I can't figure you out, and the trouble is that I'm beginning to like you. You have a charming way about you and I like your company, but I need to keep my distance if I know what's good for me.*

I looked over at him. "Mike, I can't do that. We need to keep it on

a professional level. I'm not your friend. I shouldn't even have gone in for coffee."

"It has nothing to do with me. My mother wants to meet the guy who is responsible for my life, and she's not only worried about me, but she's worried about you. She said she feels that we are a lot alike in many ways. Believe it or not, my mother prays for you. She's very religious."

"What do you mean, she prays for me?"

"She prays the rosary three times a day, for me and you." "Huh, I thought all Arabs were Muslims. Not so, huh?"

"No, not at all. There are many Christian Arabs in the Middle East.
We're not all Muslims."

"Well, I learned something new today. But, I still can't come to dinner, so she can pray all she wants."

"Trust me, Frank, she will. She prayed for my older sister and she still died of breast cancer. She prayed for my older brother and he still died of stomach cancer. She prayed for my father and he died from a heart attack. She prays for me and I get arrested. I told her, 'Ma...stop freaking praying!'"

"Mike, you know I'd laugh if it weren't so sad. Please tell her to stop praying for me too."

"You know, a lot of the old Arab ladies pray. I guess it's part of our Christian culture. Who knows?"

I was beginning to realize there was more to this guy than met the eye. He was observant, intelligent, and intuitive, and he knew how to talk to people, which is a real art.

Baraka looked over at me looking at him.

"What?" "Nothing, just trying to figure you out."

"Nothing too complicated. What you see is what you get. Listen, you really should come to dinner. My mother's a great cook. She wants to cook for you, the ultimate Jordanian compliment. It'll be a wonderful evening, trust me."

There's that word again, trust. Only five freaking letters, but what a word! It's not really one word—it's more than that. It's friendship, honor, respect, faith, dependency, and maybe other words I can't even think of. It's what I learned growing up from my folks. It's the way I want to conduct my life, but sometimes get distracted, and then something happens and brings me back to what I've been taught and believe in.

The question for me was: Who did I really trust? Did I trust Joey? Absolutely, only because he was a lot like me, we'd been through the same personal ringer with our ex-wives. Did I trust Helen? Absolutely, but she wasn't around, so that didn't count for much. Did I trust Denise? Nah, we hardly had a relationship, so she didn't count either, at least not yet. Maybe that would change, but getting burned once was enough for a while, even though the whole fucking mess with Helen was my fault, not hers. Didn't matter; the burn marks hurt just the same, no matter whose fault it was.

So you want me to trust you Mike? You spit the word out so easily, but it hits me between the eyes like a stray bullet. So do I take a chance and trust that you won't try to burn me?

"Tell you what, Mike, I'll think about dinner."

"Well, that's a start, but think fast, because my mother has to get to the market before the good stuff runs out, and she needs to know if you're coming."

"Hey, I'm just one guy here. I don't eat much, so if I don't show it's no big loss."

Mike gave a big grin. "You've never seen an Arabic feast in honor of a guest. We'll be eating leftovers for days."

"Okay, Mike, I'll come. What time, and what can I bring?" "Don't bring a thing. Come around seven."

"I'll be there."

"I'll call my mother and tell her. She's really going to be excited." I thought it might do me some good to get out with someone other than Joey, as much as I loved that guy. Right then I felt I was in a rut and needed a change. Besides, it got me out of my shitty apartment. I wondered what made me say yes. Perhaps I was tired of playing by the rules. Or was it the rebellious side of me always wanting to push the envelope? Either way, the dye was cast. That night I'd be dining at the Barakas'.

I was getting hungry and asked Mike if he wanted to grab a bite to eat.

"Sure, I'm hungry, let's stop."

We weren't too far from the Saw Mill River Diner in South Yonkers. We arrived around 3 p.m. The place was nondescript as diners go—brightly lit, with the typical off-white, speckled Formica counter and imitation leather counter stools. We sat in a booth away from the counter so we could talk without being overheard. We both ordered cheeseburgers medium, fries, and Cokes. One thing I was looking forward to was the cherry pie. The pie was baked on the premises, and it was to die for. The waitress brought our order over in record time, placing the plates down in front of us. We sat and ate in relative silence, enjoying the food. Over pie and coffee, I told Mike to try to set up a meeting with Zisser at Fellini's Restaurant on Columbus Avenue in Manhattan for the following night, if he could. I gave Mike my cell phone number, telling him that from then on he should only call me on my cell. It wasn't that I didn't trust the guys in the office, but you never knew who'd pick up the phone. He nodded yes and, through a mouthful of cherry pie, said that he'd try to get in touch with Kareem that day and have him set up the meeting for the following night. I called the waitress over for the check, paying the bill as we left. I dropped Mike back at his apartment, telling him that I'd see him at seven.

On the way back to the office, I thought about my meeting with Zisser the next night. Not that anyone was immune to the business of dealing drugs, but dealing with an Israeli was a first for me. If there was a Jewish drug ring around, I hadn't heard about it, so I wondered how Mordechay Zisser was connected, and to whom. Although a lot of people use drugs, I'd never come across a Jew who sold kilo weight. I had to do some research on my friend-to-be Mordechay.

After studying a myriad of intelligence files for three hours, I was beginning to get a headache. I turned nothing up on Zisser; no known associations linked him to any drug syndicate. I thought that Mordechay might be a newcomer to the drug business. Just then, Mike called, telling me that a meet was set with Zisser for eight o'clock the next night at Fellini's. Then he asked if I was still coming to dinner. I told him that I was running a little late, but I'd be there by eight. He said that was fine, and told me that he had another lead on a drug guy, and would tell me about him at dinner. I wondered why he hadn't mentioned the lead at lunch, but who knew? Maybe he hadn't had all the information on him yet. Anyway, I loved it. He was keeping me busy.

Realizing that I needed to get it together if I was going to get to Mike's house by eight, I knew I'd better pack it up and leave. I needed to get to the florist before they closed and then get home to clean up, where hopefully I could find a freshly starched shirt and a clean set of sport clothes.

I almost made it to Mike's place on time, five after eight—still socially acceptable, I guess. Mike answered the door when I rang the bell, smiling as he invited me in. He wore a starched white shirt, open at the neck, a pair of light gabardine slacks held up by an expensive- looking, hand-etched belt, and brown tassel loafers. I wore the same clothes I wore when I tried to visit Helen and the kids, but truthfully I didn't have a closet full of dress clothes to pick from.

Mike took the pink roses, thanking me, and gestured that I should follow him into the living room and take a seat on the sofa. He brought the flowers into the kitchen, where squeals of delight came from Hanna and Mike's mother Adel as the stems were cut, placed them in a crystal vase, and then they were carried out by a smiling Hanna and placed on the coffee table in front of me.

Not that I was tense—that would be the wrong word to use in this situation—but I'd certainly been in any number of situations where I'd felt less awkward. It wasn't every day you had dinner with a confidential informant, his family, and the daughter of the man you sent to jail for life. Boy, I really knew how to step in it. And I was trying to figure out Baraka. But how about figuring myself out? I really must've been fucking nuts.

While Mike was in the kitchen, I peeked into the dining room and saw only place settings for two. I thought that was odd. I wondered what was up with that. I thought we were all sitting down together for dinner. Mike came into the living room, offering a cold beer out of the can. He asked if I wanted a glass and I told him that the can was fine. He was drinking a can of Coke. He took a seat on the couch next to me as an elderly women came into the room, and set a plate of hors d'oeuvres on the coffee table. I guessed that she was Mike's mother, a short plump woman in her mid-sixties with hair that was obviously dyed brown, cropped just below her ears, and dressed in a plain black dress. She said something to Mike in Arabic before retiring from the room and heading for the kitchen.

I asked, "Aren't your mother and sister and Cindy going to eat with us?"

He popped a piece of cheese in his mouth as he said, "No, it's an Arabic custom for the women to eat in a separate room, serving the men first." He explained that customs die hard, even in the new country, and that the remnants of Jordanian society, which is strictly patriarchal, are still adhered to even in second-generation Jordanian Americans.

The beer began to relax me, along with knowing I didn't have to make small talk with Cindy Galgano. Although I hadn't met her yet that evening, I could hear her voice coming from the kitchen. I had nothing to say to her, and I doubted she had anything to say to me. I finished the first beer in record time. Mike, seeing that I needed a refill, asked me if I would like another.

"Is the Pope Catholic?"

He got up and went into the kitchen for another beer, and returned with the beer and another Coke for himself.

"You not drinking? I'm curious, because I know you drink, so why not tonight?"

"My mother doesn't like us to drink in the house, and I respect her wishes. She's okay with guests drinking, because they can leave at any time, but both my father and mother felt that alcohol ruins so many lives, and they didn't want to witness their kids drinking, especially in the house. That's just the way they felt, and we respect that."

"So what's a good kid like you doing hanging around with dirtbags? You sure know enough of them."

Mike took a sip of Coke and then set the can on the coffee table. "That's a hard question to answer. I guess it started when I began working at Club Zazu. Somehow when I meet these guys, they like me. They open up to me. I know there's an underground society of Arabs dealing drugs all over New York, using fake storefronts for all sorts of illegal activity, from scamming food stamps to importing and distributing heroin. If you asked me locations, I couldn't tell right now, but just give me some time. It's not what I want to get involved in, but now, because of my circumstances, I have no choice.

I glanced over at him. "Well, the Cruz case was a good case, but just so you know, I wanted to work my way up to Lopez. I was overruled. Look, Mike," I continued, "I want you to be careful out there. It may be that Hector got word to Lopez that you set him up with the cops."

"I know. I'm always looking over my shoulder now. If it's okay with you, I'd like to stay away from Hispanic drugs dealers for a while."

"Sure, it's fine with me."

"Thanks. Frank, I gotta ask you a question." "Yeah, what is it?"

"You've mentioned that you like to wear your brown suit because it brings you luck. Why's that?"

"I don't know. I guess I'm superstitious. I've worn it for almost ten years on field operations, and it hasn't failed me yet. So why upset a good thing? I feel it keeps me safe, so I intend to keep wearing it until I retire. It's lightweight worsted wool, so it's good to wear in any season. Does that answer your question?"

"Yeah, but don't you believe in a higher power? Don't you believe in God?"

"I don't know what I believe in. Anyway, tell me about this other drug guy."

"I thought I'd save it for tonight when you came over. I met this Italian guy, Louie DeFalco, at Petra's nightclub in

Manhattan the other night."

"Man, you get around."

Adel entered the room. She didn't say anything—just looked at me and smiled, and then she turned and left.

"She's just happy that you're here. Anyways, I was standing at the bar next to the guy and we struck up a conversation. The guy thought that I wanted to score some heroin. He ends up telling me that his heroin is the best around, and that he can take care of me. He owns a laundromat on Eastchester Road in the Bronx and told me I should drop by some time. I said that I had a friend who's connected and would be interested in what he's got to sell if the product was as good as he said it is. Louie told me that he doesn't want to deal with a third party; that he wants to keep it simple. I convinced him otherwise, so I need to contact him to set up a meet. I wanted to talk to you first about the timing of it. I told him I'd meet him at Petra's on Saturday night around 11 p.m. for a drink to set something up."

I had to ask him. "This sounds good, but why not tell me this at lunch today? You're not hiding anything, are you?"

From the Calise investigation I knew that Sami Hassan hung out at Petra's, and that Yousef Nebor owned the place. I figured that Yousef might be up to his eyeballs in drug-dealing. Now that Mike was in the place, I might get a chance to find out what Yousef and Petra's was all about.

Mike looked squarely in my eyes. "Look, Frank, I didn't think it would make a difference when I told you. I'm not hiding anything from you." Just then, Adel came into the room, spoke softly to Mike in Arabic, and then left the room. Mike told me dinner was served, and his mother hoped I would enjoy it.

We went into the dining room, where the table was so loaded with food that it reminded me of Thanksgiving. Dishes of chicken with tomato sauce were still simmering on hot plates; sliced steak in garlic marinade was on platters; and stuffed cabbages, grape leaves with rice, falafel, and dishes of lamb and potatoes were arrayed around the table. I was surprised there was any room for the place settings. The three women came into the room to serve us as we sat at the table. Cindy said good evening, smiling at me with no malice in her face, me relaying the same, and we both left it at that. Mike told them thanks, explaining again to me that the women would eat later, and Cindy gave him a friendly scolding.

"Don't get too used to it, Michael."

Then they all retired to the kitchen, leaving us to ourselves, a tradition I found slightly demeaning.

I asked, "Can't they join us for dinner? If not, maybe we can invite the entire building to join us, as there's enough food for an army here." Mike laughed. "No, my mother's a stickler for tradition, and Cindy and Hanna, at least in this house, will follow her lead. So it's you and me. See, I told you it wouldn't be such a big deal. It's just like eating in a restaurant, except the food's better."

I grabbed another beer from the large, thoughtfully iced bowl on the sideboard. I began to relax more and more in the friendly atmosphere of Mike's home. I guess it made me realize what I'd been missing. I hadn't had a home-cooked meal at my mother's house in quite some time. We helped ourselves, buffet style, and then sat down to enjoy the fruit of Adel and Hanna's labor. Mike explained that Cindy was learning his mother's cooking, but for now was mainly responsible for the salads.

It was inevitable that Mike had another question up his sleeve. I could feel it coming as we dug into the mountains of food.

"Frank?"

"Here we go again. What's on your mind now?"

"It's something you said a while back, and it's been bothering me ever since."

"Oh, what's that?"

"You said, 'They can kill me, but they can't eat me.'

I don't understand that. What do you mean?"

"Look, Mike, it means that they can't feed from an empty plate, so the worst that they can do to me is to kill me. Do you get it now?"

"No, I don't."

"I got nothing to lose. Being afraid is one thing, and not really giving a shit what happens to you is altogether different. I've lost everything I care about—my wife, my daughters, Francesca and Catie, and my home. I guess I lost who I am. I shoulda realized a long time ago that my wife and kids were the most important thing I had. But I didn't. I let the job come first. So now my plate is empty. The bad guys can't eat off it. What hurts the most is I got no one to blame but myself. Do you understand what I mean now?"

"I understand what you mean now, and I'm sorry. Is there anything I can do?"

"No, I think that it's a done deal for now." I reached for another beer, twisting the cap off and taking a hefty swig.

Mike, noting how much I was drinking, asked, "Is that why you drink so much—to forget?"

"Why are you so interested in what happens to me?"

"I feel sorry for you, Frank. Like I said, if there's any way I can help, even if it's only to listen, I'd like to be able to do that. You're a good guy, Frank; you just don't know it. My mother is never wrong about a person, and I always listen to her."

"What you mean? Your mother doesn't know me, so how does she know what kind of person I am?"

"Let's just say she's intuitive."

I was annoyed. "If you always listened to her, you'd have graduated from college and have a decent job, instead of working off a ten-year beef, so who's kidding who?"

Mike looked down at his plate. "You've got a point there, but that wasn't her advice I failed to follow, it was my father's. We had some major arguments about that, and I should have listened to him, I'm not denying that. But the money was too good to pass up, so I took another route. And you're right, look where it got me."

Just then Cindy brought in a cart filled with all kinds of desserts, including baklava, a Turkish pastry made with layers of baked phyllo dough filled with chopped nuts and dates, and sweetened with honey. Also on the cart was that Turkish coffee that I had had when I was last there. Cindy rolled the cart up to us and asked if we wanted her to pour the coffee. We said no thank you, that we would get to it in a minute. She smiled and left the dining room. Mike and I couldn't help but hear the conversation from the ladies around the kitchen table. As Cindy spoke no Arabic, Hanna translated.

As Mike and I dug into the baklava and poured ourselves a cup of the Turkish coffee—not forgetting that it had already been sweetened, on my part—I asked Mike how things were going with him and Cindy.

He replied, "Fine. She's still living upstairs, and my mom will take care of her until the baby comes. Then we'll see."

"Are you going to get married?"

"My mother wants me to marry an Arabic woman. She says I've got nothing culturally in common with Cindy. But nights like this are good for us, because it gets my mom to get to know Cindy on a personal level instead of seeing Cindy as just that girl, Nick's daughter. That's why I'm glad that you came over tonight, Frank—maybe my mother will see Cindy in a different way."

"Huh, I see your point, and here I thought tonight was all about me."

Mike asked if I wanted more dessert, and I told him that I was tuffed. The women entered the room and cleared the table. Cindy then brought another tray of the baklava, some cookies, and a bottle of arrack into the living room, placing them on the coffee table. Adel then motioned for us to go into the other room. We entered the living room and took seats on the couch, next to the coffee table, for easy reach. Observing the bottle of liquor, I asked him what exactly it was. He said it was a

Middle Eastern after-dinner drink with a licorice flavor. Mike told me that you mix it with a little water and it turns cloudy, and that most Middle Eastern men drink it that way. He asked if I wanted some, and I nodded yes. He poured me a small glass; I took a sip and told him that I liked it. Knocking it down, I grabbed the bottle and poured myself another.

Mike then began to speak about his cousin Ayman. He said that his mother had been in touch with her sister in Jordan, and she was putting pressure on her sister to have her son come back to the states to face the music. I was a little taken aback.

"It's not that easy, Mike. Remember, you've been convicted. It's not like the charges can just go away."

Mike leaned towards me, whispering so no one but me could hear him. "Listen, if he comes back, I'll figure out a way to get him in front of a judge. But I'll need your help. Will you help me, Frank?"

"That's really for lawyers, Mike. I'm not sure what I can do. You've already been convicted. This is for your lawyer and a judge to decide. Just so you understand, I'm not the most appreciated guy in the office, so if I were you, I wouldn't hold out too much hope for any help from me."

Adel walked back into the room, shyly sitting in a chair at the other end of the room. She said something in Arabic, clutching a small white jewelry box in her hand.

"My mother wants to give you a gift."

"Mike, I can't accept a gift, but tell her thanks just the same."

Adel said something else to Mike. He then told me, "It's not the type of gift one would normally think of. This one's to keep you safe, and she says you're not leaving without it."

She got up from the chair and handed me the box. I took it and opened the lid. There lay a handcrafted, wooden rosary on red velveteen lining. I could only stare at the beads, not really knowing what to say. Then Adel spoke again in Arabic, as Mike translated.

"They are from the Mount of Olives in Jerusalem. They were her sister's. She wants you to wear them, as they are more powerful than a bulletproof vest. Between that and your lucky brown suit, you'll be safe."

Not knowing what to say, I placed the box in my pocket. "Did she add the part about the suit, or was that you?"

Mike smiled. "Me."

I took another sip of the Arrack as Cindy came into the room. She took a seat in another armchair opposite the couch. I looked over at her and realized how drop-dead gorgeous she really was. Michael was a lucky man, or at least I thought that at the moment. I guess it was time to break the ice.

"How's your dad, Cindy?"

She looked over at Mike and me.

"Stubborn as ever, but thank you, Frank, for asking. I know you know our situation. When I told him that I was pregnant, he was angry, but I think he's coming around. We just had a long discussion about it recently, and eventually he'll have to accept it."

I really didn't know how to respond to her. The only thing I could think of was, "Good luck with the baby, and I hope that your father comes around."

"Thank you, Frank, and thank you for working with Michael."

It was time to go, so I told Cindy and Mike that I had to leave. As I got up from the couch, Hanna, a spitting image of her sister Delia walked into the room. I thanked them all for the delicious dinner and their hospitality. Adel came over to me with her arms wide open, placing her head sideways on my chest as she wrapped her arms around me. When she let go, she muttered a few words in Arabic—words I later found out were the rosary to protect me. I walked over to Cindy, who was now standing, and offered my hand, saying, "I hope your father recovers and that he comes around."

She took my hand and we gently shook. She said thanks

and that she hoped for the best. Mike walked me to the door, telling me that he would call me the following day, midmorning. I walked down the stairs, out to the street, and into my car. I wasn't looking forward to another night alone, so I decided to call Denise to see to see if she was dancing at the Melody Club that night.

It turned out that she wasn't. Since it was only around 10 p.m., I asked her if she would like to go out for a drink. She said yes, that she'd just been wondering when I was going to call. I apologized, saying that I'd really been busy the last few weeks and I really wanted to see her, explaining I'd just come from a friend's place, where I'd had dinner. She said that instead of going out for a drink, why didn't I just come over to her place for a drink. I told her that I would be there in twenty minutes. If I got lucky, maybe I'd be waking up with Denise in the morning. It looked like things might change for me after all.

Chapter Seventeen

Mordechay Zisser had a healthy head of white hair parted in the middle and combed to each side. He wore an expensive, black pinstriped suit, a reddish pink Countess Mara paisley tie with an expensive gold pin, and cufflinks to match; a Rolex with a diamond bezel completed the ensemble, along with a perfect tan that made me think of him more as a Miami real estate magnate than a drug dealer. The tan made him look a lot younger, softening the crow's feet around his hazel eyes. His face crinkled when he smiled, showing off his teeth, which were cosmetically whitened. He looked like a character out of a movie from the Roaring Twenties.

The restaurant was typical old-school Italian, decorated in lots of red and black, with ornate mirrors hung everywhere against gold velveteen scrolled wallpaper. It resembled a Sicilian whorehouse. But the food was supposed to be exceptional.

Mike pretty much kept his mouth shut during dinner. He was learning that there was a time and place for his continual stream of questions. Having finished dinner, Mordechay and I agreed over coffee and cannoli that we would meet later that night at the Days Inn up on west 94th Street and Broadway to conclude our business. I gave him my cell number and told him to call me. Before getting up to leave, Mordechay slipped me a sample of his heroin in a packet of tinfoil under his napkin. I reached under the napkin and placed it into my suit coat side pocket. I got up and pulled out a roll of hundred-dollar bills from my pants pocket, peeled two of them off, and threw them on the table to cover our portion of the check.

"Frank, I got this, put your money away."

"No thanks, Mordechay. This is the way I do business."

"I respect that; maybe another time. See you later,

when I get things together."

We all stood by the table as Mordechay called for the waiter and paid the bill. We shook hands and walked outside, where it was pouring rain, so we had the valet get the cars as we waited under the portico in front of the restaurant. It was one of those awkward moments where the business of the evening was concluded and no one really had anything to say, except Mike, talking about the weather, that the rain during the year had set a record, and that the Yonkers drainage system was so overtaxed that his street was often flooded. He said that the fucking politicians were doing nothing about the problem. Zisser seemed to enjoy the conversation, and I prayed that Mike wouldn't say something that might scare Mordechay and nix the deal. When his car, a late-model, white Bentley, pulled around the block, we shook hands again, and Mordechay gave the valet a generous ten-dollar tip before getting into his car. Five bucks was all the valet guy was going to get from me, rain or not.

Once in the car, I told Mike I needed to make a few calls. Driving west on 57th Street, I pulled the Lincoln over and called Captain Christopher from my cell phone. I told him of a potential buy that night and apologized that it was last-minute, but the guy was anxious to get rid of two keys of heroin that he had stashed in his girlfriend's house. I asked if he wanted me to call Shake and Bake, or would he? I explained that I didn't want to deal with that guy right then unless I had to. Christopher asked if Howell had been briefed on the case yet. I said that he had, but I hadn't thought that things were going to move this fast. Captain Christopher said he'd call him, that he completely understood, and since he was in charge of the narcotics squad, he should be in the loop anyway.

"Frank, just bring me up to speed, so if Howell has any questions, I'll know how to answer them."

"Okay. The guy's name is Mordechay Zisser. The buy is supposed to go down in a couple hours at the Days Inn on

West 94th Street and Broadway. It's 11 p.m. now, so figure 1 a.m. I got a sample at dinner. I'll need to test it later."

"Where are you now?"

"I'm with the C.I. on West 57th Street."

"How much money we talking about?"

"The guy wants one hundred and twenty-five thousand a key."

"A hundred and twenty-five thousand a key? That's low."

"I know. Something's wrong. Look, Cap, I'd like to call Joey."

"Frankie, I got no problem with it, but the Chief will."

"Fuck him. It's my ass."

"You're right. So, I need to get $250,000 together?"

"Cap, do we got that much money in the office to show him?

"Yeah, I think so."

"Good."

"Frankie, are you driving the black Lincoln?"

"Yeah, and Zisser is driving a late-model Bentley."

"Okay, I'll call Howell and set it up. You'll need the props, right?" "Of course. I need to put a show on for the guy."

"So what's he look like?"

"He's average height, about sixty, snow-white hair, black pinstriped suit, fancy red tie—trust me, you can't miss him. He looks like he just walked off Miami Beach."

"Okay, consider it done; we're going with the usual." "Thanks, Cap."

I then dialed Joey, hoping he was around. Nulligan picked up on the second ring.

"Hey Frankie, what's up?"

"Joey, you sober? I need a favor. I've got something going down tonight. Can you be there?"

"Yeah I'm sober. Thanks for asking."

"Joe, I just got a bad feeling about this one. Something isn't right; can you be there?"

"Absolutely, buddy; I'll be there. Do the bosses know?"

"I told Christopher that I was going to call you, just so you know." "Fine—so what's the deal?"

I explained to Joe the reasons why I felt uncomfortable about the case, and that Mordechay was calling me in an hour to let me know that he was on his way over to the hotel. Joe said that he was leaving his apartment immediately, and would be at the hotel in thirty minutes. I pulled the car back onto West 57th Street and drove directly to the Days Inn, parking in the underground parking lot. Had I been looking for a tail, I would have noticed the five or so cars following Mike and me to the hotel. But for some reason they weren't on my radar, and I didn't pick them up.

We took the elevator from the basement up to the lobby. Once in the lobby, I was waiting for familiar faces to show up to let me know things were under our control. I told Mike that we were going to do it by the numbers, as we did with Cruz, and for him to hang in the lobby until Mordechay was in handcuffs. In short order, Chief Howell, Captain Christopher and a team of detectives entered the hotel booking several rooms. I gave them a minute to get settled, and then called Howell for my room number before taking the elevator up to room 503. He told me to pick up the keycard at the front desk. He said their command center was in the adjacent room. I saw other detectives positioning themselves around the lobby.

I told Mike to have a seat, picked up the keycard, and took the elevator up to room 503 to check on the lab equipment and to make sure that I was wired with a transmitter. Everything seemed to be working fine, with all personnel able to communicate with each other via handheld radios. Once everything was tested and ready to go, I tested the white powder that Zisser had slipped to me at dinner. It tested positive for heroin. Almost at the same time my cell phone rang. It was Mordechay.

"Frank, Mordechay here. Do you have the money together?" "Yeah, I'm all set on my end."

I knew that this guy was slippery, so I expected that he might try to pull a fast one and he did.

"Frank, why don't you come down to the hotel at Kennedy Airport and we'll meet in the parking lot to make the exchange?"

My blood began to boil and there was heat in my voice.

"Mordechay, I'm not traveling anywhere with the fucking money.
We agreed that the deal was going to go down at the hotel, and now you're changing the location!"

"I just thought it would be easier to do it at the airport—less people around."

I exploded. "Look, don't waste my fucking time, you hear me? I'll come down there and put you in a fucking dumpster, you understand me?"

"Okay, okay, don't get excited. Where are you?"

"I'm at the Days Inn, West 94th Street and Broadway, just like we discussed. I'll meet you in the lobby in an hour. If you're not here, I'm history."

"I'll be there; just stay cool. We'll get this done, and that'll be the end of it. See you in an hour."

He hung up. Deputy Chief Howell and Captain Christopher then walked in from the adjoining room. Captain Christopher, the gentleman that he was, and understanding the pressure I was under, delicately said, "Frankie, you don't want to be threatening the guy over the phone like that." Howell just stood there glaring at me.

I looked at them, understanding the meaning of Christopher's comment, knowing that my outburst could bite me in the ass if the case went to trial. I shook my head yes.

"Okay, Cap, I understand what you mean." I then took the elevator down to the lobby to wait for Mordechay. Mike was where he was supposed to be, sitting on one of the couches. Detectives posted in the garage and in the street in front of the hotel were to notify us when Zisser pulled in.

Sure enough, at 1:30 a.m., Mordechay walked into the

lobby alone. Mike got up from the couch, and we walked over to Mordechay, shaking his hand. Then he and I repeated the Cruz scene in the men's room. Unlike Hector, he was clean, but I was watching him like a hawk. Not that I felt comfortable with any of them, but something about Mordechay really didn't feel right. We then took the elevator up to the fifth floor and entered room 503.

Joe later told me it was quite a scene in the underground parking garage where Zisser parked his car. He told me the whole story, down to the verbal exchanges, over drinks we had the next day at Jake's. He said that he spotted a dark blue sedan near one of the elevator entrances in the garage that seemed to him to be out of place, so he approached the car from behind, crouching low, careful not to be observed in the side- view mirrors. As he rose next to the car, at the same time drawing his weapon, he noticed semiautomatics in the laps of the two occupants through the driver's side open window. He placed his gun on the temple of the driver and yelled, "Police, freeze! Keep your hands off the guns and where I can see them!"

The driver yelled back, staring straight ahead, "DEA! We're DEA agents!"

"Yeah, and I'm Mary fucking Poppins!" "We have ID!"

Nulligan hissed, "Take it out and hand it to me. With one hand! You breathe wrong and I'll paint the inside of the car red."

Joe looked the ID over, realized it was legitimate, withdrew his gun from the man's temple and, hearing the chatter on the agent's radio, immediately transmitted the following to the command center. "It's Nulligan, we got a problem down here in the garage. The garage is loaded with DEA agents. They're just about ready to take the door down on the fifth floor. I think it's us."

It must have surprised the hell out of Howell, hearing Nulligan's voice over the radio.

"Nulligan, is that you? You're not assigned to work tonight."

Joe didn't answer the Deputy Chief; instead his attention was focused on the two agents, who were now standing outside of their vehicle.

Joe was tense, his deep blue eyes on these cowboys. "What a clusterfuck this is. Don't you assholes ever talk to anybody? Stay here until we get this sorted out."

Seconds after Joe's radio transmission, there was a loud bang on my hotel room door, then lots of radio traffic coming from the hallway. I stepped back away from the door, confused, stunned, glaring at Mordechay, yelling, "What the fuck is going on?"

I heard a voice screaming from the hallway, "Don't hit the door!
The guy's a cop!"

There was more yelling. Captain Christopher shouted, "Police, police! Everyone stand down! We have another agency on the set!"

Sergeant Cook opened the door to the buy/bust room and walked in. "Frankie, DEA almost took the door down; they're out in the hall. We almost had a tragedy tonight."

Fucking Zisser stood motionless and mute in the middle of the room as detectives and agents poured into the room, including Deputy Chief Howell and Captain Christopher. I realized what just had happened. I was pissed; you could see the veins in my neck pulsating as the blood and adrenaline in my body boiled over.

"DEA? What the fuck is going on?"

Captain Christopher looked over at the Deputy Chief, then over to me. "Frankie, we're in the process of straightening this mess out. DEA was about to take the door down."

Mordechay didn't move an inch, standing pat. The DEA agent in charge entered the room. The Deputy Chief asked, "What the hell happened here?"

The agent replied, "Special Agent Dan Bender, DEA, Manhattan, Group 33."

Captain Christopher snapped back, "Westchester County District Attorney's Office, Narcotics Squad. Care to explain?"

SA Bender, looking as surprised as we were, replied, "We thought your guy was a legitimate target."

I piped up. "What do you mean legitimate target? I'm a cop, for Christ's sake!" I then asked Christopher, "Larry, how could they give me a sample of heroin and think I'm a wise guy? Don't they have to vet me?"

He replied, looking at Bender, "They should absolutely know who they're keying on; we do."

Then I got up into Bender's face. "How the fuck could you not know I was a cop? And you gave me a fucking gram of heroin. How could you not know?"

Bender looked embarrassed, which to me and everyone else in the room led us to believe he didn't do his homework.

"I'm not discussing it further; I'll contact your commander in the morning."

Just then Nulligan walked in. I was still in Bender's face yelling, "The fuck you will. If it wasn't for Joe here picking up on the village idiots in the garage, we'd all be picking up the pieces now."

For the first time, Bender looked me in the eyes. "Take it easy, Detective."

"Fuck you, I'll take it easy all right." I grabbed him by the neck and shoved him against the wall. "I want some answers, dipshit!"

Deputy Chief Howell, for once attempting to calm the situation, shouted, "Back off, Frank! That's enough."

I let go of my hold, wishing I'd had two hands around his neck instead of just one.

Bender stepped away from the wall, trying to gain some semblance of composure; his self-respect was in the shitter. He huffed, "I'll take the sample of heroin back."

"You want the heroin back? Fuck you! I'm not giving it

back until I get some answers." Then I pointed to Zisser. "And who the fuck is this guy?"

Bender looked over at Mordechay, who still hadn't said a word. "He works for us."

"He's an agent?"

"No, he's a C.I."

Just then Captain Christopher interrupted, saying, "Frankie, give him the sample back. That's an order."

Respecting the Captain and calming down somewhat, I said, "Yes, sir. I'll give it back, but I want a fucking receipt!"

Nulligan picked up a notepad from the nightstand and handed it to Bender, who signed it for the return of the gram of heroin, and then I exchanged the heroin for the paperwork. Bender took the heroin and stormed out of the room in a huff, with his team in tow.

Then leave it to Howell to step on his dick, confirming everyone's opinion of the shaky bastard. He turned to Joe accusingly.

"Nulligan, what were you doing on the set tonight?"

My jaw dropped. I actually wondered if I was really experiencing this or if I'd been dropped into the movie *Who Framed Roger Rabbit*. At that moment I realized what a jackass this guy was.

I looked directly at him, square in the eyes.

"Chief, I asked him to watch my back tonight, for Christ's sake. I can't believe you. If it wasn't for Joe, a lot of us might not be going home tonight." I then stormed out of the room, Nulligan behind me. The next day was going to be an interesting day in the office.

Chapter Eighteen

Captain Christopher told me to take a couple of days off and relax. No doubt the powers-that-be didn't want me to come back to work unless I had a clear head.

On the first day back, I was seated in ADA Jacob Staton's office along with Chief Daniels and Mike Baraka. I still had a pretty good burn going on from the Mordechay fiasco, and wanted some answers. But I knew that the questions I had weren't going to be answered, at least at that meeting. I'd learned that when the Chief called for a meeting, he'd already decided its outcome. So all the questions I had about the other night didn't really matter. Now for Mike, who didn't have any experience dealing with Daniels, the best thing he could do was to sit there, listen, keep his mouth shut, and take up any issues he had with his attorney.

I figured that I'd start the meeting off with a sensible question. "So, Chief, any word on what happened the other night, other than we know that the DEA fucked up?"

Daniels, who was sitting next to Mike and I, looked at me with distain, but he held his temper. The familiar red hue was beginning to rise in his neck as he replied, "Since your ass was on the line the other night, you have a right to know what went wrong. Jacob spoke to Pat Donnelly and John Kenny about the matter. It seems that Special Agent Bender wasn't happy about the mix-up either, and gave Donnelly an earful of shit. I know that there's no love lost between you and Bender, but you should know that Bender was given the green light by Washington to go after you and Mike. He was just doing his job, and he has the same issues that you have. Unfortunately, Mike came up as a heavy hitter in DEA's intelligence database. For some reason he wasn't flagged as a C.I. This shouldn't have happened, but it did. The DEA is investigating the slip-up, and Mike's file has since been tagged so that what happened the other night won't happen again."

"Jesus, Chief, a lot of guys could have been killed. I can't believe the DEA didn't know that Mike is cooperating—no wonder no one trusts the government."

"Like I said, it won't happen again, Frank. I'll see to it that we're all on the same page from now on. And by the way, in your last report you indicated that Mike has another target?"

I wanted to pursue the issue of the DEA dropping the ball, but Daniels made it clear that the matter was closed.

"The other night Mike was a Petra's, an Arabic restaurant in Manhattan, and met a guy by the name of Louie DeFalco. It seems that DeFalco is in the heroin business."

Mike couldn't stay silent and I couldn't blame him. It was his life we were talking about.

"Frank and I are supposed to meet Louie at the restaurant tomorrow night."

Jacob sat behind his desk taking it all in as Daniels continued, "Well, if you're going to pursue this guy, I want you working with the DEA. Detective, is that understood?"

I lost it. "Christ, Chief, after what just happened, you want us to climb into bed with these cowboys? I can't work with them; I don't know them, and I'm not comfortable with anything they do."

Mike was physically upset by what was just said.

He said with conviction, "Look, my lawyer and I agreed to work with you guys, not the DEA. I've had enough experience with them. As a matter of fact, I'll make you a bet that I wouldn't be in this mess if they did their homework. It seems to me that they only care about making arrests, and don't give a rat's ass about who they arrest."

One thing about Mike—he wasn't stupid. I noticed the Chief and Staton were paying attention to his comments.

The Chief then said, "Look, Mike, that's exactly why we're going to work with the DEA to avoid another scene like what happened the other night."

Jacob jumped into the conversation. "Look, you two have no choice. I've already spoken to John Kenny and we're all in agreement that both agencies work together."

The Chief closed the door on the matter. "I'll set a meeting up with Special Agent Bender this afternoon so you can discuss the DeFalco investigation. Now let's get back to work."

It was decided—we would now being working with the DEA.

Taking the back elevator down to the basement of the courthouse with Mike, I wondered what Baraka's cooperation agreement said, and if it was being violated. I knew that he never agreed to work with the DEA; I was sure of that. I figured he should discuss the matter with his attorney. If Mike refused to work with the DEA, the U.S. Attorney's Office might throw him back in jail. They could say that it was up to them who Mike worked with. So we might both be fucked if we didn't go along with them. We'd have to see.

We got into the elevator, taking it to the sub-basement of the courthouse, and exited the building through a rear door into the reserved parking lot, where the car was parked. As we walked towards the car, Mike's complexion was ashen gray. He didn't say a word, but I knew he wanted to talk. Before we reached the car I grabbed his arm, turning him towards me.

"I know you're upset. Let's get lunch. We can talk."

Mike started in as soon as the car door closed; he was determined to make the twenty-minute trip to the Saw Mill River Diner hard. His face was flushed, his body tense. "Just so you know, it was my intent to only work with you, no one else. Jesus, how did this happen?" He pounded the dashboard with his fist.

"Listen, it's not like I won't be there, and it's not like I won't be calling the shots." Christ, I hoped that was true. "Mike, nothing's changed really, just the addition of another agency on the set, so don't go getting yourself upset. You've gotta trust me. I have no choice—I have to do what I'm ordered to do, and if you refuse to work with them, Kenny might revoke your bail and have you remanded."

He sighed, beginning to understand that he had no alternative. I asked him the question that I'd wanted to ask at the meeting with Daniels and Staton.

"What exactly is in the cooperation agreement you signed? Did it say which agency you are to work with?"

He looked over at me, with any glimmer of hope extinguished. "No, it just said in cooperation with law enforcement, or some other worthless bullshit."

"Well that's it then. As Daniel's said, we'll be working with the DEA now."

We actually had a pleasant lunch, as Mike calmed down after I kept reassuring him that I would be by his side every step of the way. He made me laugh when he got on to the subject of his mother and Cindy and their most recent interaction in the kitchen. He said the other night Cindy had made moussaka with squash instead of eggplant, and his mother spit it out on the first taste at the dinner table. Cindy didn't know what happened and got scared. She thought that his mother had a stomach bug. Apparently, Cindy had grabbed the wrong vegetable off the counter and cut it up, thinking she was on a roll to a great dish.

"Now she knows the difference between an eggplant and a squash," he said.

After we finished our burgers and fries and plowed through the cherry pie, the waitress came over to ask if we wanted anything else; we both said no thank you, we'd take the check. We got up from the booth, walked over to the register, paid the check, and left the waitress a good tip. I put the receipt in my shirt pocket, needing it for Mike's informant's expense account. Captain Christopher had previously called me, telling me that our meeting with Bender was scheduled for 3:30 p.m. in room 1002 at DEA headquarters in

Manhattan. As we walked towards the car, which was parked in the diner parking lot, I told Mike we probably should head for Manhattan to meet with Bender. He reluctantly nodded his head yes.

We were lucky we left early, as a truck had overturned on the Cross Bronx Expressway and had traffic tied up west into New Jersey and east all the way to the Long Island Sound. That in turn jammed everything up to the Major Deegan north and south onto the Cross Bronx Expressway. The Hutchinson and the Henry Hudson parkways were also affected. As the Deegan had no breakdown lane, we pushed along until we came to an exit and were able to take the side streets to the Willis Avenue Bridge and into Manhattan, arriving at DEA headquarters about 3:15 p.m.

The building is located at 99 10th Avenue between 15th and 16th streets, in what had previously been known as the Meatpacking District. The area was being revitalized and now featured the new Chelsea Market, Mario Batali's restaurant Del Posto, and Morimoto's, operated by the famous Japanese "Iron Chef" Masaharu Morimoto. I parked the car in a lot on 10th Avenue and we walked the few blocks south to the building. When we entered the building, a receptionist seated behind a bulletproof glass-enclosed station greeted us. I identified myself, telling her that we were meeting with SA Bender. She then buzzed us through a secure door to the lobby, where we took an elevator to the tenth floor. Once we got off the elevator, I had to look to see which way the numbers ran for room 1002. I had to squint at the numbers on the doors because of the poor lighting in the hallway, but eventually found room 1002, down the hall to the right. Besides the poor lighting, the corridor was painted battleship grey, and that made it even more difficult to see the numbers inscribed in black on the office doors.

I knocked on 1002 and was told to enter by a female voice. A redheaded secretary who looked to be in her fifties told us to have a seat, and that Agent Bender would be with us shortly. The secretary's red hair was about the only lively color in the room. Everything else was drab gray or brown. She was even wearing a gray sweater, perfectly matching the décor of the whole building.

We sat in two wooden chairs, facing her desk and dreading the meeting. After a few minutes Bender walked out of his office, and told us that we should follow him to the conference room next door. Just as we left the office, a large man walked past us, looked at us, and continued down the hall. Mike froze as he was closing Bender's door; his face lost color as he glared at the guy who just passed. I wasn't paying attention and followed Bender into the conference room, taking a seat opposite him. Bender was a big guy, about fifty, 200 pounds, light skin, with sharp facial features and deep set blue eyes that gave him a Celtic look. He stood about five eleven, with jet black curly hair that he kept short but not combed in any fashion. Dressed in blue jeans, an opened, button-down, blue-striped white dress shirt, and nicely shined brown loafers, the guy definitely knew how to dress.

Mike hadn't followed us into the conference room. He was still in the hallway unable to move. I called out to him.

"Mike!" No answer. "Mike!"

He finally walked into the room with a twenty-mission stare. "Yeah, sorry," he said, and took a seat next to me.

Bender began speaking. "Thanks for coming in. Chief Daniels spoke to me this morning about this guy DeFalco. I'll have men inside Petra's tonight."

I shot back, attempting to keep control of the investigation, "No. No agents. I don't want DeFalco to get hinky because of strangers in the place. I want to see where this is going first. Then, when it's appropriate— if it's appropriate—you can be there."

Bender sat up in his chair, took an assertive posture, his face contorted.

"Detective, that's not the way we do things."

I replied bluntly, "Well that's the way I do it. As soon as our meeting with DeFalco is over, I'll let you know what went on." Mike was sitting there, not saying anything, staring into space.

Bender leaned across the conference table. He was fuming. "Santorsola, why do you have to be such a hard-ass? I know all about you. Remember, we're on the same side, Detective." He then took a calming breath and I guess he resigned himself that it was going to be my way. "Okay, Frank. Let's see what happens. Just keep me informed. As soon as the meet with DeFalco is over, call me. Here's my cell number." He wrote his number down on a small piece of paper and slid it across the table. An understanding had been reached between us. We began to go over a few things about Petra's and Yousef Nebor, the club's owner.

But Mike was distracted, looking around the room, and apparently not even able to wait to get the hell out of there. I wondered what bug got up his ass. He should be focused here, I thought, not looking around the fucking room like he didn't give a shit what we were talking about. Finally I turned to him, raising my voice.

"Mike! Mike—pay attention! What the fuck is wrong with you? This shit is important; listen up. Our asses are on the line here, so listen to what's we're talking about!"

He nodded his head yes, but he was restless, fidgeting in his seat, and he wasn't paying attention to the conversation. I thought it best to leave, as we were nearly done. I wanted to find out what was bothering him. So I told Bender that we would talk soon, and that I'd be in touch. We stood and shook hands. He walked us out of the conference room and escorted us to the elevator. He waited until the elevator arrived, and as we entered the elevator, he motioned goodbye. Mike and I left the building and walked the few blocks to the car. I felt that it was better to find out what was going on with him in the car while we headed north to Jake's.

I looked over at him as he buckled his seat belt.

"Jesus, Mike, what the hell happened up there? You looked like you were gonna puke."

He turned to me. "I saw someone in the hallway—Agent Donnelly.

He's the reason I didn't want to work with the DEA." "I don't get it. What do you mean?"

Mike's breathing was heavy. "Do you know him?"

Driving through the toll on the Kapok Bridge, I said, "I never saw the guy in my life. Why?"

"Frank. When I was in the holding cell with my brother-in-law and the others, I saw Donnelly. Sami took me aside and whispered that he'd been doing a deal with Yousef Nebor in Petra's basement." Mike began to hesitate.

"C'mon, you started this. Continue."

"Okay. Sami was selling two kilos of heroin to Yousef that he'd skimmed from one of Mickey's shipments. They were in the basement of the nightclub when Donnelly walked in on them. He asked was what was going on and if Yousef was holding out on him."

"Are you kidding me? You mean to tell me that Donnelly's working for Yousef?"

"No, Frank, that's not it. Yousef's working for Donnelly."

"What?" I had to steady the wheel so I didn't drive off the road. "Sami said that Donnelly took a hundred and fifty thousand off the

table and walked out, and Yousef said nothing." "Mike, are you sure about this?"

"Yes. Sami wouldn't lie to me. He has no reason to. I've seen the guy at Petra's myself. DEA must think that Yousef is one of Donnelly's informants."

Mike then asked me, "Frank, have you ever dealt with Donnelly?" "I told you, I never saw the guy in my life. Do you think I'd try to

148

set you up with him? Do you think I'm corrupt?"

"No, Frank. But I'm scared, and I need to know that I can trust you."

"You can."

"Frank, I told you I'm innocent, and I am." He looked out the passenger-side window, tears in his eyes. "I just want someone to listen."

"So, I'm listening; go on."

"Mickey must have heard us talking that night; he told me to keep my mouth shut, don't say a fucking word about this to nobody. And Nick would like to see me dead. He even pistol-whipped me for dating Cindy. The whole bunch of them are nothing but a bunch of rats in a bag, nipping at one another to get out. And Donnelly, the Number Three in the DEA, is a heroin dealer."

Mike had just dumped more shit on my plate. I needed time to think about it, and how I'd handle it. We were about fifteen minutes from Jake's.

"No talking about this in the bar. This shit stays between us. I don't want you to worry about this. I'm glad you told me. Look at it this way. Donnelly doesn't know what you know. He doesn't know if Sami told you anything about that night. If anything, he can only suspect that Sami might have said something to you. So let's keep him guessing. I need time to think this thing through. Man, if there was ever a time in my life I needed a drink, this is it."

"Yeah, me too."

Chapter Nineteen

Denise MacKenzie and I were kindred spirits, or at least that's how I viewed it at the time. But it's been said people really don't get to know each other unless they're married or find themselves in life-and-death situations. That's when you realize—sometimes too late—who you can depend on. I'll take the life-and death-scenario, because I've met spouses in my line of work who never really knew their husbands, and were totally shocked when their husbands were exposed as monsters. Not that I was ever one to my wife, but if Helen and I had known what we'd be getting ourselves into, I think a lot about how that could have influenced our decisions. Did she really know the person she was marrying? Did I really know myself back then?

They ought to pass a law that no one should be married before the age of forty. And you should have to pass some kind of exam to make sure you'd found yourself. There'd be a lot fewer divorces and unhappy children.

Having learned that I should communicate honestly with women, I called Denise from Jake's around 4:15 p.m., after arriving with Mike from our memorable meeting with SA Bender. Instead of calling at the usual late hour, I called to see if dinner in a decent restaurant had any appeal. She said of course, and I asked if 7:30 p.m. was good. She replied she'd be ready, and where to?

I said, "The Morningside's on East 51st Street in Manhattan." I told her casual, but it didn't matter, because she looked good in anything. Me? I'd try to keep the stains off my clothes for the next two and a half hours.

After I hung up, Mike seemed to be interested in the call. "So, you like this girl?"

We were in a booth in the bar area. I gazed over at him, irritated he'd stuck his nose into my business, but he was good at that.

"What the fuck? If I didn't like her, I wouldn't be taking her to dinner." I had a feeling what was coming next, and now I wished I'd made the call in private.

He looked down at his drink, mumbling, "I just thought maybe the four of us could go out sometime; you know, have a double date like normal people and a nice evening."

Mike upset me with his comment. "Look at me. Look at me, damn it!"

As he raised his head, he was focused on what I was about to say. "I can't believe after what we've already discussed that I have to talk about it again. How much do you think I want to know Galgano's daughter? What, we're going to socialize over drinks and dinner and make small talk about how her father's doing in prison? And from a practical point of view, you've got no income but what I give you. So, even if we were to do what you suggest, I'd have to foot the bill. So what's really happening here is that you're inviting yourself and Cindy out on my dime. Think about it for a minute and how fucking stupid it is. What the fuck is wrong with you? We need to keep things on a business arrangement here, *capisce?*"

He raised his head, realizing that perhaps he'd stepped on his dick.

"You're right, but Cindy and I don't really have anyone we can call friends that we can go out with, so I just thought we could all go out and have a nice evening, that's all."

"Let's put it this way—you didn't think, Mike. In my line of work, I gotta think all the time; I have to. If you'd thought through your suggestion, you'd have never brought it up. What scares me about you is that sometimes shit spews out of your mouth before you can put a cap on it. That's why sometimes I come down hard on you—because I never know what you're gonna say next. And the shit we're involved in, if you say the wrong thing it can get you dead. You need to keep your brain in front of your emotions. You'll live longer that way."

Knowing Mike, though, he wasn't going to let his wanting to double-date die a natural death. In the back of my mind I knew that this wasn't the end of this. Watch—he'd try an end run, maybe another invitation over to his mother's for dinner, or he'd orchestrate a situation where I'd be forced to have drinks somewhere, and Cindy just happened to be along. It may not happen right away, but it was coming. I knew it. We drank in silence for the next fifteen minutes, and then I said, "Let's call it a day, since neither of us is up for any more conversation. Just think about what I said. It's important."

It was just as well we were ending the day early, as my mind was centered on other company, and I was getting tired of his. I drove him home, saying I'd be in touch in the morning as he exited the car. I needed to go back to my apartment for a shower and a change of clothes. After showering, I put on a pair of freshly pressed, light brown slacks, a light blue, collared sports shirt, and the same brown tasseled loafers I always wore. I grabbed a light, cream-colored summer jacket from the closet and threw it on the bed.

I sat on the edge of the bed, thoughts running through my mind. If Denise and I kept going out I'd have to divert some of the income I spent on going out towards buying some new clothes. And maybe at some point introduce her to my mother and brother. I wondered what my mother would think about a new woman in my life. As for Richie, I knew that he didn't want me to be alone. But, he'd told me that it would take a special woman to put up with my shit, so I needed to be careful who I dated. Then there was Catie and Francesca. What would they think when they met her? I didn't want them to feel that Denise was taking Helen's place, because she couldn't. Wow, this was a lot to think about. I thought I'd better stop thinking and keep my fucking head on straight or I'd ruin an evening that hadn't even begun yet. So I got up, put my jacket on, switched off the lights, locked the front door, and left the apartment.

I drove to Denise's apartment in Riverdale. She lived on the ninth floor in a large building overlooking the Henry Hudson Parkway. I arrived at Denise's at 7 p.m. The doorman asked me if I was staying or if I would like to take the car to guest parking. I told him I'd only be a minute, and that I was picking up a friend for dinner. I gave him a $5 bill to ensure the car was still there on my return. After all, I was driving an office car. Only in New York can you get nickel-and-dimed to death, going broke before the night even started. I entered the building and headed over to the lobby desk, where I told a matronly receptionist that I was picking up Denise MacKenzie from apartment 918. She buzzed the apartment and Denise, over the intercom, said that I should come up. I took the elevator up to the ninth floor; Denise's apartment was a few doors down from the elevator. I pressed the doorbell, the electronic chimes ringing several times before Denise opened the door. She was wearing a bronze, silky cocktail dress held up by spaghetti straps and matching bronze pumps with little bows near the toes. She literally took my breath away, but somehow I managed to mumble, "Hey Denise, how are you?"

She just smiled as she said, "Horny."

Now that I wasn't expecting. She grabbed my arm and brought me into the apartment, the door shutting itself, not even offering me a seat. She pushed me up against the wall next to the door, put her arms around my neck, then placed her lips against mine, forming a perfect "O." Her tongue flicked over my teeth as she disengaged her arms and began unbuckling my belt. By this time, I was at full mast. Her hand went down my shorts and closed around the shaft as she nibbled the lobe of my ear, small exclamations of lust with labored breathing coating my cheek.

She whispered, "Fuck me, Frank. Bend me over the

couch and do it from the rear."

By this time, my pants were down around my ankles. I placed my hands on her hips, gently pushing away from her so I could bend over to slip out of my shoes and socks and slide my pants off. I ripped my shirt off and then stripped off the boxers. There I was, stark naked in front of her, little Frankie not so little anymore, standing straight up at full attention. I guess Denise liked what she saw because she took both her hands and, beginning at my neck, traced her nails down my chest, along the abs, teasing me along the sides and head of the shaft, and then lightly massaged the sides of my balls, one hand occasionally cupping them just to ensure they were in good working order. I reached around and unzipped her dress. She gently pulled the straps off her shoulders and the dress fell to the floor, leaving her only in pink bikini panties and heels. She had no bra and no need for one. Her perfect breasts exhibited raspberry sprouts at the nipples centered in symmetrically round areolas, and as I kissed each one, sucking on them, small moans emitted from her throat. She held my head in her hands, kissing me again, pressing herself into me, as her left hand slid down and encircled my cock. She turned and led me over to the back of the couch, stripped off her panties, and still with her heels on, bent forward, whispering, "Fuck me, Frank. Fuck me."

I could have come right there, as I gazed momentarily at those perfectly formed buttocks, split in half by a glistening silken prize exhibiting swollen lips of lust begging entry. Her thighs and legs were tanned and taut, and the muscles of her calves rippled when she moved. I began to enter her, and she thrust back, fully enveloping me, reaching back behind her with both hands holding my hips as she propelled forward against the couch. I began my own thrust forward, and each time I did her backward motion met me, so that my pelvic region was in continual contact with her perfectly formed ass. With my hands surrounding her hips, I looked down at my member surrounded by those engorged gripping lips, reluctantly relinquishing it only to find a new assault waiting. She huffed, "Oh God, that feels good. Don't stop. Wait for me, Frank; don't come yet."

I breathed back, "Not too sure I can control that, babe." She slid a hand between her legs, and I saw a flash of knuckles as she went to work on her clitoris to help ensure we came together. For once in my life I didn't want this to stop; it felt too good. To come now meant it would be over. But she had me so aroused that the inevitable was about to happen. And then it was on me—I spasmodically jerked myself into her as deep as I could go, my hands holding her hips hard against my pelvis. Several seconds later, her entire body shook, moans escaping from her throat, as she brought one hand back, pressing on my left buttock, encouraging me to go deeper, which at that point was an impossibility. Then, almost simultaneously with the onrush, I felt lightheaded, as if I were about to faint from the pleasure of it. I had to take one of my hands from her hips and grab the back of the couch before I fell backward onto the floor. I'd never felt that way before during sex, and I knew right then and there I wanted more of it.

We stayed there, standing for a few moments. I slowly withdrew myself from her as the milky liquid began spilling out, running down the inside of her thighs.

I said, "Maybe I'd better call the restaurant and tell them we'll be late."

Denise replied, "Fuck the restaurant. No, better yet, fuck me. We'll order out later. I'll be right back."

She went into the bathroom, still in her heels, as I placed a quick call to the Morningside restaurant, telling them we'd be unable to make it after all. They said no problem, maybe another time, but thanks for calling. I heard Denise close the bathroom door and walk down the hall. She called out, "Come here, Frank, I'm in the bedroom."

I don't always do what I'm told, but in this instant, I needed no further persuasion. It wasn't until midnight that we had something to eat from a takeout pizza joint in Riverdale

Center that Denise liked. The thought crossed my mind several times that I should tell Denise that I was a cop, and before we fell asleep I finally told her. She understood why I hadn't told her when we first met, but now she wanted to know everything about me and my work.

I told her about my rough divorce from Helen, and how she was keeping my girls away from me. Denise wanted to know why. I told her that I thought it was because Helen felt I was a bad father and because of what I did for a living—that I'd be a bad influence on their lives.

"She really hates the fact that I'm a cop."

Denise said that Helen was wrong, and that the decision whether the girls wanted to see their father should be left up to them. She wanted to know what kind of cop I was. I explained that I'd infiltrated an organized crime family and was currently assigned to an undercover unit working with an informant, developing narcotics cases in the area. She said that she now understood the emotional pressure I was under, and how it must have impacted my marriage. She hoped that I'd feel comfortable talking to her about my life, and who I really was as a person. Then she wanted to know all about my mother and brother Richie. She said that both of her parents were dead, and she didn't have brothers or sisters to rely on. She wanted me to know that she wanted to be more than a one-night stand, and even suggested that maybe someday she could meet my family.

It was a little past 9 a.m. and I hoped that the five dollars I'd left the doorman was sufficient to secure my car for the night. Denise had just gotten up, thrown on a robe, and told me she had an 11 a.m. class at Columbia University that she had to make. She said, "Why don't you jump into the shower, and I'll make us some breakfast. You know where the clean towels are. And use my toothbrush if you need it. It's the only one in there."

"Okay, but I don't eat much in the morning. Coffee is fine." She stood by the bed. Damn, she was gorgeous.

"Don't you know that breakfast is the most important meal of the day? I don't want you fagging out in the middle of making love because you don't have enough energy to finish," she said, chuckling.

"No chance of that happening. All I gotta do is look at you and I become aroused."

I got up from bed, took Denise's arm, pulled her into me, and kissed her forehead. Her hand slid down my arm, cupping my testicles, giving them a gentle squeeze. She moved her body close, kissing me on the cheek, then said, "Get your ass in the shower, or we'll both be late."

I'd been living like an animal in that dump of an apartment for so long that I'd forgotten what civilized living was all about. As I looked around her bedroom, I took note of some pastel watercolors enclosed in steel-edged glass frames hanging on the walls. There was a low-rise dressing table on the opposite wall, over which hung a mirror encased in wooden gold gilding, an obvious antique that lent the room an air of elegance. The light pink, padded, mid-backed gilded chair tucked under the table complemented the mirror above it. The queen bed actually had a matching footboard and headboard, open and airy, featuring intertwined vines and leaves in off-white wrought metal, both anchored properly to the bed—so they hadn't separated during the previous night's romp.

I walked out of the bedroom and into the hallway, noticing the framed photos of various geologic formations lined up on each wall, some stunning, as the camera had caught several stages of sunlight playing off striations in the soil, which evidently defined different geologic eras. I thought I'd have to ask Denise whether she took them and where.

Her bathroom was immaculate, unlike mine, where I felt dirtier coming out than going in. I got into the tub, drew the curtain, and turned on the hot water full blast, almost reluctant to wash the night's lovemaking from me. Scrubbing up, I began to daydream about meeting Louie DeFalco, and how our meeting would go. Most of the time, like a pro athlete, I have to visualize in my head how I want things to go before the game begins. In this way, my instincts are sharpened and I'm ready to handle most of the unexpected situations that might come up. It's my number-one rule: plan ahead.

I was brought back to reality as I heard Denise yell from the hallway, "Hey, Frankie, quit daydreaming in there. I need to get in the shower too. Your breakfast is on the counter."

I yelled back, "So come on in. There's room for the two of us." She yelled from the other side of the bathroom door, "Yeah, sure, and if we start that all over again, we'll never get out of here. I've got things to do today, so c'mon, let's get with it."

Freaking women. Why are they always right? What's with that? I shut off the shower, grabbed a towel hanging on the towel rack, dried off, wrapped it around my waist, brushed my teeth, and walked out into the hallway. Denise was standing there, still with her robe loosely tied around her waist. Saying nothing, she grabbed my hand and led me back into the bedroom. She led me to the edge of the bed, sat down facing me, and unhitched the towel from my waist. She cupped the stem of my penis, looking up at me, smiling. She wiggled out of her robe, flung it aside, and sat with her legs spread on the bed as she surrounded me with both arms, placing her hands on my ass. She lowered her head, her lips forming an "O" surrounding the head of my cock as she gently played her tongue over the tip and sensitive area under the head. I looked down at her, her passion rising, as I took my forefinger and, with an up-and-down motion, gently caressed her nipples, which were now pert. I pulled on them gently and a moan escaped from her, as she enveloped two thirds of the shaft, then slowly pulled back, her mouth a suction cup; she let go of the head with a little pop, then repeated the action, slowly at first, then at a faster pace. Suddenly she stopped, gave a hop backwards, and lay on her back, her legs apart and her head against the pillow.

"One more for the road, Frankie. Now, doesn't this beat the hell out of booze?"

I entered her, the sugar walls willingly parting, as she thrust up against me, locking her legs around the back of my calves. She whispered in my ear, "Frankie, I love the way you make love to me."

We banged pubic bones together again for only a few minutes before we both were overcome with another apex of animal ecstasy occurring simultaneously, and this time it would have to hold us for at least a day. We lay there in each other's arms for a few minutes, and then she said, "I've really gotta get going. I can't be late for class. Sorry for the rush."

"Don't apologize. I understand." I propped myself up on an elbow. "But I have a question to ask you before I leave. Did you take those photos in the hallway?"

"Yes, I did. On a few field trips. Why?"

"Because they're beautiful. You really know how to take a picture, you know. I'd like to learn more about geology. It's kind of fascinating, something I know nothing about."

I could see by Denise's expression that she was touched that I cared enough to ask.

"I'll give you the names of some books you can look over, then we can talk about them."

"I'd like that; I'd like that a lot."

"It's not many guys who are interested in what I'm studying; they're more interested in the window dressing."

"Yeah, I can only imagine."

"These books, they're not too complicated. Just some beginning information."

"Sounds good. Thanks."

Denise got up off the bed, draped her robe over her arm, and walked out of the bedroom into the hallway. While she showered I began to look for my clothes. She had neatly hung them over the back of a chair in the dining area off the kitchen. Before I went to the office, I'd have to drop by my apartment to change my clothes. I just hoped the doorman had taken care of the car. I got dressed and then walked over to one of the woven-rope, high-back swivel barstools on the outside of the kitchen counter facing the kitchen. Denise had set out some Cheerios topped with sliced strawberries, and had placed the milk in a small, blue ceramic pitcher off to one side of the counter. The coffee was on the counter, having just finished perking. The sugar and light cream were placed on a small silver server on the counter next to the milk.

I poured a cup of coffee in one of the two mugs on the counter and took a sip. It was the way I liked it: strong. I didn't need the milk or cream, since I took my coffee black.

I hadn't had much of a chance to study the apartment, but with Denise in the shower, I swiveled the counter chair around, looking into the living room. It was tastefully decorated, typically feminine, with soft white furniture and pastel accents. The couch was a three-seater, with pink and blue pillows in each corner. The off-white throw rugs scattered on the floor were modern, with rectangular patterns of soft blue and pink designs in various degrees. The modern chairs along the windowed wall opposite the couch looked like designer chairs with their sweeping walnut frames contrasting soft aqua fabric. Drawn over the window were eyelet curtains covering at least a fifteen-foot width; they must have been custom-made. They were lined, so that the easterly rising sun wouldn't fade them.

Centering the room was a square glass coffee table framed in white metal that sat on one of the white throw rugs in front of the couch. On top of the table was an oriental-looking vase with a green, etched design featuring a wispy, leaved plant. At the end of the room was a fireplace with opened glass accordion windows. On the wall over the fireplace hung an Impressionistic oil painting of several sailboats docked in a harbor, its colors complementing the room décor. I loved the painting. It reminded me of the harbor on Thames Street in Newport, Rhode Island, where my brother Rich had recently bought a summer house. Maybe Denise and I could spend some time in Newport. That would be nice; we could really get to know each other.

Over the couch hung another beautiful painting. This one looked like a watercolor of a sparkling harbor with fishing boats facing a small Italian village. The painting reminded me of a picture of Positano on the Amalfi Coast that my folks had shown me from their trip to Italy they'd taken a few years before my father died. Separating the kitchen from the living room was a small dining area with a heavy glass table on a large, white-birch pedestal with six off-white padded chairs on silver metal legs. Denise had cleverly separated the two spaces with a long, cherry wood serving table with tasteful candlestick holders. She really had an eye for decorating.

She soon came out of the bathroom wearing a robe and a turbaned towel on her head. I could never figure out how women did that so the towel held the knot. She poured herself some coffee and a bowl of cereal, and sat next to me.

She smiled. "That was nice last night. I like having you here."

I smiled back, "Yeah, it was. I hope you're in those kinds of moods often. I loved last night."

Denise looked over and smiled, her teeth sparkling between those gorgeous, sensuous lips. She should have been on the cover of *Vogue* or something. How does someone this good-looking dance at a club and go to school? She doesn't even have any makeup on and doesn't need any. Someone needs to discover her. The fucking girl with green eyes was Hollywood material.

"Frankie, I'm just about done. I hope I didn't make the coffee too strong." She batted those green eyes, revealing a lusty laugh. I wanted to jump her right there on the barstool. I hadn't been with a woman for such a long time. I almost forgot what it was like.

"Frankie, why don't you leave first? I don't want people in the lobby to know every aspect of my personal life—at least not yet. So, scat, so I can get dressed and get out of here so you don't distract me and we end up in bed again or on the floor." She laughed. I laughed too, grabbing her and pulling her off the stool, giving her a kiss, telling her I'd call her later. I said that I had something to do that night, and that it would most likely be too late to get together. She placed a hand on my cheek, pulling my face into hers.

"Be careful. It'd kill me if anything happened to you. I want a rain check for the dinner I never got."

I left my cell and office number with her, and then she walked me to the door, holding my hand. We embraced once more as I kissed her goodbye and opened the door. She turned as the door closed slowly behind me. I walked to the elevator. As soon as I got into the elevator, the depression hit me. I couldn't imagine myself going back to that shithole of an apartment I lived in. I had to do something about that. I could never invite her over. I'd be ashamed to have her see it. I'd better start thinking about getting another place to live. Then it hit me. I needed to pick up my lucky brown suit at the cleaners for my meeting with DeFalco that night. When I walked out of the building, my car was in the same spot where I'd left it. Thank heaven for small favors.

Chapter Twenty

I lived in a violent world, and that world has made me hard-core. There was nothing that could shock or surprise me anymore. It's sad but true that after a while most cops become dehumanized because of the job they do, serving the public and protecting them from themselves. Sometimes it's the little things that drive you crazy—things you couldn't imagine happening, but do. You can either continually fight with what life throws at you, or you can go with the flow to protect yourself from becoming mentally unhinged. Somehow, I've chosen to go with the flow. Since I'd left Denise's place on a high note, the day had gone downhill. There'd been a fire in my building, and although my place hadn't been touched, there was a pungent smell of water-soaked, burnt wood in the building. Some asshole probably had fallen asleep with a cigarette burning in bed. From what I'd learned, no one in the building was hurt.

But there was another problem. The Chinese dry cleaner on the first floor of the building had taken a major hit, as water from the fire hoses destroyed the place, forcing them to close until they were able to sort out the mess and become operational again. That meant my lucky brown suit was in limbo, and not available for the night's meeting. That didn't sit well with me. I was used to wearing it and having a sense that it was protecting me, whether it did or not. That suit had become a big lucky charm in my small world. I still had business to attend to, and I couldn't let the fact that my suit was out of commission deter me. I'd just have to go without it, and believe that things would go well. Or at least that's what I kept telling myself.

I settled on an old blue blazer I'd had for a while. I'd had it so long it had gone out of style and then had come back in. I put on a pale green, button-down shirt, jeans, a braided belt, and loafers, then slipped on the blazer. Suddenly I noticed the

163

rosary beads Adel had given me on the night table. I picked them up, gave them a quick look, said, "What the hell, that can't hurt," and put them in my pants pocket.

I had a lot of time to kill before meeting up with Mike, so I called Joe to see if he was available for lunch. He said he was, and we decided to meet at the White Plains Diner in an hour. He was already there when I arrived, sitting in a booth looking over the menu. He got up when I walked in. We gave each other a hug before we sat down. It was good to see him; it'd been a little while. I took a look at the menu, not really hungry since I'd just had breakfast. The waitress walked over. I ordered a BLT and Joe ordered the special: minestrone soup, meatloaf in mushroom gravy, mashed potatoes, and string beans. Amazed at what Joe ordered, "Joe, didn't you eat last night?"

"I ate. I'm hungry."

"Joey, you got some appetite."

"Frankie, I'm still growing."

"By the way, how's Jessica? I haven't seen you guys in a while."

"Jessie's fine. She's working hard. I'll tell her you asked for her."

The waitress soon brought the food and set it in front of us, then went about helping other patrons. Joe dug in. With a mouth full food, he asked, "How's it going with Baraka?"

"Here we go. Can't we have lunch without Baraka sitting at the table?" I put the BLT down and looked directly at him. "This Baraka thing is really bugging you, isn't it?"

He put his fork down. "I should be with you, Frankie; you need backup. Look at what happened with the Zisser thing. What if I hadn't been there? Jesus, how can Daniels be so fucking stupid?"

"I don't know, Joey. It's like the snowball that begins to roll down the mountain. It gets bigger and bigger with nothing stopping it. Look, we need guys like Mike. I know that you don't trust him. I understand that. But right now he's bringing in the bad guys and that's all I care about."

"Daniels was wrong to reassign me with Angel. He's a good cop, but you and me work better together. I know what you're thinking and know how to react to things. Believe me, Frankie, this freehole Baraka is gonna screw you, you wait and see. You're getting too close to him, and the fucker is just looking for an opening to jam you up. You'll see."

"Look, Joey, I don't want to fight about this. There's nothing I can do about the situation, no matter what. You say I'm getting too close to Mike, and maybe you're right. He's not what you think he is. And you know what, I think he's innocent. So, you've gotta let me play this my way and if I'm wrong, well, then I'm the one who'll take it in the ear, no one else. I can live with that."

Joe's face was a blotchy red. The capillaries in his face were expanding from his rising blood pressure. He was clearly irritated.

"It's flat-out fucking wrong that I'm not with you. Period!"

"Joe, there's nothing we can do about it. You know how Daniels feels about this."

"Frankie you should say something to the Chief. Tell him that you need me. Let him know how difficult it is working alone. That's what friends do—they stand up for each other."

Oh, man, Joe really knew how to hurt a guy.

"Okay, Joey, for you, I'll do it, but it's not going to be easy, so don't get your hopes up. We already know the outcome."

"Yeah, I know. But I just needed to know that you'd try to talk to him for me. Thanks."

I really didn't want to go into it again, but I felt that Joe needed to hear it again.

"Frankly, you blew it when you gave Mike all the shit the night we first started this gig. So you think Daniels really wants you back in the fold, knowing how you feel about guys like this? He's not gonna let personal feelings get in the way of major cases that make him look good to the department and to the District Attorney. Remember, the guy serves at the pleasure of the District Attorney. He only thinks about keeping his job and the paycheck he gets every two weeks. You know, he thinks we're both burnt out, and probably can't wait for us to fuck up so he can get rid of us for good. Once that stubborn fuck gets something in his head, that's it—it's a done deal. He'll never change his mind, and his mindset is that he wants you out of all cases involving Baraka."

A slight smile appeared on Joe's face as he made a pretense of cutting his meatloaf. Then he said calmly, "Okay Frankie, I'll let you off the hook. You're right; he won't let me back in with Baraka. But the fact you're willing to speak to Daniels is enough for me. At least I know you've still got my back."

"I'll always have your back. Nothing's changed, except I have to work this guy for all he's worth. You know it was hard for me to get back into the squad after all the time away with Calise. And Baraka came along at the right time to make my entry into the unit a lot easier."

"Frankie, I understand. You don't have to explain yourself to me.
I'm your friend."

Joey understood very well that politics was politics, no matter what line of work you were in. And Daniels knew how to play the game well. As long as he could keep Harriet Larson happy and in the newspapers, he had a job. That was his main concern; in fact, that was his only concern. We all knew that.

At least our lunch ended on a positive note. Since I'd asked Joe to lunch, I grabbed the check, paid it, and led the way out the diner door to the street. I told Joe that I was going back to my place to get some rest before I met up with Mike for our meeting with DeFalco at Petra's that night. He told me to watch my back—that he'd be thinking of me, and no matter what, if I needed to call him, he'd be there. To hell with Daniels; I told Joe that if I needed him, I'd do just that. Before we got into our cars, Joe asked me if I was still seeing

Denise, and how things were between us. I told him that I saw her the previous night, and that I thought we were becoming an item. He said that sounded great; I needed to finally be with someone. Joe then headed for the office and I to my apartment, where I found a parking space around the corner from my building. I walked up five flights, opened my door, and realized that I needed a couple of hours of sleep after the night I'd spent with Denise. That was a first. No woman had ever worn me out like Denise had. I kind of hoped that it wouldn't be the last time.

Plopping down on the bed, I called Mike and told him I'd pick him up for dinner at 8:15 p.m., and then I fell into a deep, dreamless sleep. The alarm woke me up around 7:30 p.m. Even though I'd showered at Denise's, I always felt better taking a shower after sleeping. So I took a shower. After getting dressed for the third time that day, I called Mike, telling him I'd pick him up in thirty minutes. As I hung up the phone, looking around my shithole of an apartment, I realized again that it was time for me to find another place to live. I figured that the office would continue paying my rent to protect my cover as long as I continued to bring in high profile cases that kept the DA on the front page of the paper. So far, it'd been working for me.

I picked up Mike at 8:30 p.m. and we decided to go into Manhattan to a small Italian restaurant on West 48th Street and Ninth Avenue. It wasn't far from Petra's. Mike asked on the drive over, "Frank, where's your lucky brown suit?"

"Don't fucking remind me. There's been a fire in my building, and my suit is stuck in the dry cleaner's on the ground level. They're closed because of water damage."

"Frank, let me ask you another question."

"Mike, all these fucking questions! What the fuck now?"

He had a grin on his face. "Does that suit get you lucky on dates?" He then fell over laughing. I had to laugh too.

We were ten minutes away from the restaurant. I pulled off the West Side Highway onto 48th Street and drove around the block, parking in front of the restaurant on Ninth Avenue. As I was getting out of the car and about to shut the door, I stuck my hand in my pants pocket, feeling the rosary beads and remembering what Mike's mother had told me. They were more powerful than a bulletproof vest. *Well,* I thought, *we'll see.* I closed the car door and joined Mike on the sidewalk for the brief walk to the restaurant.

Our dinner was uneventful, although the food was good. I had linguine with white clam sauce and Mike had osso buco, a veal dish. He was full of his usual questions, wanting to know all about my brother, my kids, and my mother. I really didn't feel like answering him any more. I just wanted to relax and enjoy dessert. I'd finally had enough of his questions.

"Mike, you're driving me crazy with all the questions. What, you writing a book about me?"

"Sorry, Frank. It's a habit I have. I've always asked a lot of questions."

"Please break the fucking habit with me. Now let's discuss something important. Our meeting tonight with DeFalco—we're going to go about it in the usual way, no chitchat from you unless you're spoken to, *capisce*? You just do the introductions, okay?"

He nodded his head yes. I looked at my watch. It was 10:30 p.m.

"Okay, it's 10:30—time to rock and roll."

After I paid the bill, and of course getting a receipt for the meal, we left the restaurant and walked to the car. We were only fourteen blocks away, but I didn't want to be late. The traffic was minimal, allowing us to arrive at Petra's ten minutes early. I parked the Lincoln one block down and across the street on Tenth Avenue. We walked the short distance up to the club. We entered Petra's, where loud Arabic music was blaring. The club was dimly lit from ceiling lights and a few Tiffany lamps that hung over the private booths. Crossing the dance floor, we walked over to the bar while scanning the crowd. The majority of patrons were Arabs. Mike nudged me as he noticed DeFalco standing at the end of the bar. He whispered and pointed towards Louie.

"That's him."

Huh—an Italian in an Arabic nightclub. I thought that he and I were the only non-Arabic men in the joint. Louie was also looking around the room; he spotted Mike and me. He then waved us over. I thought to myself that it would be hard to talk due to the loud bouzouki band and belly dancers performing on the dance floor next to the bar. I'd never seen anything like it. Arabic men were dancing with the belly dancers, tossing bills at the them while holding onto the drinks in their hands.

Mike made the introduction. "Louie, this is Frank," he said as we shook hands.

I asked him how he was. "Fine, Frank, and you?"

"I'm good."

"What are you guys drinking?"

"I'll have Dewar's, with a little ice."

Mike replied, "Heineken."

DeFalco turned to the bartender. "Get me a Dewar's with ice and a Heineken." Then he turned to me and asked, "So, Frank, where you from?"

I looked at him before replying, trying to get a gauge on the guy. He was short, about five six, in good shape, and looked about forty-five; he had a nose like a hawk, deep-set brown eyes, and was balding, with black hair that was graying around the ears. Louie had on a black shirt with two buttons opened to show an expensive gold chain he wore around his neck.

I replied, "Fordham. How about you?"

"Flushing."

"Yeah, I got a friend on Roosevelt Avenue. He loves the Ice King on the Avenue. They make the best Italian ices ever."

"Yeah, I know. That guy's got the best."

The bartender slid the drinks over. I wondered if Louie and Yousef Nebor were friends, and who was really working for whom. If what Mike had told me was true, this could turn out to be an interesting night.

DeFalco spotted a table emptying and said, "Let's grab that table," motioning to it. We walked around the dance floor and sat down, placing our drinks in front of us. Louie wasted no time. "Mike tells me you're looking for some new product."

Putting the glass of Scotch down on the table and sitting back in the chair, I replied in a serious voice, "Mike told you right, depending on its quality and of course the price."

Just then Yousef Nebor made his way towards us from the bar. Yousef was thin, maybe 150 pounds, and approximately six feet. He was dressed all in black, his dark black hair combed back, and wore a thin, black pencil mustache. The guy looked like Satan; all the fucker needed was a pair of horns. Approaching our table, he signaled to the waiter to come over. He greeted us, telling the waiter, "A bottle of our best champagne for my friends." The waiter nodded and hustled off.

Mike turned his head towards Yousef. "Yousef, this is Frank Miranda," gesturing to me, "and my friend Louie DeFalco."

Yousef shook our hands. "Mike, it's always a pleasure. Gentlemen, enjoy the food, the girls, and the music. The waiter will be right over with the champagne." He nodded and walked away.

DeFalco was all business. "Frank. I have what you're looking for.
Do you feel like taking a ride?"

I looked at him, wondering what he was up to. "Where to?" "Brooklyn, just over the Brooklyn Bridge."
"Fine."

Louie sat back in his chair, charm just oozing from him.

"Let's order a few things to pick on with the champagne, then I'll swing by out front and you can follow me."

"Sure. We're parked down the street. We can meet you in front."

We finished some rolled grape leaves filled with rice and a few falafels that we washed down with a couple of glasses of Dom Perignon champagne while making small talk about the old neighborhoods. Then we agreed it was time to go. Mike and I got up, walked out to the street, and got into the car, and I pulled up behind DeFalco, who was driving a later model Mercedes. We then followed him towards the Brooklyn Bridge.

As we crossed over the bridge and into Brooklyn, Mike looked out the passenger-side window, catching a glimpse of the Statue of Liberty. He said, "Frank, let me ask you another question."

"You gotta be kidding me."

"Have you ever been there?" He pointed his finger towards the Statue of Liberty.

Looking over towards the statue, I said, "Yeah I've been there during a third-grade field trip. It's hollow inside with a bunch of stairs to the top."

Mike muttered, "As a young boy in Jordan, I thought it was much more than that."

I just looked over at him, not saying anything, but understanding what he meant. DeFalco was a few cars ahead of us as we drove into Brooklyn Heights. We turned onto Adams Street heading south to Atlantic Avenue, one of Brooklyn's main drags. From there, DeFalco took us east on Atlantic to Nevins Street heading south, and then turned onto Union Street, where we followed Louie into the Parkside Service Center. He parked his car nose in, in the last empty space next to a dark sedan at the far end of the lot. I pulled into the parking lot, parking the Lincoln almost directly across from his car, on the opposite side of the lot, with the nose of the car also facing into the space. By now it was almost 1 a.m. The street was almost deserted. Mike and I got out of the car at the same time Louie exited his. We stood at the back of the car, looking at Louie as he popped the trunk of his Benz, waving for us to come over. Mike and I started crossing the lot, approaching DeFalco, when two hulking men got out of the sedan parked next DeFalco and began to walk towards us. Mike and I naturally stopped in our tracks, not understanding what was going on, until a barrage of gunfire from their semiautomatic pistols blew by us, bullets whizzing everywhere.

It's hard to believe, but everything seemed to slow down to such a degree that the shooting seemed to be taking place in slow motion. I could actually see the muzzle flashes and bullets as they flew by me, and the Arabic faces of the men who were firing at us. I reached for the nine millimeter tucked in my pants at the small of my back, but before I could get a round off, Mike was hit, crumbling to the ground. I grabbed him by his jacket, pulling him back to the car as bullets flew by me. Reaching the back of the car, I pulled Mike into the space that separated my car from the car parked next to mine, and began to return fire. I emptied my gun, firing at them as Louie jumped into his car and burned rubber out of the lot. As I slammed another clip into the magazine, the two Arabs jumped into their vehicle and sped out of the lot. I was hoping I had hit the bastards.

I ripped open Mike's shirt, reveling a gaping hole in his right shoulder. There was blood everywhere and his entire shirt was nearly soaked.

I yelled, "Mike, hang on!" He was in shock and passing out. "C'mon, Mike, stay with me."

I tried to stop the bleeding by shoving some of Mike's shirt into the hole in his shoulder. He fucking screamed. Then I whipped out my cell phone and called 911 just as Mike fainted again, rolling over, his head face down on the pavement. It's a good thing I knew where we were, as I told the 911 dispatcher our exact location. A cacophony of sirens was heard in the distance. Soon an ambulance along with a number of police cars arrived on the scene. They administered first aid, and just as the EMS personnel were putting him on the gurney, I took Mike's hand, assuring him that he would be fine, and that as soon as I could, I'd see him at the hospital. He was barely conscious, but he heard me, and nodded his head yes. They then took Mike to Methodist Hospital on Sixth Street near Prospect Park.

Of course, I had no ID on me, and things had to be straightened out with the local police. I asked the uniform sergeant on the scene to call Captain Christopher so that he could verify who I was, and that I was working that night. The sergeant had no problem with that, and said that he would call when we got back to the precinct. The sergeant took my weapon and said that a uniformed officer would drive my vehicle to the station house and, if I didn't mind, I would ride with the officer assigned.

As I was speaking to the sergeant, they were cordoning off the lot for evidence, placing numbers by each spent carriage, and then photographing them. Once back at the precinct, Captain Christopher was contacted to verify who I was, and that I was working with a federal informant. I then gave a written statement as to what had occurred that night— my meeting with DeFalco, and the subsequent shooting that had taken place in the parking lot.

After leaving the 84th Precinct with an empty weapon, I drove to Methodist Hospital to see how Mike was doing. The front desk receptionist called the nurses' station on the fourth floor, speaking with the duty nurse, who said he was resting and would be okay, but had lost a lot of blood. She asked if I was a relative. I told her I was a close personal friend, and had been with him when he was shot. She asked if I was okay and if I needed assistance. I said that I was fine, but if Mike needed more blood, I was available. She said he was fine at that time, but that if he needed another transfusion the hospital would get in touch with me. I gave her my cell phone number, telling her to call if he needed more. I then told her I'd be back the following day to see him. She said that he should be awake by then, although in a lot of pain.

I now had to tell Mike's family that he'd been shot. Now that was something I wasn't looking forward to. I couldn't speak to Mike's mother because she spoke no English. Then I thought about calling Cindy and having her tell the family, but that would be taking the easy way out. So I decided that the best thing to do was to speak with Hanna as soon as I was able to get her phone number. I walked out of the hospital to the street where my car was parked. I was beginning to come down from an adrenaline high and the reality of what had just happened was beginning to set in. Baraka could have been killed, and was lying in a hospital bed, severely wounded. He'd become a friend and I liked him, in spite of the circumstances of our relationship. I really felt badly about getting a friend hurt. I should have smelled a rat, but I didn't. I was thinking more about making a case against DeFalco instead of thinking outside of the box. It was shame on me.

With these thoughts racing through my head, I called 411 for Hanna's number. Luckily, she was listed, although the thought occurred to me that maybe she shouldn't be.

It was 6 a.m. when Directory Assistance connected me. Hanna answered on the second ring. She sensed that something was wrong because her brother hadn't come home the previous night, as he usually did, unless he was staying with Cindy. But, he'd always called so they wouldn't worry. I explained that there had been an incident, that things had gone badly, and that Mike had been shot in the shoulder, but was okay. She began to cry, trying to control the quivering in her voice, asking if he was really going to be okay. I told her that he needed some blood, but was going to be fine, as I choked back my own tears, making every attempt to keep my voice from cracking. Hanna sensed my pain, telling me that things were going to work out for her brother and me. She said that Mike trusted me and that her family trusted me, and not to worry, it must be God's plan.

Now, I've heard a lot of people put a spin on things, but this was one for the record books. Here I'd called to tell her that her brother had been shot, expecting hysteria and condemnation, and Hanna ended up comforting me. Go figure. She said that she needed some time before telling her mother, but would tell her soon. I told her to tell her mother how sorry I was, and that I wished that it wasn't Mike that was hurt.

Before the call ended, I said I'd be back at the hospital in late afternoon. She replied that they'd be leaving for the hospital shortly. I gave her the address and the directions to Methodist Hospital, which she wrote down. I asked if she needed a ride, but she said they'd take a cab. I wondered whether if the shoe had been on the other foot, and it had been me instead of Mike being shot, would Helen have come running to me? It's funny that I'd think of Helen first and not Denise, but I guess some things just take time.

I got into the car and found a gas station down the street from the hospital. Then I headed home for an hour or so of sleep, knowing that I'd have to have a face-to-face with Chief Daniels soon. Now that was something for me to really to think about.

Chapter Twenty-One

I hate hospitals, mainly for never releasing any information on patients except to family members. When I called in late afternoon to ask about Mike's condition, they wouldn't give me any information. The only thing I could get out of the nurse at the station on Mike's floor was that he was stable.

Before I could make my way to the hospital, I needed to head into the office to meet with the wrath of God. And 11:30 a.m. felt too early for me to meet with the Chief after such a late night, but when his nibs called, you had to run.

Not surprisingly, I wasn't in a good mood when I walked into the Chief's office. Ruth wasn't at her desk, so I knocked on his door, hearing, "C'mon in." He was at his desk, his face a blotchy gray, as if his circulatory system was shutting down.

He looked up, peering over reading glasses that hung at the end of his nose, and motioned me to sit down with a flick of his hand.

"Sit down, Detective. There's no point in beating around the bush. The decision has been made. You and Baraka are done. I'm pulling the plug on him and you."

What a miserable fuck of an excuse for a human being. Did he ever have a mother, or was he conceived outside the womb? The heartless prick. No *How you doing, Frank? Rough one last night. Glad you're okay. Sorry about Baraka. How's he doing? Tell me about what happened and how it went down; I'd like to hear it.* There was none of that. I'd have liked to grab him around his flabby neck and thrown him out the fucking window, that fat piece of shit.

He went on, "As I said, you're directed not to have anything more to do with Baraka until we rethink this thing."

I snapped back, "Rethink what thing? I thought you've given me the green light with Baraka? What do you mean,

Chief?"

Daniels snarled, "What I mean is it's getting out of hand, first with Zisser and now with the shooting. We don't need these problems."

"Chief, you know as well as I do these are the risks. This is what we do. Please talk to Larson."

"Frank, who do you think gave the order?"

"Does the DA really think that Mike's going to stop because she says so? Trust me, he's not. As soon as I find DeFalco, we're back at it."

Daniels leaned forward, his beady eyes staring through me, hands cupped, his arms stretched out on the desk.

"Stay out of it, Santorsola. We have two detectives from this squad and two from the 84th in Brooklyn trying to get a line on him."

I couldn't contain my emotions any longer, exploding, spewing venom for him and the whole fucked up political system.

"Stay out of it! The fucking guy tried to kill us last night! Mike's lying in the hospital with a fucking bullet in his shoulder! And you want me to stay out of it! What the fuck is wrong with you, Sean?"

He screamed, "That's enough, Frank! Who the fuck do you think you're talking to? Nulligan? I'm the Chief, and you're nothing more than a has-been detective. I'm seriously thinking of throwing you back in the bag. You're becoming a royal pain in my ass. You've never learned how to play the game, especially with me. Come on. Come with me for a minute. I want to explain something to you."

Daniels got up from his desk, crossed the room in a huff, and walked out of his office into the hallway with me following. We walked into the room that houses the Intelligence Squad. There was a chart of the five organized crime families covering the back wall. He pointed to the chart, his face beet red.

"Recognize this chart?"

"Yeah, the New York five families. So what?"

"Santorsola, huh? Let's see if we can find your Guinea name up on the wall. After sleeping with these guys, I'm sure I can find your name up there somewhere. You get my drift, Frank?"

I just shook my head. "You're unbelievable. If I only…"

He interrupted and talked over me. "I'm sure we can find your name if we look hard enough. Remember, we can always find it. Do you understand me? Stay away from DeFalco and stay away from Baraka!"

"Sean, do what the fuck you have to do. I've had it!"

I spun around and left the room, to Daniels calling, "Frank! Frank!"

I left the building, called Joe, and asked him if he could meet me at Jake's. He said that he could, and that he didn't have anything going on with Angel until the evening. Hearing the sound of my voice, he wanted to know if I was okay.

"No, not really. I could use the company."

"I'll see you there in thirty minutes."

It looked like I wasn't going to the hospital to see Mike after all, at least not right that minute. I walked into Jake's at about 1 p.m. Jessica was working the bar. A little surprised to see me, she waved hi as I grabbed a booth, yelling out, "Dewar's straight up, no ice."

She brought it over, slid it in front of me, and gave me a quick kiss on the cheek.

"How's it going, Frankie?"

"It's fucking going."

"Okay, so much for asking." She turned and walked back to the bar. As I waited for Joe, the Scotch seemed to calm me down. I needed to get away from the giant headache that Daniel's had given me. I needed to remember what was important, how I was raised, and that there was normalcy somewhere in the world—away from police work. Maybe Daniels was right about one thing; I was burned out. But he had everything else wrong. What a dick he was, trying to intimidate and threaten me. I could only hope that what goes around comes around, and someday I'd have his ass backed into a corner, with me, the only one to throw him a lifeline. Like they say, it's not over until the fat lady sings.

Just then Joe walked in and slid into the booth. Jessica hurried over, carrying a Blue Point beer. She kissed him lightly on the lips.

"Hey, honey. Frankie needs cheering up."

"Hey, Jess. I know. I think we're just drinking. See ya later."

"Okay." She then turned and walked back behind the bar.

Joe then asked, "So what's going on? But just so you know, there's a lot of chatter floating around the squad room about the shooting last night. What the fuck happened?"

"Look, Joey, I know what you're thinking, but I didn't see it coming last night. Maybe I should have. Believe me, if I had any idea that we were being set up, I'd have called you in a heartbeat. This guy DeFalco planned the whole fucking thing. I gotta find out what and who is behind him."

"Frankie, whatever I can do to help. But please tell me the whole story."

I related it in detail, including the fact that Mike was in Methodist Hospital in Brooklyn with a bullet in his shoulder. I also told him what Mike told me about Pat Donnelly and his dealings with Yousef Nebor. When I finished, Joe just sat there with his head in his hand, in disbelief. We both called for another round of drinks. I started to say something, but Joe put up his hand to stop me.

"Let me think about this. I need to think through what you just told me. Maybe you're too close to it to see what's going on. You know what I think? I think you're in a nest of rats, and someone's playing you like a fiddle. Plus I think that Yousef Nebor and his club are right in the middle of everything. This guy Nebor thought he was serving you your last supper last night. He's in it up to his neck. DeFalco may or may not work directly for him, but if not, I guarantee he's working for Donnelly. Tell me something—why wasn't Nebor hit along with Calise and the rest? It's obvious there's a drug operation going on in Petra's with Nebor and, maybe—and I say maybe—Donnelly. So, Sami Hassan gets arrested. He's doing side deals with Yousef, but Nebor isn't touched. How fuckin' stupid we gotta be to not see what's going on here? Your C.I. has it right, and no one sees the forest for the trees. It seems to me that Donnelly's pulling all the strings."

"What the fuck? And I'm supposed to be working with these guys?" "Well, forget that. You can't trust anyone over there, and when the DEA asks you about what went down with DeFalco, you're going to have to be less than honest until we get to the bottom of this mess. And let me throw more shit into the mix. How close is Daniels to Donnelly?"

"Joe, I don't know."

"Well, think about it. Now, I'm not saying the Chief is dirty; I hope not, because that will put a dark cloud over all of us. And what agency needs that? But you never know—money can make people do crazy things."

With all the talk, we finished our drinks, and I didn't feel a buzz. So, I asked Joe if he wanted another drink. He replied, "Do bears shit in the woods?" We waved to Jessica for another round.

Staring down at my drink, shaking my head, and wondering what was coming next, I said, "Joey, so what am I gonna do? I'm ordered to stay away from Mike and that fuck DeFalco. I've been such a fool, after sacrificing everything for almost three years working with the bad guys, losing my wife and girls. Joey, what the fuck was I thinking? These political hacks don't appreciate a fucking thing, but that's not their fault, it's mine for not seeing past my fucking ego. I know that it's too late; it's done. Like they say, you can't unscramble eggs. Joey, please, please tell me—where do I go from here?"

"Look, Frankie, that's water under the bridge. You've gotta survive for today. Fuck them all and above all protect yourself and your pension. You've worked too hard to let them fuck you out of it. You need to keep your head on straight. Frankie, how often do you report to Daniels anyway? He really doesn't want to hear from you. And when he does, he knows that it's trouble coming his way. So my advice to you is to keep Christopher in the loop. He's a good guy and he'll cover you with Howell and Daniels. We can work under the radar and look for DeFalco ourselves. That cocksucker will turn up sooner or later."

"Joey, thank you." I checked the time; it was 3:30 p.m. "I'm going to take a ride to the hospital to see Mike."

"Yeah, I can see you're following orders." I laughed. "You're right."

Joe picked up the tab and as we parted on the sidewalk, he said, "Frankie, you know you have friends in the squad. You know who they are and I don't need to tell you. Just remember, they'll be there when you need them."

When I arrived at the hospital I inquired at the main desk as to what Mike's room number was. They said I could only see him if I was a relative. I told them I was his first cousin. They gave me a visitor's pass, telling me that he was on the fourth floor, room 410 West.

When I walked into the room, Adel was sitting in a chair next to Mike's bed, wiping his forehead with a damp washcloth. Cindy was standing by his side, holding his hand. Hanna was in one chair and Delia, Sami's wife, was in another chair at the end of Mike's bed. To my surprise, Mike was alert, and his color had returned. I was nervous and didn't know how I'd be received by his family, but they lit up when they saw me. I had a hard time looking at them, especially Mike. He was all bandaged—his arm in a sling, his shoulder bandaged all the way down to his waist. I felt responsible.

Finally, I asked, as I walked over to his bed, next to Adel, "How you feeling, Mike?"

Mike pushed himself up in the bed with his good arm

and with a slight smile he said, "I'm doing fine. Don't worry, Frank. The bullet went clean through, didn't hit any bones. I should be out of here tomorrow." "Hey, Mike, you're taking it like you've had a splinter removed. No rush to leave here. You know you had me worried there for a few minutes last night."

Then Cindy, not able to hold it in, while squeezing Mike's hand, said, "Please tell him, Mike."

I looked at the both of them. "Tell me what?"

Then Adel said something in Arabic. Mike translated. "She wants me to tell you about Ayman, my cousin. When my mother found out what happened last night, she came to the hospital to check on me, then went home, and was on the phone the entire night with her sister in Jordan."

Adel again said something in Arabic, this time with more animation, pounding her fist into her hand. Mike said, "She wants me to tell you, 'My son has suffered enough.' She told her sister that I'd been punished enough for something I hadn't done. My aunt finally agreed and is forcing her son Ayman to return to the United States and to come forward, telling the authorities that it was he who worked for Mickey Calise, and not me."

My eyes brightened, partly because of the news, and partly because I could sense no blame from any of them.

Delighted, I said, "That's wonderful news; you should set up a meeting with your lawyer."

Then Cindy said, very seriously, "Frank, we need you to take Ayman's confession."

Mike continued, "If I go to my lawyer, the government will think I paid my cousin to take the blame."

Hanna joined in. "It's true. You're a detective, Frank; you have nothing to gain."

Hanna and Delia got up, standing beside Cindy as they looked down at Mike. Cindy said, "We'll wait outside while you and Mike talk this over." She turned to me. "Can I get you something?"

I'm thinking, *Yeah how about a Scotch, eight ounces in a*

tumbler, no ice. I said, "No thanks."

Adel got up and joined Cindy and her daughters, but before they left the room, Adel took my hand, leaned over, and kissed it, saying something in Arabic. Jesus, how could I say no after that? My eyes filled up with tears as I looked away from Mike, trying not to cry.

"I guess my mother was right."

"What do you mean? What did she say?"

"She said that because you wore the rosary beads, you were kept safe and her son is alive. She said it's a happy day, a happy day."

Tears began pouring down my face. I was sobbing and could hardly speak. Here I thought I'd be facing a firing squad when I walked into the room, and all I found were thanks and celebration. With all I'd been through in my life—personal problems, disappointments—maybe I'd lost sight of what was important in life; what I'd been taught growing up—that regardless of life's tragedies, one needs to see the good in people, and that your family comes first above all else.

Mike took hold of my hand. "Frank, it wasn't your fault. Trust me, I know the risks. I'm willing to live with them. I'll find that fuck DeFalco. I'll put my feelers out as soon as I get out of here. We'll get him, don't worry."

Wiping the tears off my face I shouted, "Hold it, you're not going anywhere until the doctor says so!"

"Yeah? Well, we'll see about that. My mother is something. She says we're two of a kind; you believe that? Twin souls, she calls us, both restless. I don't know about all her religion and stuff, but she's right in one way, and that's that we're in this together. You've got nothing to feel bad about. You understand?"

"I appreciate the sentiment, but you're my responsibility and I dropped the ball. I was only interested in making cases so I could continue working as a lone wolf in the squad, instead of looking out for the people I'm supposed to keep safe. I was looking out for me, and that's got to change. Staton was right; maybe we should have stopped after Cruz."

"You know, it's not like you two have the only say here. I didn't want to stop; I didn't want to go back to jail, and in spite of what happened, you're the only person I trust in this whole fucking mess. So I'd still rather be taking my chances out in the street with you than rotting in jail, bullets or no bullets. So quit feeling so fucking guilty about the whole thing. It's not on your head, it's on mine. And guess what? When I'm well and I get this mess behind me, maybe we can have a real friendship. How's that? But I need you to take the confession. I need you to do that. Will you do it?"

I squeezed Baraka's hand so hard I think I hurt him. He grimaced and I heard a muffled "Ouch."

"I'll see what I can do on my end first. You know, this is gonna get a little dicey, so we gotta go easy. Let me talk to some people to get a vibe on this. It's really between the legal beagles to decide to take the confession or not. I gotta think this through. *Capisce?*"

"*Capisce.*"

"Now, I gotta go. Take care of yourself. I'll call you when I know something." I left the room, waving goodbye to Mike. I walked down the hall to the waiting room, where Mike's family was holding court. I asked them to come out into the hallway so we could talk.

Once out in the hallway, I said to them, "Look, about taking Ayman's confession, you need to understand this isn't going to be as easy as it may sound. Remember, Mike has been convicted and sentenced. The U.S. Attorney's Office is not interested in overturning a conviction, admitting they made a mistake. You know my office has a part in this, and they aren't going to be receptive to having the conviction overturned either. They pride themselves on their high rate of convictions. That's what reelection is about."

Hanna replied, "We understand. That's why we need you

to help us."

I lost focus for a moment—maybe it's just a guy thing, but Mike's sisters are knockouts. Hanna's olive skin glows, her black hair swept back into a long ponytail, her delicate frame accentuated by the swell of perfectly proportioned breasts under her light turquoise sweater. Delia is similar in build and looks, although an inch or two shorter than her sister. I wondered why my mind went there. Like I said, it must be a male thing.

Cindy spoke up. "We know you'll do what is right, Frank."

"Guys, the bottom line here is that I'd be disobeying a departmental order. Right now, I'm ordered to stay away from Mike. After the shooting, my Chief ordered me to shut it down with your brother. I need to work other angles here. If they don't work, then maybe I can figure something else out, but I wouldn't count on it. I told Mike I'd make some inquiries and feel things out in my office. That's all I can do for the moment. Now, since I have some down time, I have to go see about getting a new apartment."

Hanna held my arm. "Frank, give me a minute while I translate for my mother."

As Hanna was explaining, Adel's eyes widened. She rapidly spoke back to Hanna, who then looked at me and smiled.

"My mother says thank you for all that you are doing, and that she knows somehow it will all work out. She wants you to know that there is a vacant apartment in our building, and that she'd like you to look at it."

Now that I wasn't expecting. I took Adel by her hand, even though she couldn't understand me.

"Thank you, Mrs. Baraka, you're very kind, but I think that my department would frown on it. You know, the circumstances and all."

Hanna translated again and Adel popped right back.

"My mom knows some building owners through my father.

She says she wants to talk to them for you, and she won't take no for an answer." "Okay." I chuckled. "Tell your mother how much I appreciate her help, and I look forward to seeing some of the new places."

Hanna translated once more. Adel beamed and gave me a big hug. Hanna and Delia too grabbed and hugged me, and then Cindy leaned in and kissed me on the cheek, saying, "Thank you."

I gave Hanna a card with my cell phone number on the back, and then told them all goodbye. As I drove back to my apartment I thought about my relationship with the Baraka family. For Christ's sake, now they were my real estate brokers? What was I thinking?

Chapter Twenty-Two

I needed some down time to think things over. I knew that the powers-that-be would not be interested in overturning Mike's conviction. They had nothing to gain and might end up with egg on their face. But, I'd have to test the waters anyway and go through the motions, just to make sure that everything was memorialized in writing. It's called protecting your ass. Now the issue was how to proceed after my pitch to take Ayman Baraka's confession was rejected? I needed a game plan, but right now I had nothing. Plus, let's not forget the allegation that Special Agent Pat Donnelly was a heroin dealer with ties to Yousef Nebor, and maybe to terrorists in the Middle East. And let's hope that Chief Daniels was not in bed with Donnelly, because the reality of two agencies imploding was pretty astounding.

It was midmorning, so I decided to call Denise to see what she was up to. She said she was studying but could use a break. I asked if she had ever been to Van Cortlandt Park. She said no, but that she would love to go since it was such a nice day. I told her that the park was really nice that time of the year, and since we both were New York City taxpayers, we should take advantage of it. Denise said she'd meet me there, but that the park was a big place, so pick a spot. I replied no need; I'd pick her up. I asked her when she'd be ready.

She said, "How about now?" I was liking this girl more and more. Now, Van Cortlandt Park is not as well known as some of its counterparts, like Central Park and Bryant Park in Manhattan, probably because it's not in the thick of continual pedestrian foot traffic. But, it's almost a third larger than Central Park. It's over 1,100 acres, and you can get lost in it.

We parked on East 242nd Street and walked into the northwest side of the park, where we sat in the front row of the Gaelic football field bleachers. There was a two-team scrimmage going on and the play was rough, laced with good old Irish profanity. There was an ice cream truck nearby, and I asked Denise if she'd like a cone. She said sure, that she'd like a vanilla cone with those little colored sprinkles on top. I went the macho route—a chocolate sundae, hot fudge, nuts, whipped cream, and a cherry on top in a cup. I walked back to the bleachers with the ice cream in hand. As I sat down and handed her the cone, I said, "So this is how normal people live."

She gave me a puzzled look, her green eyes centered on mine as I sat beside her. She was wearing jeans, a white tee shirt, and green sandals with sundial decorations on top of the thongs separating the toes. "So, you don't think you're normal?"

I looked out over the field—the play was sporting but rough, as the players had no equipment on for protection. I briefly thought to myself that I couldn't do that. It's not worth the body ache and injuries. Every second on the field risks a broken bone. Then the thought hit me that it was a hell of a lot safer than what I did just to make a living. Once you put some distance between yourself and your career and look at it objectively, you get a totally different outlook on what you do. Maybe I was afraid of what I'd feel if I took a break. Or maybe I was truly an adrenaline addict. But who the fuck knew, and who the fuck cared?

You know what I think? I think the word fuck is the greatest word in the English language. Know why? Cause when you peel back the onion to a certain level and don't feel like dealing with the issues in your life that you have no answers for, you can just say, "Fuck it." It allows you an out so that you can get on with your life without blowing your brains out sitting on the edge of your bed in a one-room, dingy apartment, your only companions the roaches scurrying around between the pizza boxes.

I looked over at this beautiful woman, a woman any man would be privileged to be with, wondering at the simplicity of her life. It's true that to some extent she had to deal with the sleaze, but she was still an innocent, relative to my career. Most people were.

I said, "Yeah, I don't think I'm normal, not what I do for living. I'm a shit extractor. I try to remove all the garbage from society."

With Helen, I always clammed up when she asked me about what went on at work, partly because I didn't want her to know how dangerous my job was, and partly because I didn't want her on my ass all the time to quit. So what did I do? In essence, I ran away from her. I treated her like a separate entity in the marriage by shutting her out of my work and what made me tick. In retrospect, that was the biggest mistake I made between us. It cost me my marriage and my kids.

So, what do I tell the woman in my life about my day? *My day? Well, it was midnight and I was on the street, pretending to be a drug dealer so we could bust this guy. He gave a sample of coke, which he wanted me to snort, but I told him no. He pulls out a gun and sticks it on my forehead, telling me to snort it now. I fake it by pretending to sniff it, blocking one of my nostrils with my finger while I turn my head away from him and hoping that my theatrics works so he doesn't shoot me. And the confidential informant waits for me in the car and has just about pissed his pants because he thinks I'm going to get it right there in the street and he knows that he's next.* Do I say to her, *Baby, do you want to know how my day went?* Yeah, right.

I knew that Denise was trying to figure me out. She asked, "Thinking about changing careers?"

Still looking out over the field, but not really seeing any of the action, I answered, "Not really. I'm not ready to hang it up yet."

She asked, "Then why worry? You are what you are. Leave it at that until you don't want to do it anymore. You know, I don't give a shit what people think of me. I think you know that. The people who see me in the club, to them, well, I'm just a piece of ass they'd like to take home and have fun with. I know that and I don't care. You know why I do what I do? It's simple; I can't make the same kind of money at some part-time job. I'm on my own; I've got rent to pay and tuition at Columbia, which comes to about $40,000 a year. Those people in the club don't know me, and I don't want to know them. I'm an object to them, plain and simple. I'm the owner's money machine, and I'm the only dancer there who never fully takes her clothes off. The top, yes. The bottom, never. I don't have to. The guys know when I dance, and the place is packed with guys waiting for me. So I really don't think about what I do much. No need to. Why twist yourself up in knots when you know what you're gonna do anyway? Even after I'm employed full time, I might dance part time. It's legal, and the money is outrageous. But that's a decision I'll make down the road."

Looking over at her, I realized that she had a hard edge. This wasn't a well-manicured girl from the suburbs. This was a woman who knew exactly what she wanted from life, and was determined to get it.

Her passion was geology, specifically the formation of rocks. I asked, "Why rocks? Why not business, or medicine, or law?"

She laughed and, using a western accent, said, "There's gold in them thar hills, partner, gold, I tell you." I laughed as well. She then said, seriously, "There really is a lot of money to be made, either with the oil or mining companies. For instance, there was just a huge diamond find in South Africa and a large lithium field discovered in Afghanistan. I'd like to be on the cutting edge of some of those types of discoveries. What about you, Frankie? Why'd you become a cop, and why undercover?"

I'd never opened up with Helen about this, always kept it under wraps. But look where that got me. Maybe it was time to learn from my mistakes? Time for a fresh start. I needed to be honest with Denise. I really liked her, so instead of keeping my feelings bottled up inside me, I decided to tell her what I felt, and who I really was.

As we finished up our ice cream, I said, "Couple of reasons, really. For one, I get a rush out of beating the bad guys at their own game and putting them away. And another—and I guess the most important— reason is that I believed that people should operate by a set of rules, sorta like golden rules, and that when someone chooses to go outside of those rules for selfish reasons, it can hurt everyone."

She gently took hold of my hand. "I don't think I've ever met anyone quite like you, Frankie."

"Well, I guess that's a compliment. But let's talk about you. I really don't know anything about you. You've said that you don't have family to fall back on? What happened to your parents? Where'd you grow up and go to school? You know, the things people know about each other." "Well, Frankie, I grew up in Chicago, and have no brothers or sisters. I was raised by my mother's sister since I was eight years old. My father drank himself to death by the time I was sixteen, and my mother also chose booze over me, deciding to live on the street. My aunt's husband left her early on. She struggles to pay the mortgage and put food on the table by waiting tables at a diner near her house. So as soon as I graduated from high school I decided to come to New York, get a job, and put myself through college. And once a month, I send my darling Aunt Margret a hefty check to help her out. So now you know the story of my life."

"Gee, Denise. I had no idea. I'm so sorry."

"Don't be, Frankie. Who says life is fair and owes you something?
You just have to pick yourself up and follow your dreams, and I did." "Denise, I'm really flattered that you told me. Believe me, it goes a
long way to knowing who you are. You see, I don't trust anyone at first. It takes a long time to figure out where people are coming from and their hidden agendas. It's a process that

usually takes some time. I analyze every word they say to see who they are. But with you, it's different. Everything seems to flow in our relationship, and fits like a soft pair of cashmere gloves. Since my divorce from Helen, I now feel that relationships are based on honesty and trust. I want to learn from the mistakes I made with Helen. I never talked to her about what made me tick. I'm not going to make that mistake with you. Look, I'm not telling you not to see other guys, but I want you to know that you're the only one I've been with since my divorce."

I could feel Denise's grip tightening as she slid even closer to me on the bleachers

"I'm glad I'm not Helen, and glad that we're together now. And as far as dating, I don't date because of my schedule. I don't have the time, and frankly I'm not interested, with one exception—you. So Frankie, can you tell me about this case you're working on?" She then let go of my hand and smiled, anticipating what I would say.

"How much time you got?"

She laughed. "All afternoon, if you want."

"Well, it won't take all afternoon, so here it goes."

So, I explained the intricacies of working with a confidential informant, and how through the takedown of a crew of an organized crime family I was assigned to work with him, the Cruz bust, and now the shooting situation, along with the problems I was having with my department about breaking off my relationship with the informant, and finding the guy who shot my C.I. Denise didn't interrupt me the whole time. She took both of my hands and held them. When I finished, she let go of my hands, placed both her hands on her knees, and, leaning forward towards me a bit, anxiously said, "Holy shit!"

"Yeah, when you hear it for the first time, I guess that would be a standard reaction."

"So, what are you gonna do?"

"You know, talking it through like this kind of helps.

Maybe I should have done more talking like this in my past life. I'm gonna find a way to take the confession, even if my office and the U.S. Attorney's Office won't cooperate. I'll try to arrange it with Federal Judge Sposato. I'll have to see . . . " I trailed off for a second. "You know what? Fuck it. That's exactly how I'm going to go. I'm going through Judge John Sposato."

Denise then turned my head gently towards her and, leaning in to kiss me on the lips, she said softly, "I really don't understand it, but I feel that I know you, and you'll figure things out."

It was an easy thing to say that I'd figure it out, but much harder to do, especially when I may have been embarking on a career-ending move. Even though Mike was innocent, I'd have to get through the very people who were supposed to make the criminal justice system work, but in fact were clogging it up for whatever reasons I needed to figure out.

I then said, "Yeah, you're right. I think I've got it figured out. So tomorrow, it's the lion's den. But today it's a day off, so got any plans?" "No, Frankie, no plans. You know, there are some things I've never done in New York. I've never taken a boat tour of the harbor. I've never seen the Statue of Liberty, except from a distance. I've never been on the Staten Island Ferry, and I've never been to some of those ethnic restaurants in Queens. Let's play tourist today and do some of those things. I don't want to live in New York the rest of my life and miss the things that make it famous."

And so we did just that. We played tourist all afternoon. We went to the hollowed-out lady with a lot of stairs. She's more impressive up close than from a distance. We went to the top of the Empire State Building, took in the 360-degree view, and then stopped for a beer up the street at the Heartland Brewery. We then drove to Astoria, in Queens, and snacked on some lamb shanks at a Greek restaurant that had no set menu and no published prices, but had the tastiest lamb I've eaten in quite a while. We decided not to have our dessert at the restaurant, and instead walked down 31st to Broadway and bought a few pieces of baklava from a Greek bakery. They were delicious! Then, to top off the day, I suggested the New York Waterway Twilight Cruise. We had just enough time to catch the 7:30 p.m. departure from West 38th Street Pier in Manhattan. She said she'd love it.

We quickly made our way across the 59th Street Bridge, arriving at the docking area at 7:15 p.m. I parked on the street, displaying my official police placard on the dashboard. Luckily, there were tickets left for sale, although they were almost sold out of the five hundred or so tickets they were permitted to sell. We boarded just as the departure horn on the ship sounded. It was a balmy evening, and we made sure that we got a double seat on the outdoors upper deck, to take advantage of the New York City skyline. I asked Denise if she wanted something to drink, as they served wine, beer, and soda on board. She said that she'd like a white wine, so I walked down to the lower level of the boat where the bar was situated and bought two glasses of wine, one chardonnay and the other pinot noir. It took a while to get the drinks, as the bar was crowded with tourists. When I returned, I found Denise taking in the view as we cruised past the Statue of Liberty and into the East River.

We were so relaxed sitting there, sipping on wine, making small talk, and taking in the Manhattan skyline; we got lost in the moment. Really, there is no place as beautiful on the planet.

If you've never seen the New York skyline lit up at night from the water, it's surreal-looking, almost as if the city skyline is painted on a canvas. And now and then you can hear the engine of a small boat as it passes by, and the faint sound of people talking in Battery Park as you round the southern tip of Manhattan. It's truly breathtaking, and it makes you realize how fortunate you are to be a part of the city on a daily basis.

The ship docked at 9:30 p.m. and we made our way a

block over to where I'd parked the car. We headed up the Henry Hudson Parkway so I could drop Denise off. I then planned to drive over to my apartment. But before we approached the tollbooth, Denise asked, "Why don't you stay with me tonight?" She must have read my mind.

I'd have been nuts to say no. "I'd like
that a lot." She smiled. "Me, too."

I drove through the toll plaza and took the second exit off the Henry Hudson for her building, parking in the rear. We entered the building by way of the rear entrance, using her key card. Staying with her was the end of a perfect day. I knew what tomorrow would bring, and how imperfect that day would be. But for now I was looking forward to a peaceful evening, and to not thinking about the problems I might face the next day.

Chapter Twenty-Three

Things were looking up. Chief Daniels was attending a Chiefs of Police meeting and wasn't in. After checking in with Captain Christopher I took the stairwell up to Jacob Staton's office. He seemed to be less than his cool, level-headed self when I walked into his office. He had the word "stress" written all over his face. Perhaps Jacob hadn't slept well the previous night, or maybe he was preparing for a trial that had hair on it. In any event, I was about to throw him a curveball that would give him a case of acid reflux. I really didn't like stirring up the pot, but sometimes throwing a good curveball into somebody else's batter's box was necessary. Besides, I was really getting tired of having them thrown into mine. After I explained the allegations made about Pat Donnelly, Staton was visibly shaken, both in his body language and tone of voice.

"There's no way in hell the District Attorney is going on a witch hunt to investigate allegations from a C.I. that the third-ranking official in the DEA is a drug dealer."

"Jesus, Jacob, Donnelly might be running a major heroin operation out of Petra's nightclub, and we need to at least look into it. Baraka spilled his guts a few weeks ago about Nebor, Hassan, and Donnelly tied together trafficking in heroin, and it looks to me that their base of operations is the nightclub. It all makes sense now. If we dig hard enough, I guarantee you that we'll find they're all connected. And as far as Mike, he got swept up in it because the DEA wasn't careful enough, or didn't care enough to distinguish him from his cousin, who skipped to Jordan and is now willing to come forward and give a statement that it was he working for Mickey Calise, and not his cousin Mike."

Jacob's face ballooned into a bright red hue as he realized that perhaps I might just be right in my assumptions, although I had no hard evidence to back them up. Assumptions that I'm sure he didn't want on his plate. You know, Jacob was definitely one of the good guys, but I knew I had backed him into a corner, and I also knew that he had to do something with the allegations.

He sat there thinking for a moment, and then shouted, "You've got nothing concrete for anyone to open an investigation on Donnelly! And as for Baraka, the DA's not going to get involved in overturning a federal conviction." He emphasized the word "federal."

I fired back. "I'll find the evidence! Jacob, you've known me a long time. I don't bullshit! And as for Mike, it's the right thing to do for the guy. I understand the political implications, but when a wrong has been done, don't we have a responsibility to fix it? What the fuck, Jacob; we're supposed to be the good guys. What'd you want me to do, sweep this shit under the rug and just forget about it?"

"Frank, we prosecuted Baraka. He was found guilty."

"But his cousin Ayman is willing to come forward and tell the truth."

Jacob sat back in his chair, maybe thinking he'd reconciled the two- pronged assault I'd leveled at him. He said, matter-of-factly, "Let Baraka's lawyer worry about this shit, not you. That's what lawyers do, Frank— they work on behalf of their clients; cops don't. Cops don't have clients. They arrest people so lawyers have work to do. Don't get the two mixed up. And as for the DEA, let them clean up their own house. You're putting your career on the line, which I'm not willing to do."

Now it was my turn to make up for the distance between us by leaning forward in my chair. This was a point that I didn't want him to miss.

"You know what, Jacob? Every time I'm working on the street, my life is on the line. All that needs to happen is the wrong word said, my body language is wrong, more sweat than a situation warrants, and I'm gone. There's a hundred

197

different things that can get me killed. I lived with the Luccheses for years. I knew when the warrants were to be executed, and I never once folded. And you're telling me I'm taking a risk with my career by doing the right thing here? Jacob, it's a fucking cakewalk compared to what I do every day to earn a living. So, who's kidding who? My career? What career? Every time I walk into the fucking Chief's office, my career's in jeopardy. He wants to put me back into uniform. Pal, I don't know what you're gonna do, but I'm not going to worry about my fucking career any more!"

I guess Staton realized that I wasn't going to let this one go. "Okay, I'll speak to Larson, but I can pretty much guarantee what she'll say. She's a hard-ass about this stuff, and I've never known her to revisit a conviction, especially one that her office was only a part of."

I got up from my chair, offering my hand. I felt like saying, "Maybe that's what's wrong with the DA's office," but I bit my tongue. I said instead, "I'd appreciate anything you can do. Thank you."

Before I left his office, he said, "I'll call you this afternoon with what comes out of it, but I wouldn't hold out much hope."

"I understand, but going through channels first is a start. Talk to you later."

Now if Larson said no, that was the end of it in the office, but to me, it was just the beginning. I called Nulligan and asked if he could meet me at Jake's. I needed a sounding board. He said he could, and that he was having a shitty day, and hoped we could stretch it out to three or four hours. I drove over to the restaurant, parking right in front, my usual spot. Ben, the part-time bartender, was working, as Jessica had the day off. That girl put in a lot of hours, probably sixty hours a week, and I'm sure she had plenty to do taking care of her personal life. While waiting for Joe, I pulled up a stool at the bar and ordered a Dewar's on the rocks. Ben asked if I'd like to try something new—Famous Grouse Scotch, which they

198

just gotten in.

I replied, "Sure, why not? I'm adventurous."

Apparently Ben was a self-tutored expert on all types of liquor. He began to give me a dissertation on the Gloag family that started The Famous Grouse distillery in the late 1800s in Scotland. He said it was the best-selling Scotch whiskey in Scotland, and that it was made with over sixty-five different types of whiskey. Nothing unusual in that, he said— some blends have over one hundred varieties of Scotch in them. He went on to say that there now was a Black Grouse, somewhat heavier, to bring over the folks that liked single malt whiskey, as well as a Snow Grouse, meant to be served cold. Most of the other details of Ben's lecture I've forgotten, but I didn't forget its taste. I liked it. It had a sweetness other blends didn't. I asked him about its sweetness, and he said it came from the wooden sherry casks, which the family originally had bought from Spanish producers, and in which they distilled the Scotch. They'd kept the tradition through the years, with the Scotch since having become one of Scotland's main commodities. I had to hand it to Ben. The information was interesting, and he sure knew his stuff. Jake McDonald was lucky to have a guy like Ben working for him.

When I was about halfway through my drink, Joe walked in. I got up from the stool, bringing my drink as we walked over to one of the booths and slid in. Ben gave Joe a nod and brought Joe his favorite Blue Point and me another Grouse. I had some concern about what I was about to tell Joe, but it was important for me to have Joe evaluate the information. Sitting there looking into my drink, I began explaining everything, from the scene in Mike's hospital room to just having met with Staton. Joe's facial expression was painful. He called Ben over, asking for another round of drinks. Ben took the order and walked back to the bar.

"Now where were we, Frankie? Oh, yeah, you were just telling me how you're going to shoot yourself in the head, ruining your career."

"Jesus, Joe, there's no letting up with you, is there?"

"Listen, here's my take on this, so take it for what's its worth, and to you that's probably not much, cause you're so fucking stubborn. You never should have talked to Jacob. He's going to the DA, and she's going to put you on the rubber-gun squad. You were ordered to stay away from Baraka, and now they know that you've disobeyed orders. I told you that Baraka was bad fucking news, and to get rid of him so we can get back to business."

"And what business would that be? Get back to exactly what? The same old shit? I can't do that, Joe. I just can't leave it all on my plate and walk away. There are major issues here, for Christ's sake. How would you feel if you were in my shoes? Staton says let the DEA clean up their own house, but who's gonna clean up ours? You tell me."

"You know, I have to tell you, I'm glad I'm not in your shoes, because it's a lose-lose proposition. I know one thing—I'd never put my job on the line for a C.I. They're all the same, and eventually they'll find a way to fuck you, whether they mean it or not. The bastards can't help themselves. That's the way they're built. As far as the DEA, well, that's another matter, but you can't just go charging forward without something to give to the likes of Larson. Believe me, she's not gonna play ball on the word of a C.I., so to me you're pretty much fucked. I'd leave it alone."

"I just can't do that, Joe."

Joe shook his head as we tried to make some small talk. He told me that he had a problem with his blood pressure. He said his doctor put him on some medication so he wouldn't blow up. And once his medication was regulated, and as long as he stayed on the pills, he'd be able to get a hard-on again and live a long and happy life, but other than that, everything was fine in his world.

"Frankie, is there anything else you want to know?" "Yeah, will I ever be rich?"

We both had a laugh as I paid the tab and left Ben a hefty tip for my course on The Famous Grouse Scotch.

Once out on the street, Joe gave me a hug and shook my hand. "Frankie, think about this. There's a lot at stake here."

"I know, Joe, but I've gotta see this through. I'll talk to you soon." I got into my car, waving to him as I pulled out into traffic and headed for my apartment. I decided to first stop on Arthur Avenue to pick up some groceries. Pulling onto 187th Street, I passed Our Lady of Mt. Carmel Church as I headed for the Terminal Market on Arthur Avenue. The thought occurred to me to stop in. I hadn't been in a church in a long time, and maybe the quiet of the church would do me some good. I parked the car around the corner on Belmont Avenue, the neighborhood that Dion DiMucci grew up in. If you've never heard of Dion DiMucci, I'm sure you've heard of Dion and the Belmonts, the recording artists who took their professional name from Belmont Avenue.

I entered the church through the center set of the large, oak- paneled doors, and walked halfway down the center aisle, taking a seat in a pew near the main altar. There wasn't anyone else in the church at the time, and the silence was soothing.

Joe and I had done our best to stretch the lunch out into midafternoon, and when my cell phone rang, I noticed that the time read 3:02 p.m. It was Staton. He said he'd just come from a meeting with Larson and Daniels, and that Larson had said she wasn't going to entertain the thought of Baraka and me turning her office upside down. He said that she'd directed him to call AUSA John Kenny and sever our relationship with Baraka. She had also told him not to mention any of the allegations against Donnelly. Jacob said that Daniels had already spoken to me about Baraka, and for me to keep away from him. Larson finished by saying she wouldn't have the image of her office tarnished in any way by unsupported allegations.

Jacob was emphatic. "So, Frank, you'd better leave it alone." Hey, I expected as much.

"Let me get this straight, Jacob, just for the record. Not having her office tarnished is more important than a man's innocence? And Donnelly—he gets to operate like business as usual, right out in the fucking open?"

At this, I realized that I was in a church and looking at the crucifix above the altar. I silently said that I was sorry for my excessively foul mouth.

Jacob ended with, "You've no alternative, Frank. Leave this one alone. I gotta go."

I knew full well that DA Larson had slammed the door in my face, but I was about to open another, and the consequences could be lasting. Hey, I could always go back to teaching, but those poor kids.

My eyes were transfixed on the large wooden cross suspended above the altar with the tortured body of a crucified man nailed to it. Maybe by thinking about what this man stood for, not yielding his principles to save himself, somehow I might be strengthened by his strength to correct this injustice, regardless of the personal consequences. Somehow, sitting there, the decisions I needed to make on how to handle things seemed a lot clearer. Looking up at the stained glass images of the many saints above the altar, with the sun playing off each shade of color, I hoped that God was real, and that He would help me work through this system of so-called justice. After all, the justice was why I'd become a cop in the first place.

Suddenly the thought of my girls, Catie and Francesca, flooded my mind. Living without them had torn me apart, and after crying myself to sleep on many nights, I no longer had any more tears to shed, but they would always have a special place in my heart. Perhaps someday things would be different, but I now understood why Helen had shielded them from me. I believe that Helen somehow felt that I would infect them with the aura of criminality that continually surrounded me, and that somehow it might rub off on them.

I realized that the life I lived had changed me dramatically from some sort of normalcy into a negative, untrusting, and sometimes violent person. I believed there was a fine line between love and hate, but before that moment, I'd never realized it could turn so fast from one to the other. I could live without being married to Helen, but to keep the kids from me was something else. Who'd do that? A woman who hated you, that's who.

Tears of guilt and self-pity coursed down my cheeks. And, at that point, I didn't try to stop them, as it seemed that I was heaving loose some pent-up emotions, and it felt good. After about ten minutes of dehydrating my tear ducts, I decided it was time to head for the Terminal Market. I got up from the pew, looked around the church one more time, genuflected, crossed myself, and left.

I made my way to my car, now knowing the course I was going to take, and somehow feeling a lot better about myself. My girls were another issue, and maybe things could never be worked out with them. But I'd try, that was for sure.

After picking up some canned tomatoes, garlic, and homemade pasta, I drove home with the intention of cooking myself dinner and then giving Mike a call. He should have been home by then, hopefully taking it easy and recovering. But knowing him, he was probably out on the street already, looking for DeFalco. I hoped not.

As soon as I got in I called Mike. "Hey, you're home. How you doin'?"

He said that he was fine, but there was still some pain, and the doctor said he'd heal in a few weeks, with no lasting damage to his shoulder.

"Hey, that's great; just follow the doctor's orders and don't be like me and ignore everybody who gives you sound advice." We both laughed. I continued, "Listen, I told you I'd get back to you on your cousin. I've run it through channels and, sure enough, no one's going to help us out. Just so you know, I thought as much."

He sighed. "I'm innocent, Frank."

"I know you are. That's why I'm going to help you."

There was silence on the other end of the phone. Then he said, "But, Frank, you said no one wants to help us out. How are you going to handle this by yourself?"

"You let me worry about that. You just let me know when your cousin arrives in New York. I'll take it from there."

"He's due in soon. My mother will be speaking to her sister."

Evidently, his mother, Cindy, and Hanna were in the room, so he related my conversation to them. The next thing I heard over the phone were voices celebrating in the background, with Adel yelling, "Sha-la, sha-la," loud enough to be heard down the street.

"Mike, it sounds like there's some excitement going on there." "Yeah, my mother is screaming that God has answered her prayers, and that you are like a son to her. The rest of them are jumping around the room, hugging one another."

"Listen, call me as soon as your cousin arrives. I assume he's coming in at Kennedy Airport?"

"Yes."

"We don't want your cousin getting cold feet and disappearing into the woodwork. We'll pick him up at Customs."

"Frank, thank you."

Mike ended our conversation by telling me that his mother had a lead on a nice apartment in Bronxville that she wanted to talk to me about. I told him that I'd love to look at it, and that I might be getting a leg up in the world by getting out of the Bronx and back into Westchester County. I was really looking forward to a new apartment, and maybe a new start in life.

Chapter Twenty-Four

Nothing in life is ever as simple as it seems. It turned out that Baraka's cousin was not as forthcoming as Mike's mother had hoped. In phone conversations with Mike over the next several weeks, I learned more than I wanted to know about the Jordanian tribal structure and its accompanying social hierarchy. Mike told me that Adel's sister had become frustrated with her son's obstinacy in coming forward and doing the honorable thing, even though he'd made that previous commitment to his mother. Knowing his habits in Jordan, she couldn't physically go into the neighborhood where he lived, as it was too dangerous for her to go into what literally was a den of thieves.

After Ayman's father had died some years back, his mother had always had her hands full with him, basically washing them of him when he had become eighteen. He'd been pretty much on his own since then and, like a lot of kids everywhere, he had let the attractions of the seamier side of life, with its quick money, rule his life. She'd had little control of him then, and she had little now. But one thing she did have was a connection to one of the respected tribal leaders of the Maayeh, one of the larger Christian tribes in Jordan. His name was Bachir, meaning "Good Tidings."

As a regional tribal elder, Bachir wielded power and commanded respect throughout Amman. Mike explained to me that, even in the modern day, to dishonor the tribe was to dishonor all its members, and that every member of the tribe was responsible for instances where a member brought disgrace upon anyone else in the tribe. Ayman had committed the cardinal sin of allowing another to assume his debt to society, distancing himself from his family and operating outside the dictates of the tribe. Bachir could not let this stand, and told Adel's sister he'd take care of the matter. Bachir had then contacted ten or so of his fellow tribesmen to go into the slums of Amman to explain tribal etiquette to Ayman. These were no ordinary tribesmen in Maayeh robes. These were battle-hardened soldiers in the Jordanian army who'd had experience fighting jihadists and al-Qaeda terrorists in the desert. They told him that if he wasn't on a flight to New York within two weeks, he would be taken out to the desert in a military transport and shot. They also told him that if he didn't follow through with his agreement once in the United States, they'd follow him to the ends of the earth to exact vengeance. They then cranked up the loudspeaker in their jeep, broadcasting to the slum that Ayman from this time forward was an outcast, that he had a debt to pay, and failure to do so would mean retribution from the tribe, and that anyone who came to his aid would also be dealt with.

Ayman refused to contact his mother with any flight arrangements, so no one knew exactly when he was coming into the United States. He may have had a commitment to keep, but evidently he was going to fulfill it his way. This presented a problem for me, as I was under the impression that I would pick him up at the airport, escort him to a hotel, and take his confession there. So it became a waiting game. Mike finally called me, telling me that his cousin was in New York, but Ayman wouldn't let him know where he was staying. He said that his cousin needed some time to get his affairs in order, as he expected to be sent to prison once he made the confession.

In the meantime, I had time to look at the apartment that Mike's mother mentioned. It was on the top floor of a six-story building in Bronxville, not far from the Bronx River Parkway. The rent was $1,800 a month. I wasn't sure about renting another apartment, especially when I didn't know if I'd have a job to pay the rent. I asked Denise to come check it out with me. I made arrangements with the landlord for a walk- through when I knew Denise was off. So on a Monday afternoon we met the landlord at the apartment for a walk-through.

As soon as we walked in, Denise said, "Frankie, this is beautiful— it's really clean, and you have a view of the park along the parkway. Look, there's plenty of closets for storage. It's a two-bedroom with a den, and you even have a terrace, so you can sit out and enjoy your coffee in the morning. Hey, there's even an area for a kitchenette. I think it's perfect. What do you think?"

If she only knew what I lived in, there'd be no discussion. "I think I'll take it."

"Frankie, that's great. I know you'll be happy here."

The landlord seemed pleased as we shook hands. I was set to sign a one-year lease in a few days, and planned to move in at the end of the month. Denise then suggested that we explore Bronxville to get the lay of the land. We found Bronxville to be a delightful, upscale village, situated between Tuckahoe, Yonkers, and Scarsdale. I knew of a good Italian restaurant, Scala's, which was just down the street from my new apartment. Heads turned on the street as we entered the restaurant, and I guarantee they weren't looking at me. Jeans, taupe sandals, white designer T-shirt, dark aviator glasses, and a bag slung over her shoulder made Denise look like she'd just stepped off Rodeo Drive in Beverly Hills. I was dressed in my usual jeans, button-down white shirt, and a dark blue sports jacket. The one indulgence I allowed myself was dark Armani sunglasses. Even though I'd never particularly thought much about my looks, we weren't an unattractive couple.

We sat at the bar and I ordered a Dewar's on the rocks and a chardonnay. Just as we took off our sunglasses and placed them on the bar, my cell phone rang.

"Yeah, what's up?"

It was Mike. He asked, "Did you take the apartment?"

"How'd you know I was looking at it today?"

Mike laughed. "My mother asked the landlord to call after you looked at it."

"Tell your mom that I took it. It's great. Please thank her for me."

"I will. She's happy for you."

Denise was trying to get my attention; I was so focused on my conversation I was ignoring her. Then the bartender said, "Sir, please take the phone outside in deference to the other customers here. They really don't want to hear your discussion."

I shook my head yes, and went outside to finish my conversation. We said that we'd be in touch, and that we'd probably talk the next day. When I walked back into the restaurant I apologized to the bartender for being inconsiderate. He said no problem, and thanked me for understanding. Sitting back down, I finally sipped my drink, and asked Denise if she wanted to go back to her place, where I could cook dinner. I said that we could stop by the grocery store on the way home

She batted her lovely eyes. "Sounds great; I'm beginning to get hungry. What you got in mind?"

"I don't know yet, but I'll figure something out."

"Can I ask what the call was about?"

"My informant found out that that I was looking at the apartment today, and wanted to know how I'd made out. His mom was excited that I took it."

"When are you going to introduce me? Maybe we can go out sometime?"

I laid my hands on the bar and put my forehead down on them, ready to scream. At that moment, I wanted to crawl back into that hole of an apartment, lay down in bed, pull the sheets over my head, and sleep for thirty hours, flaking ceiling, stained wallpaper and all.

I said to the floor, "We can't do that. It's against departmental rules. I just can't go socializing with him; professionally, it's wrong. You know, I've just recently had this conversation with the guy too. He didn't call you with the suggestion, did he? 'Cause I feel like I'm talking to him all over again about this."

She huffed, "Of course not. It's just that he's filling such a large portion of your life that I just thought we could meet."

"Look, it's all about appearances in my business. Did you ever/ hear the expression 'guilt by association'? I'd automatically be suspected of being on the take, of taking and receiving favors . . . the list goes on and on. I can't put myself in that position. You don't understand the rules I play by. All my life I've worked to keep my family name from being tarnished. I put bad guys away, and I can't risk being compromised by socializing with my informant. If there's anybody I want us to go out with, it's my best friend Joe Nulligan and his girlfriend Jessica."

"Oh, I've heard you mention Joe. He works with you, and I think that Jessica bartends at Jake's, where we met."

"Hey, you've got some memory."

Denise laid her hand on my arm and said, "I understand. Let's get together with Jessica and Joe soon. What d'ya say?"

"Sounds like a plan. Joe can't wait to meet you."

We finished our drinks and I signaled the bartender for the check. As we made our way out, she said, "Now don't forget to set something up with Joe and Jessica."

We drove over to Stew Leonard's, located off the Major Deegan Expressway, where I bought clams, mussels, and calamari. Denise said she had the other ingredients, including the linguine, to make the zuppa di pesce. We parked in the back of her building and entered through the back entrance, taking the elevator up to her apartment.

I was in the middle of making the dish when my cell phone rang. I was hoping it was a social call and not business. It was Baraka. Knowing him, he probably smelled dinner on the other end of the line, and wanted to come over. But dinner wasn't on his mind. He was excited, telling me that his cousin had called him, and was ready meet with me. Thankfully, it was still early in the evening, and I could still reach the people I needed to reach to set things up for the following day. I told Mike to hang on; I needed to make a call from another phone.

I called the technical supervisor, Sergeant Steve Cook, on his cell. I got his voice mail, and left a message for him to call me right back. In less than thirty seconds, Denise's phone rang. It was Steve. I told him that I had an interview in the morning, and asked if he could set up the interrogation room for audio and video at 8 a.m.

He said, "Sure, no problem. It'll be ready when you get in." "Steve, I owe you one," I said, then hung up and got back to Mike.

I told him that he and his cousin should meet me the following morning at 7:45 a.m. on the courthouse steps, and for them not to be late.

I could feel the excitement in his voice.

"Frank, we won't be late, I promise you. Thanks. See you in the morning."

"Frankie, can I ask who that was?"

"That was the informant. We got things to do tomorrow."

As I stirred the sauce, Denise came over, grabbed hold of my arm, pulled me into her, and kissed me passionately. She said, "I know where I'd like to be led. Can that sauce wait?"

I immediately turned off the burner. "Are you kidding me? What sauce?" She took my hand as we left the kitchen and walked down the hallway to her bedroom. Hey, tomorrow was another day, and it was sure to be an interesting one.

Chapter Twenty-Five

The morning came too soon. As usual when I was with Denise, I could have lounged around her apartment all day relaxing, but that was for another day. Being with her was a reminder of what life should be, rather than what it was. It was an effort to leave. But leave I did. That day my fingers were to test the sharpened edge of the sword of justice— not just to see if justice would prevail, but also if I would have a future in police work.

I've got another saying: it isn't easy being easy. I hope you understand it. It means that nothing in life that's easy is easy to come by. The state of life, by its very nature, makes living difficult.

I arrived early to the office to check the interrogation room out before the bosses arrived for work. I was really nervous, and wanted to get on with the meeting with Ayman. Just like a pro football player, when the referee blows the whistle for the game to start, all the jitters would be gone. I was ready for this game to start. That's the way it was with me. I was ready to get it on.

Joe happened to be in early too. Popping his head into the interrogation room, he said, "One of the court officers told me that you were in."

"Hey, you're in early too. Couldn't sleep?"

"Sometimes the blood pressure medicine fucks me up, so I wake up early. Listen, before I left last night I overheard Staton talking to Daniels. I didn't want to call you last night and upset your time off. I figured we'd talk today." Jacob had told Joe that Baraka had bought a phony passport, and it looked like he was planning on leaving the country.

I'd felt that I'd just been hit in the belly with a two-by-four. I needed to sit down. Jesus, didn't it ever stop with this guy? My color must have left me.

"Frank, you okay? You don't look good."

The news emotionally deflated me. "How'd Jacob hear about this?" "Evidently through another informant who happens to know Mike.

Kenny told Staton to drop the hammer on Baraka. They've had enough of his shit."

Joe pulled up a chair, sitting next to me. He continued, "Back off from this guy, Frankie; he's bad news."

"Joe, what the fuck am I supposed to do now, lock him up?" "Look, Frankie, I'm just warning you. Don't leave your ass out on a limb."

I was mad. I said, "You've no fucking idea. My ass is already out on a limb. I need to think for a minute."

Joe tried to say something, but I put my hand up for him to stop. "I don't have time to discuss this right now. I need to think this through. Nothing you say now is gonna make the difference with what's coming down the road."

Joey got up, and as he was walking out he took a parting shot. "I just hope you know what you're doing. I really do."

"So do I, Joey. So do I."

Thoughts were tumbling through my head like a runaway freight train flying off the tracks, the cars all jumbled on top of each other. Jesus, I'd really walked into this one. I needed to examine this for a minute. Mike bought a counterfeit passport that he thought I didn't know about, but I did. Maybe I could use this information somehow? That was number one. Number two, Joey was right. He'd said that Mike would fuck me, and it seems he was planning to. Mike had shown his true colors. He couldn't be trusted. Was he was really planning to leave the country, or was he just panicking? What about Cindy? He wouldn't leave Cindy. Number three, this was a personal insult. I did believe he'd bought the passport before I agreed to take his cousin's confession. Did I know this for sure? No, but I'd have bet on it. Trouble was, he'd hung on to the passport as a safety net. I needed to deal with the personal issues later and deal with the situation at hand. So, I'd take the confession, if he'd give it to me. Mike was innocent; I knew that much, and I wouldn't go back on my word to anyone.

I knew this wasn't going to sit well with Chief Daniels or anyone else in the office, but what the fuck, I was going to take it anyway, even if I was brought up on charges and suspended. So the bottom line was that I would take the confession and let everything play itself out. The night before, when the thought occurred to me that it would be an interesting day, I had had no idea just how interesting it would be.

Mike and his cousin were waiting in front of the building. Ayman was dressed in an open white shirt, black slacks, and square-toed black shoes, with Louis Vuitton sunglasses perched on his head. I did a double take, unable to distinguish for a minute who was who. They looked like identical twins. The only difference I could see was that Ayman sported a thick mustache. He even combed his hair like Mike did. Now Mike was wearing a light blue shirt, open at the throat, light tan slacks, a dark brown summer sports jacket, and brown loafers. They were about the same height and weight. I couldn't believe that they weren't identical twins.

I gave Mike no hello. Instead, I directed my attention to Ayman, and said, "I'm Detective Santorsola. I'll be talking with you this morning. You ready?"

He even spoke like Mike. "Yeah, I'm ready. Take me to my own fucking funeral."

I took a second look at him, realizing that he was tough as nails. I replied, "Okay, let's move it before the brass gets in." I took the lead into the building, clearing them with courthouse security. Then we all crowded into the elevator, taking it up to the fourth floor. I walked Mike and Ayman to the interrogation room and got them situated. Then I told them that I had to take care of something, and would be back. I walked into the squad room, then into the tech office, where Cook was viewing his monitor, looking at images of Mike and his cousin sitting there chatting in the interrogation room.

I asked Sergeant Cook if we were all set to start. He said, "Ready as rain, Frankie."

"Wonderful. I'll sign the original tapes into evidence later, but I'll need a copy of both tapes as soon as the interview is over."

"Sure, no problem. Are you ready to go?"

"Ready to rock and roll. And hey, I appreciate this."

"Anything for you, Frankie. I'm ready when you are."

I walked out of the tech office and back into the interrogation room. Mike and Ayman were making small talk around the four-by-six foot, light brown, rectangular oak interview table. They were seated side by side. A tape recorder had been placed in front of them. I took a chair opposite them, turning on the tape recorder and stating my name, date, and the purpose of the interview. I then began by asking Ayman to state his name, date of birth, and how he was related to Mike.

I asked Ayman about his relationship with Sami Hassan. He said that Hassan was Mike's brother-in-law, and that Sami had introduced him to Mickey Calise. He said that Calise sometimes supplied them with heroin to sell in America. He also said that, on occasion, he would meet the Jordanian sky marshals at the Holiday Inn Queens to pick up heroin that they'd brought into the country. He said that he would then turn it over to Nick Galgano. I asked Ayman if Mike, his cousin, ever imported, distributed, or sold drugs of any type that Ayman knew of. He said he was certain that Mike had not. I then questioned him about whether Mike had ever worked with Sami, picking shipments of heroin up from the Jordanian sky marshals or making deliveries to Galgano. He confessed that it was only himself, and that Mike had had nothing to do with any of it. I asked him about the heroin found in Mike's apartment during the execution of the search warrant. He said that Sami told him that he had stashed the heroin there because Sami's wife hadn't wanted it in her house, and that Mike had had no idea that Sami put the drugs in his bedroom dresser. I then asked Ayman if he was the person who should have been convicted on the charges of importation, distribution, and possession of a controlled substance, and not his cousin Mike. He replied yes, that he should have been arrested and convicted, and not his cousin Mike. He again said that Mike had nothing to do with the drugs or Michael Calise and his associates.

After some back and forth and further clarification of Ayman's relationship to Sami, Nick Galgano, and Mickey Calise, I was able to wrap things up in less than one hour.

We'd just completed the easiest part of what lay ahead. I shut off the tape recorder and then we all stood. I shook Ayman's hand and said, "It took a lot of balls for you to come forward. Your cousin has been through hell. It's about time things got straightened out." He nodded. Ayman and Mike hugged, kissing each other on the cheek. I guess blood is still thicker than water. But let's not forget Sheikh Jamal Bachir, the tribal leader of the Maayeh, and the pressure he'd brought to bear. I'm sure that Ayman's conscience alone wasn't bothering him enough to have him come forward and fess up to the truth, knowing that he was destined to go to prison.

I left the room, soon returning with a copy of the video and audio tapes, which I handed to Mike, telling him to give them to his attorney. Then I said to Ayman, "Let me know where I can find you. This isn't over. It's just the beginning. But for now, you're free to go." Again he nodded; evidently the reality of what he'd just done was beginning to set in. I turned to Mike. "You and I need to take a ride. How'd you get here?"

"I drove my sister's car. It's a block over. Why, what's up?"

"We've got some business to attend to that doesn't involve your

cousin. Why doesn't he drive the car back to your place and you come with me? We need to talk."

Mike fished in his pocket for the car keys, handing them over to Ayman. Then he asked me, "You mad at me?"

"You could say that. Let's get out of here before we run into someone we don't want to see."

We took the elevator down to the courthouse lobby and out to the street. I shook Ayman's hand and gave him a business card, telling him to keep in touch. Mike and I walked across Martin Luther King Boulevard and got into my car. I had a destination in mind, and it wasn't warm and fuzzy.

Mike asked, "What's wrong? Why are you mad at me? Where're we going?"

"Look, just sit there and keep your mouth shut." He asked again. I yelled, "Shut the fuck up. You'll know when we get there."

I drove south on the Bronx River Parkway, exiting on Pelham Parkway eastbound, and drove to the New York City garbage landfill off Pelham Parkway. Pulling into the dump, you could see the thousands of seagulls swarming the fill, feeding on garbage. It looked like Alfred Hitchcock's movie *The Birds*. I parked my car alongside one of the many mounds of garbage, telling Mike to get out of the car.

Bewildered, he asked, "What the fuck's up?"

I shouted, "Get out of the fucking car or I swear I'll shoot you right here."

He reluctantly got out, walking to the front of the car. I did the same. Again he asked, "What are we doing here, Frank?"

I screamed, "I fucking trusted you. I stuck my neck out for you, and you're going to run away, leaving me holding the bag. What d'ya think, I'm the fucking village idiot, or Jimmy the fucking dunce?"

He looked at me in shock, his face ash white. "What are you talking about?"

"Did you fucking think I wasn't gonna find out that you bought a phony passport?"

Mike's eyes widened as he realized he'd been caught being dishonest and not up front with me. "I was scared, Frank; scared for me, my family, Cindy. I had no one to turn to, looking over my shoulder every minute of every day. What else could I do but leave at a moment's notice if things didn't work out?"

"You could have come to me, instead of crying in a fucking landfill, that's what you could have done. I've put my whole fucking career on the line for you, and this is how you repay me? Fuck you!"

"Frank, I didn't know what to do. You gotta believe me. I'd never try to hurt you. It's just that . . ."

"You've fucked me, Mike, in a big way."

"I'm so sorry."

"So where's the passport?"

"It's at home. I'll give it to you."

Tears pouring down his face, Mike, his arms extended, gesturing for me to forgive him.

"It's too late; it's gone to Staton, and the pressure's coming down to throw you back in the slam. Frankly, I don't blame them. Now you're a flight risk. You really fucked things up, Mikey boy. You broke the rules, and that's gonna be hard to fix. Not only with the powers-that-be, but with me."

"I'm sorry. I panicked and didn't realize the fallout."

"So tell me, where'd you get the passport?" He didn't answer. I screamed, "Where'd you get the goddamned passport?"

I could barely hear him as he whispered, "I bought it from DeFalco."

Leaning back on the front hood of the car, I hadn't expected what Mike had just told me.

"DeFalco, now all the pieces of the puzzle are coming together for me. I gotta find this guy. There are people hiding in the background, pulling the strings, and we're being played like puppets."

"Please tell me how I can fix this, Frank, and I'll do

it. I'll do anything. You're the only friend I got, so please don't turn your back on me now." Mike leaned on the car, his head down, his tears splashing onto the fender.

"Mike, look at me. Look at me. I've made a commitment to myself about you, and I plan to see it through, no matter the outcome. You know, I'm not naive in all this. I knew what I was getting myself into, but what you've done just complicates things. Why couldn't you have seen that?"

"I'll make this up to you, I swear."

I grunted, "Yeah, provided you get the chance. Now get back in the car. I'll drive you home."

I turned the car around, driving out of the dump and back into Yonkers. We drove in silence to his building, where I let him off, his sadness evident as I watched him walk through the door.

Well, if nothing else, that'd give him something to think about for a while. Now, what was next on the agenda? It was time for a visit with Jacob Staton. That promised to be an interesting visit.

I drove back to White Plains, pulled my car into the rear parking area of the courthouse, and took the private elevator up to the fifth floor. I walked into Jacob's office without knocking, catching him on the phone, jotting down notes as he spoke. I heard him say, "Okay, I'll start writing the warrant. Who's the affiant?" I guess some dirtball was about to have his life turned upside down.

I had obviously interrupted his conversation, as he said to whomever he was speaking with, "Hang tight; I'll get back to you," and hung up. Standing in front of his desk, Jacob looked surprised.

"Jacob, I don't want you to hear this from anyone else."

I guess I had Jacob's attention. "Uh oh, I have a feeling I'm not going to like what you're going to say."

"I just finished video and audiotaping Mike Baraka's cousin's confession. He admitted that it was him and not Mike who was working for Calise, distributing heroin. The

218

government convicted the wrong guy."

Staton stood up abruptly, his face a shade of gray. "You did what?" "Just what I said, Jacob. I gave Mike a copy of the confession, and told him to give it to his attorney. I signed the original tapes into evidence, if you want to check them out."

Jacob began to shout. "What the hell is wrong with you, Frankie?" I replied calmly, "You gotta make choices, Jacob, and I've made mine." I then turned around and left, leaving him standing there. I took the stairs down to my office, where I placed a phone call to Judge Sposato's law clerk, who logged me in for a late-afternoon meeting. Just then Chief Daniels walked into the squad room with a contemptuous look on his face as he walked by me. I knew where he was heading.

I also knew that the proverbial shit was about to hit the fan, with me its recipient, so I thought I'd better leave before the fat fuck cornered me. I called Nulligan to see if he was around. He said that he was, and wanted to know what was up. I told him that I didn't want to discuss it on the phone, and that I'd meet him at Jake's around 1 p.m.

I walked into Jake's at about 12:45 p.m. and Joe was sitting at our usual booth nursing a beer. As I was about to sit down, my cell phone rang. It was the Chief's office calling, so I let the call go to voice mail. Joe then asked what I was drinking, and I told him that I wasn't.

"What d'ya mean you're not drinking?"

"Joey, I'm not, that's all."

Joe then asked, "So what's going on? Is this about the passport?"

"No. Mike's cousin confessed to me this morning."

Joe's eye's widened. "Damn, who else in the office knows about this? Does Captain Christopher know?"

"By now, everybody knows."

My cell phone rang again. It was the Chief's office calling again. They were calling me every five minutes or so.

"Frankie, it looks like you're up to your ass in alligators. This is heavy shit."

"Tell me about it. I'm meeting with Judge Sposato this afternoon, and I plan to tell him about the confession, and I'm going to tell him about Donnelly."

Joe leaned back in the booth. "You're going to need proof, Frankie."

"Look Joe, I need your help, but I'll understand if you don't want any part of it. It seems that everything is coming out of Petra's: DeFalco, Yousef Nebor, Sami Hassan, and Special Agent Donnelly. I want to start looking at the place to see what's going on."

Joe straightened up, clasping his hands around his drink. "What, do you have a fucking death wish?" I just stared at him, not saying a word for a moment. I guess the silence was more upsetting to him than the thought of working with me without the office's blessing. Sounding a little anxious, Joe said, "Yeah, what the fuck. I'll do it."

We then ordered lunch and discussed how best to surveil the nightclub. I told Joe that I'd talk to him after I met with Judge Sposato, and that I'd call him when the time was right to begin surveillance. It was now almost 3 p.m. and, not knowing what the traffic was going to be like, I told Joe that I should leave for Foley Square. I left Joe drinking his beer, giving myself plenty of time to get to the courthouse.

I parked in the underground parking garage of One Police Plaza and walked over to the courthouse. I approached one of the U.S. marshals in the lobby at the security checkpoint, identified myself, and said that I was expected in Judge Sposato's chambers. The marshal escorted me to a small room off the lobby, where I checked my gun, placing it in a weapons locker. He then directed me to room 313, on the thirteenth floor, and gave me a visitor's pass, which I stuck on my sports jacket.

The elevator was crowded and I had to squeeze out when it stopped on the thirteenth floor. The floor directory pointed to the right for Sposato's chambers. I knocked on the door and walked in, introducing myself to his secretary. His secretary said that he'd be off the bench in a few minutes, and escorted me into his chambers, which butted up against the courtroom he presided in. She told me to take a seat at the conference table. The walls were lined with law books. The deep green carpet was an attractive accompaniment to the polished walnut walls. I was only sitting there for a minute or two when the Judge came through a door from the courtroom, greeting me with a handshake. He offered me coffee as he took off his robe, making coffee from an electric coffeemaker on the dark walnut credenza behind his desk.

The Judge was about six foot, but the light shining off his thinning gray hair made him somehow seem taller than he was. He was dressed in a dark suit and white dress shirt, with a light blue tie that hung past his belt. His brown eyes seemed to sparkle with kindness as he walked over to the conference table with two cups of coffee, sugar, and a creamer on a silver tray that he placed in front of me as he pulled up a chair opposite me at the table.

I explained everything I knew to the Judge, including the issue surrounding Pat Donnelly. The Judge raised his eyebrow and said, after I'd finished, "I've known Pat Donnelly for years. He's highly respected within the DEA."

I replied, "With all due respect, your Honor, you never know when someone is gonna go bad."

"Um, will your office investigate these allegations?"

"Your Honor, they want nothing to do with it. Detective Joe Nulligan and I are going to investigate it ourselves."

"Well, I can't tell you what to do, Detective, and I can't tell you what not to do."

Just then a phone rang in the Judge's chambers. He picked up one of the phones sitting in front of us, and excused himself.

"Judge Sposato here."

There was a pause as he listened to the conversation. Then he said, "Fine; I'd like all parties concerned in my chambers tomorrow at three." He hung up and said, "That was John Kenny. It seems your agency and the United States Attorney's Office are pushing for Mr. Baraka's incarceration. I want you to attend tomorrow as well, Detective."

"I'll be here, your Honor. Thank you for hearing me out on this."

"Evidently, some things need to be said, Detective. Now, if our business is concluded, I'll see you tomorrow."

I stood up as my cell phone rang. I ignored the Chief's call, shook the Judge's hand, and left his chambers, nodding goodbye to his secretary.

I made my way to the lobby, picked up my weapon from the weapons locker, then headed down to the underground garage where I'd left my car. As soon as I started the car, my cell phone rang again. This time it was Mike.

"Hey Mike, what's up?"

"Frank," I could hear the concern in his voice, "my lawyer just called me. She said that there's a hearing in Judge Sposato's chambers tomorrow. John Kenny wants to put me in."

"I know, Mike. I just left the Judge."

"Frankie, I'm scared. You'll be there, right?"

"Yeah, I'll be there. Just stay calm, and make sure that your lawyer brings the tapes."

"Okay, I'll make sure. But what did the Judge say?"

"I don't want to talk about it on the phone. You never know who's listening in."

"Can we meet somewhere?"

"Yeah, but I need to take a shower and put some clean clothes on. You know, the fucking dry cleaners still has my brown suit. Let me think, um. Why don't we meet at Jimmy Rota's restaurant on Schley Avenue in the Bronx at 7:30 p.m.

It's by Saint Raymond's Cemetery."

"Yeah, I know where it is. I'll see you there."

I hung up and headed for my apartment. I couldn't wait until I could move into my new digs and feel like a human being. It was close to 5 p.m. by the time I arrived home. I had to circle the block several times to find a parking space. Low and behold, a car pulled out of a space in front of my building. I realized that the guy pulling out was the owner of the dry cleaners. I beeped the horn as he was attempting to drive away. I guess he didn't recognize me as he gestured that he was moving as fast as he could, and for me have a little patience. I pulled in front of him, blocking him in and backing the traffic up on Hughes Avenue. Car horns started beeping, the stupid bastards not realizing that this was an emergency involving my lucky brown suit. I motioned for the Chinese dry cleaner to roll down his window and he did after he recognized me. He gave me a big, toothy smile. Man, if I had teeth like that, I'd sew my lips shut. I doubted they'd been cleaned in years. Since his English wasn't good, I gestured to my own outfit, saying, "I need my brown suit." He just laughed and replied, "We closed now, open tomorrow. All fix." That made me laugh. "That's just great."

"Very good. Very good. We all fix now. Suit tomorrow."

I then backed up so he was able to drive from the space. At the same time, I heard a booming male voice shout out from the car behind me, "Hey, you stupid son of a bitch, move your fucking car before I move it for you. Ya got the whole street backed up, ya asshole!"

I pulled into the space as the car peeled around me, the driver's middle finger thrust out his window, high in the air. Several more cars went by with windows down, drivers screaming more insults, middle fingers flying. I couldn't help myself, so I replied in kind—shooting each car that passed the bird.

As I approached my apartment I could hear my telephone ringing. It continued to ring as I entered, but I ignored it. I knew what was coming down the pike for me, so putting myself on the cross could wait until tomorrow. I showered, changed, and then decided to lie down for an hour to collect my thoughts. My mind at ease, satisfied that there was no other course to take, I rested for about an hour, then realized that it was time to head over to Rota's.

I decided to take the side streets, knowing that the Cross Bronx would be a parking lot at that hour. In actuality, it was a parking lot at most hours, and I avoided it at all costs. I arrived at the restaurant around 7:20 p.m. My cell phone rang three times before I reached the restaurant. This time the calls came from Deputy Chief Howell. I thought about shutting it off, but didn't want to leave Mike out in the cold in case he had a hard time finding Rota's. It was good thing I'd left it on. I'd just ordered a Scotch at the bar when Mike called. He was in a panic. He shouted into the phone, "Frankie, I'm being followed! They're trying to set me up."

I left my drink at the bar and walked outside to talk. "Calm down, Mike. Where are you?"

"Uh, off the Major Deegan," he paused, probably to look around and get his bearings, "on 233rd, two blocks east of the Expressway."

"Hang on, I'll be right there." I walked back into the restaurant and told Jimmy Rota that I'd had an emergency. I gave him ten dollars for the Scotch, told him I'd be back, and to please hold the reservation if he could.

When I arrived at 233rd Street, I found Mike propping up the spare tire against the car, getting ready to use the jack to change the right front tire.

"What the hell happened?"

"I lost control of the car and the tire blew when I hit the curb. The fuckers were following me."

"How do you know you're being followed?"

"Believe me, Frank. I know when someone's following me."

"Did you get a look at them?"

"No, the car had tinted windows. I know they're gonna try and plant drugs in my car and arrest me." He was so agitated that he could hardly speak. He had to lean on the fender to keep from falling to the ground.

"Mike, calm down. No one's going to plant anything; you don't even know who's following you."

"It's Donnelly. I know it!"

"Look, if you're being followed I'll find out who it is. Trust me. But for now, let's change the fucking tire and grab some dinner."

"Sure. But, I know it's Donnelly. He's gonna fuck me one way or the other."

Just then my cell phone rang again. It was Howell. Doesn't this asshole have a life? I asked Mike to hand me the lug wrench so we could get the fuck out of there. Working together, we had the tire changed in ten minutes. Mike, a little calmer, jumped into his sister's car and followed me to the restaurant. We looked for a tail, but neither of us saw anything. We parked up the street from the restaurant, and then walked down to Rota's.

After washing up in the men's room, we took a table by the window and settled into our seats opposite each other, each ordering a double Scotch. Jimmy Rota came over and handed me back my ten dollars, saying I hadn't had a chance to finish the first one, and that these two were on the house for keeping my reservation. I thanked Jimmy for his consideration. The drink seemed to loosen Mike up, so that after the second double, he was himself.

We each ordered Kansas City strip steaks, mashed potatoes with garlic. I had the creamed spinach, and Mike had the broccoli. We also ordered a bottle of Caymus Cabernet. There's nothing like self- medicating, and all in all we had a pleasant evening. It was now after 11 p.m., and time to head home. I told Mike that I would follow him home. I was hoping to confront the people tailing Mike, if there was a tail. Trying to pick up a tail during the day is one thing, but during the night it is almost impossible.

I picked up the tab and thanked Jimmy for the great food and the good wait service. We walked out of the restaurant into a mild night with a slight breeze. We made our way up the street to where our cars were parked. I followed Mike to his building, and saw nothing to indicate that we were being followed. As Mike parked his car up the street from his building, I saw a large black sedan slowly drive by, as I was double-parked behind Mike's car. The occupant on the passenger side was definitely staring at us through an open window. I didn't get a good look at him, but whoever it was, he was taking too much interest in us. I tried to get the license plate number, but the car sped up and quickly turned right at the end of the block.

Mike jumped out of his car yelling, "See, I told you—the fuckers are after me."

"Mike, we don't know anything yet. Take it easy. Tell you what, you got an extra bedroom?" He nodded his head yes. "Why don't I stay at your place tonight? We'll go to the meeting tomorrow together."

"That's great. Then maybe I'll be able to sleep tonight."

We went upstairs to Mike's apartment and just as we entered, my cellphone rang again. This time I answered it. Of course I knew who it was. It was an agitated Deputy Chief Howell.

"Where the fuck have you been all day? I've been calling you all day long. You've got a lot of explaining to do, Detective."

"Chief, sorry. I didn't realize that my phone was turned off."

"That's bullshit, Frank!"

"What can I say? My phone was off."

"Well off this, Frank. The Chief wants you in his office tomorrow morning at 9 a.m. sharp. You got that?"

"I'll be there, John."

There was a loud click on the other end of the line. I hoped Howell had broken his fucking thumb slamming the receiver down. I knew he was pissed off, because it was way past his bedtime, and I'm sure that Daniels had ordered him to speak to me, even if it took all night.

Mike asked. "Who was that? You look upset."

"It was the Deputy Chief. I have to be in Daniels's office tomorrow morning at nine. It looks like I'll have to meet you at the courthouse instead of us riding there together."

"Are you in trouble?"

"I'm probably going to be suspended."

"Jesus, Frank. They never let up on you. I'm sorry for jamming you up like this. I never wanted this for you."

"Don't worry about it. Just make sure you're not late tomorrow. It's the only chance for both of us."

"I'll be there; you can count on it."

Adel then walked into the living room. Mike explained to her what was happening as she stood there looking dejected. She then shook her head and walked out, going to the linen closet to make sure I had fresh towels in the guest bathroom. I told Mike to tell his mother not to fuss, that I'd only be there for a few hours. She wouldn't hear of it, even making sure that the soap was new ... the things one does for a special guest. I told Mike that we were lucky to have mothers like that, and he agreed.

We sat on the living room couch for a few minutes while Adel tidied up the guest room. I told Mike that before I went to bed I'd better call Denise to let her know I was okay. I hadn't spoken to her in a day or so. He thought that would be a good idea. He said that Cindy would be freaking out if she hadn't heard from him in a couple of days. Mike then showed me to the guest room, where I said goodnight and told him to stay in the house until it was time to go to the hearing. Before turning off the nightlight I called Denise and had a short conversation, telling her that I'd be in touch in a day or so. Naturally she wanted know if I was okay. I told that I was right as rain, that I missed her, and that we'd see each other as soon as I got past this tsunami.

Chapter Twenty-Six

Sitting in the outside of the Chief's office with Ruth Williams was like waiting to be taken to the scaffold to be hung. Ruth's knowledge of the situation was evident by the deafening silence I'd encountered since I got there. The only noise in the room was her perfectly manicured nails clacking against her computer keyboard.

Exactly at 9 a.m. the intercom buzzed. "Is Santorsola here yet?"

"Yes, Chief, he is."

"Send him in."

"Yes, Chief." Ruth jerked her head towards his door and said, "The Chief will see you now."

"Thanks, Ruth."

The Deputy Chief was sitting in a chair on the left side of the room facing Daniel's desk as I walked in. I pulled up a chair next to Howell, and for some crazy reason I wasn't nervous at all. Daniels was looking through a folder containing what I assumed were departmental charges, when I remarked, "Good morning to you too, Chief."

The Chief placed the folder down, the veins on his neck dilated, and the first act hadn't even begun yet. God, how this prick must hate me. The feeling wasn't even mutual. But I couldn't think of anyone I disliked more.

Howell sat there smirking. The fuck always had a smirk on his face when others were in the fire. Sean just glared at me. His face was now a purple hue. Jesus, he basically skipped pink and crimson and went directly to purple. Maybe this would be the day that Big Louie called him to his just reward.

Then he began, "You're suspended without pay, effective immediately. Turn over your gun, shield, and car keys to the Deputy Chief."

I slid my gun across the desk, fished my shield out of my pants pocket, and took the car keys out, placing them next to my gun, then pushed them towards Howell. Howell looked at me with disdain, grabbing them off the desk, placing them in a plastic basket, and then put the basket down on the floor next to him.

Daniels opened the folder and began to read the charges, his reading glasses suspended on his spider-veined nose. "Charge one, General Order 1179, Article 123, Subdivision 53: Failure to comply with a lawful order. To wit: Chief Daniels ordered Detective Frank Santorsola to avoid contact with confidential informant Ayman 'Mike' Baraka."

Howell grinned, his face stuck in an *I told you so* posture. Daniels continued, "Charge two, General Order 1102, Article 86, Subdivision 16, Conduct unbecoming a police officer. To wit: Detective Santorsola took a videotaped statement from Ayman 'Mike' Baraka without authorization from the District Attorney's Office."

He went on, but it's funny—my mind began to wander, not really giving a damn about whatever followed the second charge. It was all bullshit, as the charges were all trumped up to get me out of the way so they could continue their silly bureaucratic nonsense. Maybe it was time to retire and do something else? But what else? All I knew was policing.

The Chief then ended with, "Well, Frank, what do you have to say for yourself?"

"Chief, I've got nothing to say." I turned to Howell. "It's pretty obvious you're having a good time with this." I then turned back to Daniels. "Now, if you'll excuse me, I've got something important to do," and walked out, slamming the door and scaring Ruth so that she jumped up from her chair. I went back downstairs, cleaned out my desk, and took care of some phone calls.

Joe called. "So, what happened?"

"I'm suspended. I'll talk to you later."

"Okay, Frankie. Hang in there."

I looked around the squad room as Captain Christopher stepped out of his office. I was sure he knew that I'd just been suspended. He didn't say anything, just nodded his head hello. Too bad there weren't more guys like him in our business—professionals doing their job. Right then, for me, it was time for the chips to fall where they may.

When I got down to the street, I called Joe and told him I needed a ride, that they'd taken back my office car. He said no problem, he wasn't working until late afternoon, and he was nearby at Jessica's apartment, so he'd pick me up in twenty minutes.

He pulled up in front of the courthouse, driving that beat-up Crown Victoria, smiling as he rolled to a stop. I ran around the front of the car, jumping into the passenger seat.

"Joe, let's get out of here."

"No problem. Where to?"

"Drop me off home."

Pulling out into traffic, Joe said, "So tell me what happened."

"I'm suspended without pay until there's a formal hearing on the charges. Daniels is trying his best to get rid of me. Shit, I guess I'll have to call my brother and give him the bad news."

"Ah, Richie will understand. He knows you've had problems with Daniels all along. Besides, you'll beat the charges."

"I don't know if Rich will understand. He's pretty straitlaced. Fuck! They got me tied up pretty good, Joe. Everything has to fall into place for me now."

"So what's the next step?"

"I want to begin looking at Petra's. Maybe DeFalco will show up." "Oh, shit. That's what I was going to tell you. The NYPD harbor police found DeFalco early this morning floating face-down near the Statue of Liberty. Someone put two bullets in the base of his skull."

I stiffened up in the passenger seat. "Are you fucking kidding me? He's dead?"

"Yeah, someone didn't want him around."

"Well that someone is pulling the strings, and I've got to find out who it is."

"Who do you think it is?"

"Maybe Galgano? Maybe Donnelly? I don't know. But I do know that I have to resolve this. Everything is on the line for me." We exited the Bronx River Parkway at Fordham Road westbound. "Hey buddy, I'm almost home, and out of your hair."

"Hey, Frankie, I'm with you all the way. Fuck them all."

"Yeah, Joey. I know that. The meeting today, I can't wait to see Daniels's face when he sees me. I hope the fat fuck blows up. I think the Judge is the only one that knows I'm coming."

"I wish I could be a fly on the wall."

Joe then pulled up in front of my building. As I got out of his car I told him that I'd let him know how the meeting went that afternoon. He asked, "How the fuck are you going to get there?"

"Look, Joey, I don't want you any more involved than you have to be. I'll take a cab, then a train down to Foley Square."

"Okay. Keep me posted. Good luck, Frankie."

"Thanks." I walked into my building. I needed to get my mind straight for the meeting.

It was about 2:45 p.m. when I entered the courthouse, and I noticed Daniels and Staton standing in the lobby. I would normally check my gun with security, but I had no gun to check. Jacob started towards me, but Daniels blocked him with his arm.

"I'll take care of this." He approached me rapidly and, from a couple of feet away, yelled, "What are you doing here?"

The pupils in his piggy eyes couldn't be smaller; his face was menacing. I shot back, "Judge Sposato directed me to be here. Take it up with him."

He squinted. "Someday you'll be going through a door, and there'll be no one there to back you up."

"Well, Chief, you know what? Fuck you!" I pushed my way past him and made my way to the Judge's chambers. I was invited by his secretary to take a seat in his conference room, where Adel, Mike, Cindy, Joan Connelly, and John Kenny were seated at a table. I took a seat next to Mike. A stenographer was seated off in the corner, ready for dictation. Daniels and Staton entered moments later, soon followed by the Judge. We all stood. I noticed Mike was nervous and about to lose his lunch.

Judge Sposato said, "Please be seated. I want to thank everyone for attending. I think we all know each other with the exception of Mr. Baraka's mother Adel and his girlfriend Cindy Galgano."

I looked over at the Chief, who was smirking, as if to say *Just wait. After this is over, you two shitbags are out of my hair for good.*

The Judge sat, with everyone following suit. He said, looking at Mike, "I understand that Mike's family is here to give him moral support." Mike gave a slight nod as he sat nervously twitching his right leg; that was obvious to everyone. The Judge continued. "Since the United States Attorney's Office requested this hearing, I'd like you to begin, John."

Kenny leaned forward in his chair, his hands clasped in front of him. "Thank you, your Honor. I'll get right to the point. Mr. Baraka's efforts, for the most part, have not been productive. In fact, they've been problematic, jeopardizing the lives of officers. The U.S. Attorney's Office requests that you evaluate Mr. Baraka's work, and that he be remanded forthwith to the United States Marshals Service for inmate processing."

I glanced at Mike, who looked like he was going to puke. His face had turned pure white, as beads of sweat poured from his forehead.

The Judge was taking notes, then looked up at Kenny. "Anything else, John?"

Kenny replied, "I would like the record to reflect that Mr. Baraka was convicted at trial, your Honor." Kenny then picked up a file and read, "In addition to conspiring with the other defendants, two ounces of heroin were seized from his bedroom. We also have statements that confirm that Mr. Baraka recently purchased a counterfeit passport with plans to leave the country. Therefore, your Honor, we consider Mr. Baraka to be a flight risk, and want him incarcerated."

"Duly noted, Mr. Kenny. And, Mr. Staton, where does your office stand on this matter?"

"Your Honor, Mr. Kenny has expressed the position of the District Attorney's Office."

The Judge then scribbled a few more lines on his notepad and directed his attention towards me. "Detective Santorsola, I'd like to hear from you."

I stood to ensure all could hear. Facing the Judge, not wanting to be distracted, I began, "Judge Sposato, I've been working with Mike Baraka for some time now, and he's never lied to me or knowingly compromised me with the bad guys. Yes, he did purchase a counterfeit passport before his cousin agreed to come forward, confessing that it was he who was working for Michael Calise in the heroin trade and not Mike. As for the two ounces of heroin, it was put in his dresser by Sami Hassan. I believe that Sami is willing to make a statement to that affect."

Joan Connelly interrupted. "Your Honor, although not admissible in court, Mr. Hassan will take a lie detector test in that regard."

I continued, "Your Honor, yesterday morning I videotaped a confession from Mike's cousin Ayman Baraka."

This time it was Daniels who interrupted. "Judge Sposato, before Detective Santorsola continues, you should know that, as of this morning, this detective was suspended for . . . "

The Judge interrupted Daniels. "Just one moment, Chief Daniels. Let the Detective continue."

234

"Thank you, Judge. Mike's cousin confessed that it was he who conspired with Calise, Galgano, Sami Hassan, and the others to import and distribute heroin in the United States. With all I've gone through and with all I've seen, I'm confident in saying that I stand before the court today with the belief that this person sitting next to me has been wrongly convicted."

I then sat down as the Judge said, "Thank you, Detective."

Joan Connelly then said, "Your Honor, I have a copy of the confession for your review."

Chief Daniels, John Kenny, and Jacob Staton looked like they'd just been kicked in the balls. Daniels, now breathing heavy, exclaimed, "That tape was obtained without the authorization of the District Attorney's Office!"

Connelly handed the tape to Judge Sposato. The Judge replied, "I'm aware of that, Chief. In light of this confession, I'll need some time to review the matter. I'm sure the United States Attorney's Office would like to do the same."

Connelly interjected, "At this time, your Honor, I would like to make application to the court to file a writ of coram nobis, vacating Mr. Baraka's judgment of conviction."

The Judge replied, "So noted. I would like everyone back in my courtroom at the same time one week from today."

Judge Sposato stood, everyone else in the room followed suit, and then we all filed out of the conference room. Kenny, Staton, and Daniels took one elevator, and the rest of us took the other. Down in the lobby, Daniels just glared at me as I walked off the opposite elevator car. Mike asked me to escort his mother out of the building, while Cindy and Mike followed behind us. I heard her say, "Michael, I can't lose you too. I've already lost my father."

"Don't worry, Cindy. Everything will work out."

Outside, standing in front of the courthouse, I said, "Look, at least the Judge has the tape and didn't refuse it. He could have, you know. He could have bounced it back to Kenny and let him handle it, but he didn't. That's a good sign. So now we just have to see. Now translate all this stuff to your mother. I'm not sure she understands what went on up there. By the way, they took my wheels. Can you give me a lift home?"

Cindy said of course they could. She then embraced me, giving me a kiss on my cheek. "Thank you, Frank. It's not everyone who'd stand up for Mike like you just did."

I just wished I knew what lay ahead. At that moment the future was very uncertain for me, as it was for Mike.

Chapter Twenty-Seven

I called Joe as soon as I walked into my apartment. I asked him if he could break free that night, and that I'd like to take a ride down to Petra's. He said that he'd work it out with Angel, so just let him know what time I'd like him to pick me up. I told him to come by at 8 p.m. and to bring me a gun.

I was standing in front of my building when Joe rolled up. As I got into the Crown Victoria he handed me a Smith & Wesson nine millimeter that I shoved into my waist, in the front of my jeans. Joe said that he thought that he had a tail following him on the way over, but thought he'd lost it.

"Is that right? You know, Mike drove me home from the hearing and we had a tail too, but I didn't see it when he dropped me off."

As Joe and I headed down to Manhattan, we spoke about the tails, and figured it was either Daniels or Donnelly. If Chief Daniels had assigned guys to follow us, we were both in trouble with the department. We arrived outside of Petra's about 8:30 p.m. I'd been nursing a large coffee we'd picked up at a deli on the way. The street was well lit in front of the club, which made it easy to see the comings and goings of the patrons of the club. It was about 11:30 p.m. when I hit Joe in the arm, yelling, "Joe, Pat Donnelly just walked in carrying a small gym bag!"

"Are you sure?"

"Yeah, I'm sure. It was him."

"You check out the nightclub, and I'll check out the alley and the back."

We got out of the car and I watched Joe go in the front door. I ran to the alley, noticing a light go on through a small basement window. I peered through the window; inside I saw Nebor pull a briefcase out of a file cabinet and place it on a wooden desk overhung by an illuminated naked light bulb.

237

Yousef opened the briefcase and took out two bricks of what looked like narcotics, and packets of U.S. currency. He placed the stuff on the desk in front of Donnelly. When I saw that, I knew I had the prick. I then ran around to the front of Petra's, practically bursting through the front door. As I headed for the kitchen, I caught Joe's attention; he was standing over by the bar. Waving my arms frantically, I yelled for Joe to follow me.

"They're breaking open shit in the basement. I'm gonna take 'em."

As Joe caught up with me, he yelled, "Are you sure about this? Are you sure?"

"Yeah, I'm sure; c'mon."

We blew through the kitchen's double doors, Joe running behind me. I yelled, "There," pointing to a trap door leading to the basement. We drew our weapons as I pulled the trap door open. Joe and I ran down the stairs to the surprise of Donnelly and Yousef. We yelled, "Freeze!"

Joe screamed, "Don't move a goddamned inch! You're under arrest!"

Donnelly and Yousef were in such a state of shock that they readily complied. Joe put the cuffs on Nebor. I took the cuffs off my belt and tossed them to Joe, who then cuffed Donnelly.

Donnelly began to compose himself. "Do you know who I am? I was just about to arrest this man."

I walked over to the table and unzipped the gym bag, which revealed stacks of hundred-dollar bills held together by rubber bands. As Joe patted them down, retrieving Donnelly's gun, he placed it in his outside jacket pocket.

Donnelly screamed, "I'm a DEA agent. You're fucking up a federal investigation!"

I shot back, "Tell it to the fucking judge, pal!"

Yousef stood behind the desk, visibly shaken, mesmerized by what had just occurred.

Donnelly yelled, "You idiots got it all wrong!" As Joe and I turned around, the sound of heavy footsteps running down the stairs got our attention. Two huge Arabs landed on the cellar floor, pointing semiautomatic pistols at us. They looked familiar and, in that split second, I placed them at the shooting at the gas station in Brooklyn. Donnelly yelled to Joe, "Get these cuffs off me!"

Joe had no choice but to uncuff him. Donnelly grabbed his gun from Joe's pocket, turned to Yousef, and yelled, "You're under arrest!" Donnelly then barked out to the Arabs, "Cuff Yousef, take them all out back, and we'll sort this out!" Could these two guys be DEA agents?

They followed Donnelly's orders and cuffed Yousef. They marched us up a set of steps, out the basement door, and to the back of the nightclub. Guns pointed at our backs, we were then ordered around the building to the alley, as Donnelly followed in the rear of this procession.

I yelled, "Okay, Pat, if these guys are agents, one of them shot Mike!"

"You just couldn't let it go, Frank. You had to stick your nose in my business."

Joe yelled, "So you're all fucking dirty!"

One of the Arabs raised his weapon towards Joe and I when two huge men burst out of the shadows of the adjoining building with pistols drawn. They looked like guys out of the World Wrestling Federation. One had a clean-shaven scalp and the other a full head of black Italian hair. Baldy said at once, "Okay, fellas, don't even think about it. Drop your weapons and throw your fucking hands in the air."

I guess one of the Arabs had second thoughts, making the mistake of hesitating for a few seconds; the dark-haired Italian slammed him in the face, dropping him to the ground. His gun slid down the alley. The Italian then proceeded to land a kick in the Arab's ribs; a loud crunch was heard. The Arab was now in the fetal position, moaning in agony. Donnelly and the other Arab had dropped their guns to the ground. Baldy then told Donnelly not to move.

I didn't care who these guys were. They saved Joe's and my ass. I yelled to Joe, "Cuff them all! You're all under arrest!

Donnelly vehemently protested. "Frank, you guys are making a big mistake!"

"Yeah, what about the fuck who was about to pull the trigger on Joe and me? Is that what they teach the agents at the academy? To kill cops? Like I said, Pat, tell it to the Judge."

Joe picked up Donnelly's gun and held it on him while I ran down to the basement to get mine. As I returned, Joe walked over to the two bruisers.

"Thanks, but who the fuck are you guys?"

The dark-haired one replied, "Mr. Galgano sends his regards. He asked us to keep an eye on you."

Baldy continued, "Frank, he thanks you for doing the right thing by his future son-in-law. Are you going to be okay with these fucking degenerates? Or do you want us to hang around?"

"We'll be fine. So it's been you following us?"

They both smiled. Then Baldy said in Italian, *Sii buono*, which means "Be good." They then walked back down to the street and out of sight.

I looked at Joe. "Can you believe this? They saved our skins." "Frankie, you can't make this shit up. It's unbelievable."

I then flipped open my cell phone and called Captain Christopher. I thought to myself, *Ha, this ought to be good. Well, what can I do? I've got to go through channels, otherwise I can't get these guys picked up and brought back to the office.*

After several rings on Christopher's cell phone, a groggy and somewhat confused Christopher picked up. After a few seconds he was fully awake, and asked, "Frank, what's up? Why are you calling me at this hour? It's almost three in the morning."

"Well, Captain, Joe and I have a situation here." I explained what had gone down, and that we needed transportation back into town for prisoner processing.

His exact words: "Holy shit, Frank. You've been suspended, and you're arresting a DEA agent?"

"Cap, as I said, it's a long story."

"Frankie, I don't know what to say. Are you sure about this?"

"Yes, Cap, I am."

"Okay, then, I'll have a van there in an hour. Are you okay with these guys?"

"Yeah, Cap. We're fine."

"Shit. You can sort this out with the Chief. I guess I'll see you guys tomorrow. I'm going back to bed."

It seemed that night wouldn't end. I tossed and turned into the morning, thinking of how Donnelly had protested during his fingerprinting and photographing. He said that he was going to ruin me, and that this was going to be the end of my career. I thought of Donnelly screaming at his attorney during his one permitted phone call, demanding that his attorney speak directly to the District Attorney about his unlawful arrest. I thought of how one of the Arabs needed medical attention because of the attitude adjustment given to him by Baldy. I had to laugh, remembering him limp out of the holding cell to be photographed. Unfortunately, the Arabs couldn't be identified through their fingerprints. They weren't agents. We'd have to go through the FBI to determine who these guys were, and where they came from. Right at that moment the only thing we knew was that they were in the dope business, and maybe working for a terrorist organization like al-Qaeda or Hezbollah. But mostly I tossed all night because I knew that I'd have to deal with the politics of my office, which I knew was on the agenda for the day, and it wasn't going to be pleasant.

The next day saw Nebor and Donnelly in two separate interrogation rooms. I watched and listened through a two-way mirror while Joe and two FBI agents paced as they zeroed in on a sweating Nebor.

Yousef yelled, "I told you!"

Joe shouted back, "You're facing twenty five years, just for possession."

Yousef, shackled to the floor, looked up at Joe from his chair at the far end of the small table, which centered the room, asking for a towel to mop the sweat off his forehead.

"I'll get you a fucking towel, but first answer my questions." "I told you, I'm not talking. I want a deal!"

Joe lunged into Yousef, grabbing him by his collar, yelling, "You're facing twenty-five to life just on the possession charge. We'll also charge you with attempted murder of a police officer. I know that you were behind the shooting in Brooklyn."

One of the FBI agents pulled Joe off Yousef. "Take it easy, Detective Nulligan."

Yousef, physically shaken and dripping with sweat, looked up at Joe. "Okay, Detective, I want assurances that I won't spend the rest of my life in jail."

"You come clean about your relationship with Pat Donnelly, and I'll go to bat for you with the U.S. Attorney's Office, and with anybody else. How's that?"

"Okay, okay. I've been working for Donnelly for almost five years, peddling heroin under his protection. And as far as shooting Baraka in Brooklyn, Pat was behind it. He thought that Frank was getting too close to our operation. As far as DeFalco, since he fucked up with the hit on Frank and Mike, he had to go. Donnelly came into Petra's with DeFalco early one morning, served him coffee from behind the bar, then pulled out his gun and shot him in the head."

"Right now, it's one liar's word against another's. Prove it. And tell me about the two Arabs. Who are they, and what are they into?"

"Detective Joe, they work for Donnelly, and I know that the heroin that comes in is from their connections in Afghanistan—and they may be tied to al-Qaeda."

"So Donnelly's supporting terrorism?"

"I don't know. But now I want a lawyer before I continue." Joe then said to the agents, "You heard the man."

I walked over to the other interrogation room, where Donnelly was seated, surrounded by two more FBI agents and his lawyer Justin Weiss, who was seated at the end of the table, taking notes. I entered the room, but didn't sit down.

"Nebor says you killed DeFalco."

Donnelly looked up, the anger apparent in his face. He yelled, "Yousef is a goddamned liar."

Weiss interrupted. "Detective Santorsola, you're fooling yourself if you think anyone will believe what Nebor has to say. You have no evidence, which means you have no case."

"He'll testify that it was your client that killed DeFalco and had Mike Baraka shot."

Donnelly sat with his arms stretched out, the picture of innocence. "I told you, he's an informant. I suspected he was providing me with information while conducting his own drug operation."

I shot back, "Yeah, I was there when you had those two guys take us out to be shot. Remember that?"

"Frank, I don't know what you're talking about. All's I know is that I went to check up on him, and I caught him with cash and the heroin. Then you two cowboys came in and fucked the whole thing up."

"That's bullshit! You wanted to have us executed! You prick!"

Just then Annette Larson walked into the room looking like she'd lost her best friend. She spoke to me angrily. "Please step into the hallway, Detective." I followed her out into the hallway. "You got anything, Frank?"

"We got a statement from Yousef Nebor. He wants a light sentence in exchange for his testimony."

She put her hands on her hips, as if to indicate that she didn't want to hear anything I had to say about Nebor or

Donnelly. "The only thing you have is hearsay, Detective— from a drug dealer, no less. You know what that's worth in court. Nothing! Absolutely nothing!"

I cut her off. "Do you really believe Donnelly was there all alone to arrest Nebor? Why are you trying to protect this guy?"

"Detective, this is an order. Release him. Don't make me say it twice! Do you understand me?"

"I got it! But you're making a mistake!"

I had no choice but to release Donnelly. Releasing this scumbag was like being forced to swallow acid. But I did what I was ordered to do, and cut him loose. My ace in the hole was Nebor, and I needed to get the office to cut him a deal.

It took a full day for Yousef's lawyer, Hyrum Shuler, to contact his client, but eventually we all met in the interrogation room once again. As Joe slid a piece of paper to Shuler, I looked the lawyer over. He reminded me of a weasel with an oversized head. Shuler peered through his glasses as he studied the paper.

"Satisfied?" Joe asked.

Shuler handed the document to Yousef, who asked, "I'll do no more than five years?"

Shuler replied, "That's right." Shuler then leaned over and whispered into Yousef's ear.

Yousef straightened up, focusing his attention on Joe and me. "You can't trust anyone, especially in my business, but one thing that keeps everyone honest, even if they don't want to be, are video cameras. Over the bar and at the far end of the lounge are hidden pinhole cameras. They captured Donnelly murdering DeFalco at the bar. For insurance, I've kept the tapes in my office safe."

That was all we had to hear. We got a search warrant that morning, and soon thereafter the FBI arrived back at the squad room with a box full of videotapes and a dismantled VCR monitor. I happened to be sitting at my desk, packing up a few personal things, when Joe walked in.

"Hey, we got the mother lode! We got Donnelly's cameo

on tape!" The agents walked past my desk, bringing the cardboard box into the evidence room. All I could do was smile. It was going to be a good day after all.

Chapter Twenty-Eight

Larson, Staton, and Daniels were shocked by the tapes, as well they should have been. The DA contacted her counterpart in Manhattan, who immediately issued an arrest warrant for Donnelly. I couldn't wait to see Donnelly's face and the spin Larson put on his arrest to protect her office. He was arrested that afternoon at Union Station in Washington D.C., just as he got off the train from New York. The FBI put handcuffs on him on the platform, creating a commotion with the other commuters. He was brought back to New York later that day and placed in a holding cell at FBI headquarters in Manhattan before he was brought to Westchester for his second grilling the following morning.

When Joe and I entered the interrogation room, Donnelly and his attorney Justin Weiss were seated, along with two FBI agents at either end of the table. One was Ed Crispin, short, stocky, wearing a gray suit. He had a crew cut, sported a face like a bullfrog, and looked like he chewed nails for breakfast every day. The other agent, Tom Hillary, was taller than Crispin, wore a dark suit, and had a medium complexion, with black hair combed over to the side. Both of these guys were all professional and all business.

I stared at Donnelly and smiled. "Pat, nice to see you again." He shot me a look that could kill.

His lawyer said, "Now that you're here, detectives, we can continue with this nonsense. My client is now being harassed. He's been arrested twice in two days. You guys are really pushing the envelope."

Joe took the cassette tape from his pants pocket, tossed it on the table, and with a sarcastic inflection said, "Looks like we've got an Oscar-winning performance of Mr. Donnelly on tape, compliments of Yousef Nebor."

Agent Crispin interjected. "I'm going to offer you a deal. No death penalty. But if you don't cooperate with us, everything's off the table. Now, for starters, are you in collusion with anyone else in law enforcement?"

I interrupted. "Yousef had a nice little video surveillance system set up at Petra's, motion-activated. It was activated early one morning when Louis DeFalco stopped by for coffee."

Donnelly and Weiss went into whisper mode. Weiss hesitated for a few seconds. Then, looking around the interrogation table at all of us, he said, "My client is prepared to give a statement, but we have to be sure that there's no death penalty."

Agent Hillary responded, "That's up to the Manhattan District Attorneys Office, but they'll likely go along with our recommendation. But before any deals are made here, we have to have everything—and I mean everything."

Weiss whispered again into Donnelly's ear. It reminded me of two school kids in class, passing secret notes to one another. They pulled away from each other, with Weiss nodding in agreement.

Crispin began hammering Donnelly, gleaning information about his heroin connection in Afghanistan and the details of all crimes he was involved in, as well as who he'd conspired with in the execution of those crimes. The agents were very interested in Donnelly's Middle East connection in relation to terrorist groups.

Donnelly outlined, in detail, all the information given to him before and after Operation Black Widow. Hillary asked him about DeFalco's murder, which Donnelly admitted to and described. He was questioned as to why he killed DeFalco. Donnelly hesitated. Agent Crispin reminded him that if he didn't tell all, the death penalty was back on the table. He looked over at Weiss, trembling. Weiss told him to continue. Donnelly related that DeFalco had known too much about the heroin operation. When the hit on me and Mike got screwed up, Donnelly felt that it was only a matter of time before DeFalco would be arrested and talking, so he killed him.

I watched as the sweat poured off Donnelly's face, dripping onto the table. He knew that life as he knew it was over. Then Agent Crispin straight out said that he needed to know if there was anyone else in the DEA, FBI, or the U.S. Attorney's Office who Donnelly had conspired with in illegal activities.

Donnelly looked at Crispin, the condemnation evident in his eyes. "Before I answer, I need to know that I'm not going to be executed."

Crispin looked him the eye. "Pat, I told you, we'll see what we can do. As I've said, the Manhattan DA's normally will go along with our recommendation. Now answer the question. Tell me if you know of corruption in any of the federal law enforcement agencies, or for that matter, any law enforcement agency."

"Okay, it's John Kenny. Kenny could have cleared Mike Baraka from the get-go, but he held back from the trial some tapes from the wiretaps in Operation Black Widow that would have cleared Mike and implicated his cousin Ayman. So when Mike Baraka was arrested that night, instead of straightening out the mess, Kenny figured that it was just another Arab being busted, and who would care? But I knew we arrested the wrong guy that night and, after the trial, I brought it to Kenny's attention. From that moment on, John Kenny was in my pocket. I made sure that he informed me of all narcotics investigations that targeted any of my people. We were able to operate with impunity from law enforcement."

I asked, "So Kenny knew the people working for you?"

"Yes, he did."

Agent Hillary immediately left the room and went up to Annette Larson's office, advising her of Donnelly's debriefing. Hillary asked to use her phone to call an assistant U.S. attorney for an arrest warrant for John Kenny. I wish I could have seen Larson's face as Agent Hillary contacted

AUSA Christopher Arnold to explain why one of their own was on the ropes. An arrest warrant was immediately issued, and Kenny was arrested by the FBI later that day in his office.

With Donnelly's confession finally wrapped up, the agents left the DA's office with Donnelly. I went back to my desk to clear a few things up, and thought I'd see if Denise was available. I thought maybe we'd celebrate surviving that last few days. Joe was at his desk talking on the phone with Jessica. After he finished his call, I asked him for a ride.

"Sure—where to, Frankie? Hey, do you want to stop by Jake's to celebrate?"

"I'll take a rain check. I planned to give Denise a call to see what she was up to."

"Sounds like a plan to me."

I then dialed her number, and lucky for me, she was home. "Hey, what are you doing?"

"I'm straightening up the house. How about you?"

I told her that I'd like to see her if she didn't have to work.

"No, I'm not working. Come on over."

I told her that Joe was dropping me off, and I'd be over in about an hour. She asked me why Joe was dropping me off and wanted to know where my car was. I said that it was a long story, and that I'd explain when I got there.

The next morning Denise and I were lounging in her living room, watching TV, when Staton called me. He said there was a press conference that was to take place at 11 a.m. in Larson's office, and that Joe and I should be there.

I said, "You guys move fast. Larson's putting on a dog and pony show for the press—how can I appear at a fucking press conference with charges pending? Has anyone thought of that?"

He replied somewhat remorsefully, "Sean has dropped the charges." I spat back, "Be nice if he called and told me instead of hearing it from you. Ah, well, let me get dressed and I'll be in. You know, I don't have a car."

"Joe Nulligan will pick you up at 10:15 a.m. How's that

sound?" "Fine, Jacob. See you later."

Since I didn't have time to go home to change, they'd have to settle for yesterday's fashion.

When Joe and I arrived in the squad room, I fished a tie out of my locker that was already knotted, and threw it on. As I walked back into the squad room, an animated Daniels walked in, bellowing that we had to get up to the DA's private office.

"The press is waiting for us; we need to move it."

I thought, *Your big day in the sun, you miserable prick.*

Joe and I followed Daniels up the stairwell to Larson's office. Her secretary motioned for us to hurry and position ourselves on Larson's right, with Daniels and Staton on her left as she stood at the podium. Joe and I looked at each other with emotions of contempt for Daniels written on our faces.

Larson began the conference, and I noticed a huge grin on Daniels's face. I thought I'd puke. Larson said, "Before I answer any questions, I'd like to read a statement: 'Through months of combined effort from the Manhattan District Attorney's Office, the United States Attorney's Office, and the Federal Bureau of Investigation, we have dismantled an international drug conspiracy with tentacles that reached into the very heart of law enforcement.'"

Then the questions started, until finally the farce was over. I needed a drink to quell the bile that'd risen in my throat. Joe and I nodded to each other. It was time to get out of there. Jake's never sounded so good. I decided that it was time to take some vacation days. I didn't even ask permission; I just took them. And no one called to ask where I was. Daniels was probably relieved that I was out of his hair for a few days. During my time off I spent a lot of time with Denise, and even had a few home-cooked meals at my mother's house. It was nice spending time with her, feeling at home again and loved unconditionally. There were several dinners with Joe and Jessica, with me buying most of them. I even had a meal at

Mike's house—all forgiven, but not forgotten.

I finally moved into my new apartment. It was clean, spacious, and smelled of fresh paint. Now I could finally have friends over, especially Denise.

Soon it was time to go back to work, and there was another court hearing for Mike. I dug out my lucky brown suit and—oh yes—the rosary beads that Mike's mother had given me. With these two things, Mike was sure to walk. When I arrived in the courtroom all of Mike's family was already there, as well as Jacob Staton. Christopher Arnold was representing the U. S. Attorney's Office. Mike stood nervously in front of the Judge.

Judge Sposato began, "The confession taken by Detective Santorsola, along with the audiotapes that were seized from John Kenny's apartment, prove to this court that the defendant had no involvement in a heroin conspiracy with Calise and the others. If these tapes had not been withheld from trial, they would have certainly exonerated Mr. Baraka. In this regard, I grant a writ of coram nobis, vacating the judgment of conviction on all counts."

I thought Mike was going to collapse. He began to weep, his words barely audible.

"Thank you, your Honor. Thank you."

Judge Sposato continued, "The court also commends the efforts taken by Detective Santorsola. Had he not persevered through the many obstacles he faced, a terrible injustice might not have been rectified. And, Detective Santorsola, from my understanding, your partner Joseph Nulligan was instrumental in assisting you. I commend both detectives." By this time, Cindy was having a hard time containing her emotions. She was also sobbing uncontrollably. Finally, Mike was able to tell his mother what had just happened. Adel ran over and cradled me in her arms, taking my breath away.

Then Chris Arnold stood up. "Your Honor, the United States Attorney's Office would like to address the court for the record."

"By all means, Mr. Arnold."

"The United States Attorney's Office formally apologizes to Mr. Baraka and his family for what he has had to endure, including his false arrest, incarceration, and the defamation of his character."

As Mike was hugging his mother, Jacob Staton walked over to him and offered his hand. Mike looked at Jacob for a moment, smiled, and shook it.

Chapter Twenty-Nine

It took some time to get back into the routine of the office. First off, I wasn't used to it. Secondly, I hated it. Thirdly, I had to deal with Chief Daniels. But at least Joe and I were partnered up again.

I was in the squad room, having just been handed a cup of coffee by Nulligan, when my cell phone rang. "Frank here."

"Frankie, it's me, Mike."

"Hey, it's good to hear from you. What's going on?"

"I have some information I thought you might be interested in."

"What the hell are you doing? We're all done with all that."

"Frankie, maybe not. I just thought I could help."

"What is it?"

"A friend of mine works as a DJ at Legs Up in Manhattan. You know it?"

"Yeah, it's run by that wise guy, Johnny 'Hoops' Migliacci." "Yeah, that's it. The other night State Senator Williams and some other politicians were there with Migliacci."

"Who was there?"

"You know, Senator Williams, he represents southern Westchester and part of the Bronx."

"Okay, and . . . ?" I waved over to Joe to listen in on the call. "My friend said Migliacci's been funding the Senator from the beginning. Now he wants him to help launder heroin money through Swiss bank accounts."

"How's your friend know this?"

"The Senator is having an affair with one of the waitresses, and she has loose lips."

"No shit."

"Frankie, it gets better. The Senator is helping District Attorney Larson's bid for mayor."

Joe's eyes were now dilated. He shook his head and mouthed for me to hang up the phone.

I was silent for a few seconds, not 100 percent sure I wanted to get involved again. Mike broke my silence.

"Frankie, are you interested?"

I made a decision then and there. "You're goddamned right I'm interested. I'll get back to you."

I hung up. Joe's look was that of exasperation. "Are you out of your fucking mind? What is it with you? You must like sticking your face in a buzz saw."

I guess I must have. I got up and told Captain Christopher that I was going upstairs to the Chief's office. Ruth Williams was busy at her desk on her computer when I walked in. She said she guessed that I wanted to see the Chief and buzzed him, informing him that I was standing in the outer office.

"Send him in." I sat in my usual spot, reserved for grilling and basting. I told him straight up, "Chief, I just got off the phone with Mike Baraka."

You remember as a kid blowing up balloons, perhaps at a birthday party, and then letting them go to fly around the room? Then, all your friends would join in, with the collective sound threatening to send your folks to the insane asylum. Daniels reminded me of one of those balloons—even his lips, which blubbered together as he let out an exasperated breath. I continued, "It seems Senator Williams and his entourage were having a few drinks with Johnny Migliacci at Legs Up. The skinny is that Migliacci wants Williams to help him launder heroin money through Swiss bank accounts. I'd like to open up a case."

The Chief had turned gray. I knew what he was thinking, *How can I transfer this fuck before he kills me? Why can't he just bring in simple narcotic cases?*

The Chief learned forward and squinted behind his glasses. "Don't do a fucking thing. You hear me? Don't do a fucking thing. I'll get back to you." He got up and walked past me, out of the office, leaving me sitting there. I wondered if I should go through his desk drawers, but killed that thought as I got up and walked out of his office, past Ruth. She looked at me, a question mark on her face, as I'm sure she infrequently saw Daniels leave first while he was hosting someone in his office. I nodded to her as I closed the outer door and walked back downstairs to my desk.

Joe came over and sat on the edge of my desk. "What'd he say?"

I looked up at him. "He said, 'Don't do a fucking thing.' That's what he said. What else would the fat fuck say? I thought that Big Louie was going to whistle, and he was going to have the big one."

Joe smirked. "Yeah, what else?"

My desk phone rang. "Narcotics, Santorsola." I listened, then replied, "Give me five minutes, and I'll be right up."

Joe asked, "Who was that?"

"The Chief and the DA want to see me."

I opened the second drawer down on the right and pulled out a small tape recorder. It had a clean forty-five minute cassette in it. I put new batteries in, turned it on, and slid it into the outside pocket of my sports jacket. Joe, watching with interest, nodded in agreement, then said, "Fuck 'em." He gave me the thumbs up as I got up and walked out of the squad room.

Epilogue

Frank Santorsola (a.k.a. Frank Miranda) successfully infiltrated the mob, made countless narcotics arrests leading to convictions at trial, and during his twenty-seven years in law enforcement rose to the rank of Chief of Detectives. He was highly decorated within and outside the department before retiring in 1998.

This book is a fact-based, fictional account of one of the investigations that Frank worked, and is a story he wants told.

Oh, and sadly to write, Frank is still estranged from his daughters. If you're wondering about Senator Williams, District Attorney Larson, Mike Baraka, and the outcome of Frank's relationship with Denise MacKenzie, you'll just have to stay tuned for the next installment of *Miranda Writes*.

For sales, editorial information, or subsidiary rights information
please write or phone or e-mail

Baxter Productions Media
308 Main Street
New Rochelle, New York 10801
Tel: 914-576-8706
Baxterproductionsmedia.com
sales@baxterproductionsmedia.com

Made in the USA
Middletown, DE
25 August 2019